BRILLIANT DISGUISES

WILLIAM THORNTON

To Albert,
Thank you for being a blessing
in my life,
Bill

To order additional copies of this book, contact:
Xlibris Corporation
1-888-795-4274
www.Xlibris.com
Orders@Xlibris.com
69816

For Donna and Sophia
who keep it real

"For though I be free from all men,
yet have I made myself servant unto all,
that I might gain the more...
I am made all things to all men..."
PAUL — I Corinthians 9

"We are what we pretend to be,
so we must be careful about
what we pretend to be."
KURT VONNEGUT — Mother Night

"I have entered on an enterprise
which is without precedent,
and will have no imitator.
I propose to show my fellows
a man as nature made him,
and this man shall be myself."
JEAN JACQUES ROUSSEAU — Les Confessions

i. PROFESSION OF FAITH

PROFESSION OF FAITH

1

When I think back on the interview, it doesn't seem that it was me sitting there in that office as much as somebody else. I suppose that was the whole point.

I had a similar feeling at my brother's funeral. It was the sensation that I was a spectator, that I had stepped outside myself into some impassive, Elysian plain of existence and no longer had any control over what I was doing. Or what was happening, I should say. It wasn't really a conscious decision — just the accumulation of a manic heartbeat and senses on a trip wire waiting for whatever might reveal itself in the next instant. I have never really understood how or why events reveal themselves like this. Perhaps that too is the whole point.

I was sitting in an office, yawning, still feeling like I had the night before — a feeling that I needed to be *clean*. In reality, I needed a new job. I had an interview just after lunch. Dr. Benjamin Forster of the Forster Foundation had an opening on the public relations wing of his empire and I wanted to be part of it. It easily paid twice what I was making, and I had the keen ability not to see any possible reason why they wouldn't hire me, given my qualifications. That is, provided I got a good night's sleep, which I didn't.

The interviewer was Prescott — Charlie to his friends, though he didn't make me feel like one — who identified himself as Forster's adjutant but never quite defined what that position meant. I noticed hanging in a closet behind his desk a few suits that had just been dry cleaned, swathed in sheets of shining cellophane. I wondered if picking these up for his boss was part of the job description.

Prescott did not dress the part of what I would consider an adjutant. That is, unless the job description included no sense of fashion. The man wore a suit that accentuated his overly rounded belly, topping his ensemble off with a vulgar-looking belt buckle so shiny it must have been made of chrome. This made him look like the human equivalent of a Mack truck angling for respectability. He was a very tall man, which may have explained his ill-fitting clothes, but I would have presumed a man working for Forster would be more image conscious. I immediately wondered if I should have dressed down. On his desk, positioned for any visitor to be overwhelmed by it, was a large framed picture of a woman I learned later was Prescott's wife, though it was natural to infer so from its prominence. On a wall near his desk were two classical Greek drama masks, with a happy face and a frowning one. Though they were meant to remind me of Sophocles and Euripides, I found myself thinking of the beginning of Three Stooges movies. How strange, the connections our minds can make.

Sitting there, waiting as Prescott looked over my resume, I realized I was wearing the same black suit that I had worn for Peter's funeral. It still had flecks of dried dirt on the pants' legs.

"Mr. Leon. Am I pronouncing that right?" he asked.

"Yes. Just like it's spelled."

"Splendid." He used the word rather self-consciously, as though he wanted me to be impressed by it. "Everything seems to be in order here."

"Oh, good." I thought it might be better to act pleasantly

surprised at his observation. Then I wondered if that might not sound too vain. *No*, I silently corrected myself, *vain would be second-guessing a two-word response to a compliment during a job interview.*

Prescott stood up. He must have been about six five, and the desk made him seem even more absurdly tall. His belt bucket hit the desk top, making a sound like a bullet ricochet in an Old West movie. "There's just one question I have to ask you, Mr. Leon."

"Yes?"

He looked mildly embarrassed. "I have to say that we've had your resume for more than a month and we've been very impressed with everything."

"Good."

"I should let you know that very few people get this far. You wouldn't believe how many apply for this position, that either don't have what it takes or wash out when we get to this point."

"I see." Or I was trying to. We hadn't actually gotten to a point that I *could* see, at least one where someone would wash out.

"Do you feel comfortable? Can I get you anything?"

"I'm fine. Do I look uncomfortable?"

"Well, you do look a little tired at least. Troubled, maybe?"

My eyebrows arched involuntarily, and though I denied anything was wrong, Prescott could probably tell I was lying.

"I wouldn't want you to feel ill at ease, especially in light of what I'm about to say." Prescott cleared his throat, came around to the other side of the desk and sat down. He looked embarrassed at first, then relaxed into something knowing and fatherly. "But there is *one* thing that isn't covered in the resume." I had braced myself for what I thought he might say. I expected a short primer on the strange habits of my potential boss. Forster was largely known through his voice — he did a series of radio spots providing little homilies on how life could be lived more richly. They smacked of easy answers to difficult questions, bromides worn bare like borrowed clothes, but delivered in his sincere, booming, believing voice. He always wrapped with the same exhortation, almost ridiculous in its enthusiasm — "Have an exceptional day!" One didn't really know what he looked like, but you guessed at some majestic, unassailable sincerity. What little else was known about him was tantalizing. Legend had it that Forster thought nothing of calling employees in the dead of night and asking the most outlandish tasks of them to be completed within hours.

But then, I'm used to that already, considering last night, I thought.

"What is it?" I asked.

"Mr. Leon...Cameron... can I call you Cameron?"

"Yes. Please."

"Cameron, have you ever been born again?"

It was at this point that whatever illusions of control I had over myself left me, for reasons I'm still not quite sure about. "Excuse me?"

"Born again." He repeated the two words slowly, in a grave voice but with an inappropriate smile.

"I'm not sure I follow," I said. I remember squinting and leaning forward in my chair, probably because I felt like I needed to do ... *something*.

"Are you a Christian?"

I wanted to be sure. "A Christian?"

"Yes."

There is probably a moment in every job interview where the applicant realizes the secret agenda at the heart of the querying. The prospective boss relays through gesture or statement what the position entails, or what is expected of the would-be employee, or what kind of man the employer is, and the interviewee immediately tailors his gifts, his experience, his very life with neat scissor snips until a workable, passable garment emerges for inspection.

A more intelligent person than myself would probably have said something different from the next thing that came out of my mouth. "You mean, like, with that Jesus guy, right?"

"Yes!" he exclaimed, as a game show host might for a contestant who suddenly recalls the answer to a question. "That same guy. I presume you've heard of Christianity?"

As ridiculous as my question had been, he responded with an off-putting level of earnestness and an annoying acceptance of my flippancy at face value. I had expected him to be suitably offended, thus pleasing me. But he didn't. And so we did this strange dance, with me alternating between the kind of self-interested lying to get a job that applicants routinely indulge in, punctuated by glib, sarcastic responses to questions I was sure were none of his business.

"Yes, yes, of course. Born again?" I said.

"I'm sorry. We're sort of fundamentalist around here. It's second nature to say it like that. It's something, a term you might say we use to identify ourselves to ourselves."

"Sort of like a code word, you mean? Or a secret handshake?"

"Hadn't thought of it quite that way, Cameron. What do you say?"

"I'm not quite sure what to say, really. If you mean God, I mean, I saw 'The Da Vinci Code.' Twice." This was actually a lie. The second time I had wandered into the wrong theatre. It took a few minutes for me to realize it because I didn't remember Tom Hanks' hair being that long.

"Well, that's a start, I suppose," Prescott said, in all earnestness. "I take it you *do* believe in God."

"Was that a prerequisite for the job?"

"You see, I told you not many people make it through this part of the process. I've seen people leave here..."

"I don't see..."

Prescott held up his hand, nodding his head as if pleading for patience. "This is a foundation, Cameron, a multi-million dollar operation. A lot of money and effort goes into what we do, and we don't want to waste the opportunity. But you must also realize this is a ministry. Mr. Forster believes heavily in a sense of mission. And that means that the job you've applied for carries, in a very real sense, some of the spirit of that ...*Spirit*, if you take my meaning."

"I do," I said. I was lying again, but I suppose I wanted the job badly enough at that point and sensed it was ascending beyond my grasp.

"I would assume then, Mr. Leon..."

I didn't like the way he lapsed back into the formal. "Cam, please..."

"Sorry, Cam. I would assume then that you're not a Christian? Do you belong to a church?"

"Um, I gave some money to the United Way. Once."

"Do you remember how much it was?" Clearly, he wasn't taking the bait.

I thought for a minute. Then I realized I had pledged to send money but never actually made out the check. I stayed quiet for a second until he gave up on getting an answer.

"You're *not* a Christian."

"I did once get a Bible trivia question right when I watching 'Jeopardy!'" I couldn't quite remember what it was.

"You're not a Christian," he repeated.

"Well, no, not as *you* define it."

"How do *you* define it, Cameron?"

"Well didn't Jesus say, 'Live and let live?' That's always been my motto."

Prescott never gave me the pleasure. "No, actually He never said anything like that."

I cleared my throat. "Why do you ask?"

Prescott began talking with his hands, gesturing like an after-dinner speaker. "I'll be frank. Cameron, our benefactor, I'm sure you're aware, is a very driven, very opinionated man. He feels strongly that if our work is to succeed, everyone must be of one mind, and one body."

"One body?"

"The body of Christ, I mean."

I should tell you that some of my responses to his questions were because of my lack of sleep. But I didn't feign much of my ignorance. I don't want you think of me as a ignorant man. I suppose what follows will convince you one way or another. Let me just say that the one remove of reality I was grappling with at that moment, the darkened glass I was looking through, if you will, kept me from associating what his words were with actual meanings. And as far as that moment was concerned, I didn't truly know my *own* body, let alone Christ's.

Maybe he figured this out from the expression on my face.

"I'm telling you, Cameron, that if you want this job, you need to go home and seriously think about your salvation."

I don't think the look on my face changed.

Prescott rolled his eyes, like a man giving up at a game of charades. "I mean, you should go home, pray about this, and ask Jesus to come into your heart."

"I thought you said something about being born again. Now you're talking about my heart?"

"It's a figure of speech."

"Another code word?"

"It has very definite meaning."

"I would think so. I think I remember a song about somebody not being born is busy dying, or something like that. I don't remember if it said anything about the heart. You want my heart born in Jesus, or Jesus born in my heart, or something... I'm still not getting it. I don't have any medical training, either in cardiology or obstetrics. I thought my resume covered that."

Prescott shook his head, still not taking the bait, still not giving up on me. "You're sure you've never heard of any of this?"

I yawned, and my hand went up to cover my mouth. My eyes went down to the floor. It seemed like a gesture of shame, even though I wasn't sure what I needed to be ashamed about. "He who would distinguish the true from the false must have an adequate idea of what *is* true and false," I said, finally.

"Who said that?" he asked, knowing I had to be quoting somebody.

"Spinoza."

"Very good. Interesting that that you're able to quote Spinoza but seemingly unacquainted with Christendom." So he could give as good as he got. That kept me from thinking too long on whether, after his prying, I really wanted this job after all.

I thought he might be about to ask me to leave. I finally said, "How do I do that? This born again thing."

"I don't want to pressure you..."

"Oh, no. Not at all."

"I mean, I realize you want this job and everything."

"Well, I do, but I'm not sure what *you* want me to do."

"Come again?"

"You say you don't want to pressure me, but you tell me I should pray about this. Is there something about me that you think is ...*evil*?" I shifted in my chair because I was curious just how much this man knew about me, how much he could read from my face.

"No, not at all," he said.

"Well, you said something about me looking troubled."

"Right, right. No, look, I don't think there's anything evil about you, Cameron. I wouldn't still be interested in you for the job if I did."

"But you still think I should..."

"I just know you're a man."

"Yeah, even though I didn't mention that on my resume either."

He forged on. "As a man, we're all prone to the weaknesses of men. We struggle with ourselves. Within ourselves. We have things we aren't proud of, things we can't quite cope with. We all know there's someone inside us, someone we know closer than anyone else, that we never can quite become. But in time we see all too clearly what we really are."

"I thought this was a public relations job..."

"It's a big step, I know, but you'll never regret it."

"You mean getting the job?"

He shook his head. "Cameron, like I said. Go home and think about it. Pray about it." He gestured again, as though he expected me to get up from my seat. Actually, he looked as uncomfortable as *I* probably felt.

"You're just giving me a day on this?"

"How much time do you need?"

I looked at my watch for some unknown reason. "Today's Friday, right? Alright, let me have the weekend."

"Fair enough. Three days is plenty of time."

I remember standing to shake his hand, though I don't remember particularly wanting to. The whole thing was vaguely insulting. I still wasn't sure where or what he expected me to do. It was obvious that what he wanted me to do was important to him at least, though I wasn't sure why. He had given me vague instructions with an indeterminate goal and expected me to satisfy his requirements well enough to get the job he was supposedly offering me.

PROFESSION OF FAITH

One of the great things about living in a democracy is that you can assemble a personal philosophy from the enduring ideas of the world, like someone pulling items from the shelves of a grocery. It's not even necessary to understand the ideas or know what the words mean. They're just words. They're just ideas. And the people and circumstances behind them are just brand names, like Coke and Pepsi. If these ideas fail, you can be comforted by knowing they weren't *your* ideas in the first place. And your own misinterpretation or willful ignorance is allowed under the Constitution. Mr. Leo Tolstoy, for example, told us that when we commit an act, *any act*, we are convinced we are doing it of our own free will, but examining it among the mass of mankind, we become convinced of that act's inevitability. The more alone we are, the more unrestricted our possibilities might be. The more we are connected to others, the less free we are.

But whatever control I had over myself returned during that interview just long enough for me to ask Prescott, "They would be able to tell me what I needed to know in church, right?"

He gave me, for the first time, a skeptical eye. "It depends which church you go to."

"Tell me," I said, "Which church does *Mr. Forster* attend?"

2

I don't know how long the phone rang the night before. It was my old rotary phone, red like what one might imagine the old nuclear hotline in the White House. I had picked it up at a yard sale and I liked the retro feel of it. It spoke of inconvenient calls with weighty issues in the balance and secret intrigues.

I don't remember answering it. I just remember speaking into it, as though someone else had picked it up and handed it to me.

"Hello?"

"Cam?" The voice sounded as though it was coming from total darkness.

"Cecelia?" I thought I recognized her. There was a quiver in *my* voice. I hadn't been expecting Cecelia to call. It had been about two weeks since the funeral. Not a long time, but they felt like years, whole years, like presidential terms, makes and models of cars, Central American revolutions and sports dynasties and the careers of television news anchors had come and gone in the interval.

"Hi." Her voice paused. "Am I interrupting anything?" Her voice was shaky too, like you would expect. I heard a sniffle and assumed she'd been crying. That's what you do at those times.

I squinted at the clock on the bedtable, just above my reclining head. It was 1:34 a.m.

"No," I said, resting on my elbow. "Is something wrong?"

"No," she said. I felt like laughing, it was such a transparent lie. "I couldn't sleep."

"I'm sorry." I cleared my throat because I couldn't stand the silence. This seemed to jump start my mouth into saying something. "I'm sorry I haven't been around lately to see you. I keep telling myself I should but..."

"Don't worry," she said. "I wouldn't come around if it were me. I mean, *I* haven't. You're going through the same thing." The only sound in between her words was her labored breath. She was breathing directly into the phone, as though her nose was too clogged from crying and she wanted someone to hear how desperate she sounded. If the situation had been different, I would have simply told her to move the mouthpiece so it didn't sound like an obscene phone call. But I didn't think I had the right to correct anything she did. Finally, she stopped. "Is it Thursday?"

"I think so."

"I can't believe I'm asking that. I guess I expect Peter to still tell me what time it is."

"I know, I know." I repeated the phrase because I wasn't sure what to say.

"Just the other day I was telling Ricky that I needed his dad, and I thought he might understand. But he's just eight years old. I don't even think he understands that his Dad's dead. To think it's Thursday already. He's been dead three weeks today."

I grunted at that word, repeated twice. She was talking about my older brother Peter, my only brother, who at that moment and for every moment in the foreseeable future, was in the ground. Peter had on his blue pinstriped double-breasted suit that he hated and his hair was combed at an awkward angle and he no longer wore his wedding ring since Cecelia had taken it off in the casket. I stood there in the funeral home looking at my brother's awkward hair and waited for him to brush up at his own hairline and set it right. But he hadn't. He never did. Then they had loaded him into a hearse and I stood there while Cecelia cried holding a bewildered Ricky and watched them shovel earth on top of my brother until it was no longer possible to see the outlines of the vault. I remember his little boy walking with his right hand extended out from his body, as though he was waiting for his father to appear from nowhere and take it, reclaiming him. I remember standing in the cemetery and looking out amongst all the stones and thinking that there were countless multitudes of people who had watched the same thing done to people who were lying underneath all the stones propped up in my eye line. But those dead people were not my brother, and they didn't really exist for me the way my brother did. Those dead people had always been dead to me, but a short thirty-six hours before that funeral I had been talking to Peter on his cell phone when the line went cold and a few hours later I got another call to say that my brother was dead in a car accident. I sometimes tried to remember what he had said to me just before the line went dead. It was several months before it hit home that those had probably been his last words. He had been found unconscious in his car by medics and had died before he reached the hospital. For some reason, I had expected some final statement worthy of my brother, or at least, a joking movie quotation from him, like "Rosebud" or "This is where we change cars" or "The horror! The horror!" It didn't seem that would be the last I would hear from him. He always had a way of getting in the last word.

And now when I thought of my brother, and where my brother was, I thought of the brother who was under all those mounds of dirt down in the cemetery. I had strange thoughts of going down there and clawing through it all until I could get down there and throw open the vault to let him out. And Peter would be there, I told myself, his toothy grin behind his mustache, offering out an arm to be pulled out of his mortality, as though he'd fallen into a ditch and had to be helped back up to keep walking...somewhere.

"Thanks, Cam," he might say to me if he were alive. "I don't know how much longer I could have stood that." Peter would laugh too, as though that was all death was — something to be laughed off like a hangover or a bad meal. "Are Cecelia and Ricky still okay?"

It was three weeks later. Peter was *still* dead. Strangely enough, it had really happened. I was still dumbfounded by it, separated by time and yet still conscious of it and my brother. My brother was no longer a presence, but an absence, and that absence was somehow more profound than Peter had been in real life.

"Do you think..." I began.

"Three weeks was nothing when he was around. Some days now I don't think I'm going to see the next hour get here fast enough."

"I know." I repeated the words again, though this time I did feel like I understood what she meant.

"One minute, it would be Monday and he would be, you know, coming out of the shower and getting ready for work, and then it was Friday and we were arguing over where we were going to eat that night."

I thought I should probably say something during these pauses, but I could only repeat *I know* so many times before she might rise up and remind me of how little I *did* know about my brother. Cecelia's grief, what was audible over the phone, seemed desperate, as though teetering on the brink of civility.

"You know, the hardest thing..."

I let a moment pass before I realized she wanted me to respond. "What? What is the hardest..."

"It's when Ricky wakes up in the middle of the night and I have to go in there and talk him back to sleep. Just me."

I nodded, as though Cecelia might see me agreeing with her. You must understand, I was still very sleepy. I had had moments in bed over those weeks where my eyes were closed, I did not move, yet I was still awake, my mind alive with thoughts of Peter.

"You know sometimes Peter would get up with Ricky when he was a toddler and I wouldn't even know it until the next morning? He just wanted me to get some sleep. That's all."

"Really?" I understood I was fulfilling a role here, as the brother

13

who might not believe his dead brother was capable of such tenderness to his wife. This would make Cecelia feel better in her grief, or so I thought.

"That was so like him. He did so many things I'd never know about until much later." Actually, the more I thought about it, the more I wondered if I should be doing my best to highlight my brother's selflessness. Cecelia's voice, her pleading, keening voice, drew out the syllables of the words as though that was the only way to get across just how much she needed her husband. "That's why I was thinking about him now. I had to get up with Ricky and I felt like he should have been here."

I transferred the phone from one ear to the other. "You mean Peter."

"Yes, yes," she said, her voice deteriorating into a whisper. She sounded like she was surrendering to an idea rather than welcoming it.

"Cecelia, I'm sorry. What can I do?"

She cried for a minute or two, and I listened patiently, wondering if I should say anything. I thought against it. "It's alright," would have been a lie, and "I understand," would have been the same. Cecelia's grief was the loneliest in the world, that of a widow. Whatever private seconds she shared with the man were alien to anyone else, and they were all now dust and memories. While I knew Peter as he had been before he became a grown man, and understood what civilization and education had done to him, I really didn't *know* him as she did, and never could.

I tried again. In reality, I felt my sleepiness tugging at me, wanting me to wrap this conversation up, since I saw no point to it other than to give Cecelia someone to cry with. And I honestly didn't feel like crying. My brother, if he were still alive, would have thought this silliness. *Just get over it*, I could hear him say.

"Cam, I need you to do something for me. Would you?"

"What do you need?"

"I need you to do *him*."

"I'm sorry?"

"I need you to *do* him. *His voice*," she said.

"His voice?"

"I need you to imitate Peter. I need you to sound like him." It didn't help that she started that breathing thing again, faster and more intensely, all the time her breaths rushing in my ear.

"Do his voice," I repeated.

"Remember, back at Christmas? We were all sitting around having coffee and you started mimicking him? Remember?"

"Cecelia, I don't..."

"Cam, you're the only one who can do this. *Now*, I mean."

It had been a game. It's hard to talk about this now, coldly and objectively, as so much has happened since. One of the stupid vain things I used to silently pride myself on — before it ever became a tangible outward portion of my life, came to dominate my every move — was my ability to mimic people. And I was nothing compared to my brother. One of our games at Christmas was to imitate actors from old movies — not the matinee idols but the bit players who flitted from John Wayne to Clark Gable to Humphrey Bogart pictures for a steady studio paycheck and appeared in hundreds of movies. Both of us could do the stars, and do them well, but the trick was to do the smaller players, and do them so well it would be obvious which one was Walter Brennan and which one was Ward Bond. Anyone can do Elvis, from the rumble and mumble and menace to the hips and lips and shuffle, but can just anyone approximate the nervous laughter in Jim Backus' eyebrows? Or recite Edward G. Robinson's actuarial tables speech from "Double Indemnity," note-perfect in his unmistakable voice? Or John Marley's staccato Italian denigrations from "The Godfather?" We placed gargantuan value on these absurd talents, and we entertained each other through our teenage years and beyond as though we had spun straw into gold.

I was good, but everyone agreed Peter was much better. The reason he was better, and the reason I envied him bitterly but would never tell him, was that Peter could improvise with the voices, act out the parts, have just the right gestures, and have the voices speak things they had never said in the movies. He could run rings around me without ever rehearsing any of his routines. I had a few things on Peter though, since I am — was — about 75 pounds lighter. Thin people can approximate fat, but weight is much harder to shed for an impersonation. Close your eyes though, and Peter was undeniable.

And since this little gift of ours turned into my life's work, I still treasure the piece of advice my brother gave me. I noticed early on the gift Peter had, so one day, I just brazenly asked him what the secret was. I felt like there was some kind of alchemy that Peter might not be willing to let go of.

Instead, he spit it right out. "To do somebody, you have to realize that some of you is going to come out anyway," Peter said. One thing he had a gift for, even as a teenager, was the ability to sound like someone many years past his education. It served him well as a salesman. "If you listen to an impersonator, one of those guys on TV, and you listen like you want to pick it apart, you're going to realize after a short time that it's really *their* voice, not the person they're imitating. Some things you can't mask. You have to hit the audience right from the beginning with something really close, and then they'll accept you as whoever you're supposed to be the rest of the way."

At Christmas, after watching Peter do voice after voice without practice, entertaining them all, I decided to upstage him. I stood up, grabbed a pillow and shoved it in my shirt.

"He's going to do Marlon Brando," Peter said. "Or Orson Welles." That only made it better. *My brother*, I thought. *You'll never forget this day.*

I opened my mouth and gave the family fifteen minutes of my brother, remembering from the first breath his vocal tic of saying, "Hey, hey..." when he wanted to get the attention of everyone at the dinner table. I then remembered something Cecelia had said earlier in the day about how Peter was a master at losing his car keys. I remembered that too, from his teenage years. Peter would enter the house with his keys in his hand, put them down somewhere, and immediately forget where they were.

"Hey, hey," I said, opening my mouth and summoning Peter's voice, "anybody seen my keys?" The rest came bundled out of me

and for the first time, I felt myself improvising a brilliant shadow of
my brother, letting the laughter of our family wrap around me. The
best part, the part that warms me even to this day, was the look on
my brother's face. Peter had worn an amused smirk, a pride mixed
with admiration for his younger brother's talent. Suddenly, I think we
both knew that however many voices Peter had done, everyone would
remember *me* doing *him*.

Sitting there in my bed, months later, I couldn't remember what
Cecelia had done that day, other than laugh with the rest of them.
Perhaps louder than anyone else, but it was hard to be sure.

"You want me to..." I said, trying to make sure I understood her
correctly. Of course I did, I just wanted to hear her say it one more
time.

"I wouldn't ask this if I didn't *need* to hear his voice again."

"Are you sure?"

"Cam, I'm afraid. I didn't think it was possible, but he's been
gone and I can't remember what his voice sounded like. It's killing
me. I was sitting here with Ricky and I was thinking about Peter and I
was trying to remember what he used to say to me. But I couldn't ... I
couldn't *hear* him saying the words."

I felt my heart quivering as much as her voice on the other end,
and I became aware of a feeling in the air, as though a presence had
entered the room.

"Please, I feel so horrible," she said. "I feel unworthy of him. It's
like I've forgotten him."

"No, Cecelia," I said. "That's not it. Your brain's fried. You're not
sleeping, you can't think straight, and you're just worn out with grief.
And it's late now and you're desperate."

"It wasn't supposed to be like this, Cam," she said. "He wasn't
supposed to..."

"I know."

"Please. Do him."

"Cecelia."

"Do it for *me*." The words unsettled me. There was a hunger in
the voice, something that I didn't recognize, but I had the feeling that

Peter, if he were still alive, would have. The husky way she said the four words had a familiarity about them reaching out for a slumbering intimacy that was not supposed to reawaken.

"What should I say?" I asked the words, not even sure if I would do this. I felt like I could, and maybe should, just for a moment, just to send her off to sleep. Just to get her through another night.

"Just talk to me like Peter would have."

"What would he have said?"

She let out a sniffle. "Sometimes I tell myself that he's not really dead. That's he's in another town on business. It's just that his plane is late and he hasn't gotten to his hotel yet. He used to do that. He used to call me, no matter how late it was. Could you do that?"

"You mean act like it's late..."

"Yeah. Just hang up and call me back like you've just gotten in."

"That's all?"

"That's all. Could you do just that?"

I paused for a second. Even before I opened my mouth, I could hear my brother's voice already, in my mind. *Don't you think this is sort of like ...cheating, Cam?*

I felt myself responding: She's lonely, Peter. You're not here. Somebody's got to be there for her.

Yeah, but it can't be me.

Why not?

"Listen, Cecelia, before I do this, I have to ask one thing. You're not going to try to keep me... I mean him... on the line? I mean, even if it sounds like Peter, it's not really him. You know?"

"I know. I know. I just need to remember."

"Okay."

"You'll do it?"

"Yeah."

"Oh, thank you," she said, her voice convulsing into sobs again. I waited for her to calm down, wondering just how I might go about this.

"You okay now?"

18

"Yes, yes," she said, sniffing again and taking a breath, as though to compose herself. "You hang up and then call me right back and do it, okay?"

"Cecelia..."

"Yes?"

"Was there anything Peter used to call you, when he called, I mean?" I could feel myself warming to the idea, taking it like a challenge. How far could I take a voice and make someone dead come alive again, and yet fool that person's most intimate connection? I even felt, once again, that pride in knowing I could do it, and with a little detail added in, could make it flawless.

Cam, do you really need to do that to me?

"Oh," she said, as though she might break again but forced herself not to. "Oh, yes. He would call me Beauty."

I shifted in the bed. I felt as though I was trying on my brother's ill-fitting clothes.

No. It felt like I was breaking into my brother's home.

"How did he say it? Did he say it cheery or..."

"He would say it slowly," she said, drawing the word out herself. Cecelia's voice was low and throaty, scratchy after hours of crying, and sounded nothing like her dead husband's, but I knew what she meant. It was just as I had suspected.

"Okay," I said, and hung up without another word. I got up from my bed and walked to the bathroom, splashing cold water on my face. I looked up into the mirror and saw the outlines of my face in the twilight. For some reason, I didn't look anything like my brother at that moment.

My breathing was shallow. That's good, I remember thinking. Peter was a big man who breathed heavy just walking across the room. It would add to the realism.

Again, I had that strange feeling. Hard to say what it was. *Unclean.* That's how I felt. Unclean.

I picked up the phone and dialed without trying to think too much about it.

3

A little more than twenty-four hours after my interview, I was
in church. I dressed in the same suit I wore to Prescott's office,
acting in much the same way in that pew as I did waiting in the outer
office before my interview. It is strange, strange indeed, that I felt
as though I was being watched. Personally watched, that is, though
not by Prescott, nor by the minister. I looked around for Prescott
and couldn't find him, not in the choir or what I could see of the
balcony. That surprised me, but I also didn't see Mr. Forster, or what I
remembered he looked like from pictures I had seen.

I found a seat midway up the pews facing the left side of the
pulpit, stood for every hymn, sang the words even though I was
unfamiliar with the tunes, placed money in the collection plate, bowed
my head for every prayer, and clapped when the choir finished its
music. There were several very uncomfortable moments for me, not
necessarily for what was being said, but when I was forced, I felt, to
interact with the people around me. The music minister encouraged
the congregation to shake hands and welcome each other, and I found

several hands thrust in my face, coaxing me. This happened several times. People smiled and I was compelled to smile back, however insincerely. It seemed there was one of these moments at every stop along the way to the sermon. What little I knew of Protestant worship, and I knew extremely little, convinced me that the whole service was laid out much in the same way as a show, with the sermon being saved for the end, like the big finale.

It was Easter Sunday. The minister's name I have forgotten. He wasn't the usual preacher, who I learned later was somewhere else. This guy was good. His voice trembled in all the right places. He held his Bible aloft at times for effect and pounded the lectern with his fist, I supposed, when he sensed he was losing the crowd. His sermon, as I recall, was about love. I didn't listen to it all that much. I looked at him, but I didn't see him or hear what he was talking about most of the time.

I saw Cecelia, and I heard Peter.

"Peter?" When I had called her back, she picked up the phone and desperately shouted the name at me. It was a reminder, I understood. A threat. *You have promised me you will be my husband, my dead husband. You will not break this promise to me. You will be Peter. Now, be Peter.*

I had cleared my throat before I picked up the phone so all she must have heard before I began was the short, sighing breath I let out before I gave myself up to my brother. "Hey, Beauty," I heard him say. "I'm here. I just wanted you to know everything's fine."

"Everything's fine..." she repeated, in a child's voice, as though every wish she had ever had in life was being satisfied at that moment. "Are you...?"

"I'm okay. They got me a nice room and everything's fine. I'm a little tired. How are you?"

She sniffled. "Oh, baby, I'm so, so tired."

"Well, get you some sleep. Is Ricky okay?" I thought I would need to do this, to remind her of the boy. *Transfer some of this to the boy, okay? You can't keep holding on to me.*

There was something strange about that moment. Not the

telephone conversation, I mean. That *was* strange, more, much more than strange. No, I mean the sermon. Just as I was remembering what we had said, or what *he* had said to her, I suddenly heard the minister speaking of Jesus. It was a story I had never heard before, of how the risen Jesus, fresh from his tomb, was encountered by Mary Magdalene. She was overwrought with anguish and when she realized that he was alive, she wanted to embrace Him.

The minister said that most translations have Jesus say to her, "Touch me not." However, he said it should read something more like, "Don't cling to me." In other words, *You can't keep physically holding on to me forever. One of these days, I will be somewhere else.* If I had not been sitting in a church, I would have been very satisfied to say it was a coincidence that the resurrected Jesus and my resurrected Peter should say roughly the same thing. But events in such settings speak with a different voice, and the menace of the random seems much more exacting when it feels guided by some great, hidden hand.

"Let me tell you something, baby," she said. There was a pause that seemed to me like a razor blade severing my spine. "I'll be waiting for you when you come back."

I shook my head. I wasn't going to break character, but somehow I knew she would do this. For some reason, I wasn't as scared of this as I should have been. "No, Beauty. You need your rest. You need to go to sleep."

"But how can I sleep when you're not here?"

"I'm still there," I said. "You've still got me. You don't need to hear my voice to know what I'm saying."

"Oh, but I do. You have no idea."

"Yes, I do. It's hard for me too, being apart like this."

I could hear her make a sort of wounded sound, an open-mouthed utterance that startled me with its depth. It was as if she hadn't considered such a thing possible, as though Peter had left town with someone for the weekend and hadn't given a thought to his family. The idea that he might be pining away for her as much as she for him seemed never to have occurred to her.

This was what upset me most of all. It was bad enough that I was doing my brother's voice. With every syllable, I felt myself missing him more because he wasn't there to hear how well I was doing the job. I felt a satisfying warmth pass over me when I said the words "hard for me too," because I nailed the way Peter would have bitten off the end of the word "for" and exaggerated the word "too." Thinking again on it, sitting in the church, I couldn't escape how wrong it seemed at the time, and how much worse it felt in retrospect.

"Oh, baby," she said. "I'm so, so sorry."

I cleared my throat. This was too much. I had to end it. "Don't think about me. Think about yourself. Get some sleep. When you wake up tomorrow, it'll be a new day."

I heard nothing, but I assumed she was nodding her head in obedience.

"And know that wherever I am, I'm thinking about you."

Her voice collapsed. "Peter, I love you so much." Her voice shook and shattered under the sobs.

"It's alright," I said. I could say it, as Peter. She would accept it. "It's alright." This kept on for a few minutes until the line was silent. I was unsure what to do next. Cecelia didn't say anything, and I wondered what had happened. Finally, I heard something, a rustle that I didn't recognize. Then another. Then a noticeable gap in time, and another. I realized she was snoring. She was asleep. I hung up the phone, went to the bathroom, and threw up.

I could still hear the sound of that too, sitting in the church. And I remember feeling alone when I hung up the phone, and before I hung it up. It wasn't like I had Peter on my shoulder or whispering in my ear. He was dead, and somehow, he was more dead because I was trying to make him live, for whatever reason. The fact that I thought I was helping his wife cope for just a few minutes was no consolation at all. I felt unapproachable because of this, that no one could understand what I had done. I couldn't explain it, not even to Cecelia. In the days since that conversation, I had had terrible daydreams of her having swallowed sleeping pills and being dead in her bedroom, my having facilitated her departure from the world. When I didn't hear anything, like a news report or a call from someone who knew her, I supposed all was well. But I still shook every time the phone rang. Not long after I got off the phone with her that night, it rang again. I hesitated picking it up, not sure who I was supposed to answer as. It was a telemarketer, asking me if I needed protection from unauthorized credit card charges.

"Do you know what time it is?" I asked.

The person on the other end, who sounded as though he was calling from another country, guessed. He was wrong. I told him.

"I'm so sorry, sir," he said, through thickly accented English.

"Just be careful when you call here at this hour," I said. Then I added, "You're liable to wake up the dead."

So I could understand someone saying he didn't want to be touched, or someone telling a loved one not to cling to him. And when they got to that part of the service where the minister invites anyone who wants to come and kneel and ask God's forgiveness, I did what I had already resolved to do in Prescott's office. I got up, walked down, and quietly and deliberately joined the church. I said everything that was required of me, bowed my head during the prayer, and smiled when it was over. And that is where it all began. Because whatever it was that Prescott had told me I needed to do, I had convinced them all I had done it, and somehow I had accomplished this *without* doing it. I gave them my body, but I did not give my heart. I joined the church, but the body of Christ, however constituted, did not include me.

I don't want you to get the impression that I was some vapid idiot who didn't quite know what he was getting into. At that time, I believed I lived in a world that was built on the foundations of Rome, Athens and Jerusalem, but those foundations were long built over with new pillars from Marx, Darwin and Freud, imperfect oracles though they were.

I lived in a world of class struggle where thinking beings driven by their own internal urges are involved in a struggle that propels history forward. Nothing but impersonal forces catapult us ahead in time throughout our lives. Not toward some irresistible destiny or grand theological narrative, but only in the pursuit of our own selfish urges. A vast boiling cauldron that we choose to give names to, like destiny or providence or karma, but which, in reality, is nothing more than *nothing* — nothing on a vast scale. So you can see that what I did was merely ceremonial, or at least, I told myself this. Yet, in the years to come, whatever I believed about the world and myself and the faith that somehow called me its own on that day were only partially understood, if at all.

So you see, when I was talking with Prescott that day, my naiveté about that "Jesus guy" was as much a pose as everything that followed. It was me having fun at the expense of a 2,000-year-old religion and the absurdity of someone holding out the carrot of a job in hopes that I would chase the stick of salvation. I had looked at Prescott and the very neat way he tugged at the knees of his pants legs when he sat down in his office and beheld him with undisguised contempt. If nothing else, joining Forster's church might allow me a chance to eventually usurp his little lackey and his capitalistic evangelism. And if I did, at least Prescott would still have his salvation if not his employment.

"See you first thing Monday," Prescott said, when I finally encountered him, shaking my hand in the sanctuary, a proud smile on his face that seemed to say, *I knew you'd come through*. I nodded my head and returned the smile and tried not to laugh at how absurd the whole thing felt. In spite of my defiance, I willingly signed up to give to the church through my credit card on a weekly basis.

Mr. Henry David Thoreau advised that one should go confidently in the direction of his dreams and live the life he has imagined. Through that prism, I simply saw whatever life — temporary life — I had with this church to be a means to an end. I wouldn't be there long. Of course, I had so totally managed to misread my own actions, deluding myself into thinking I was going in the direction of my dreams, even though my movements were hardly confident.

I know all the pseudo-psychological explanations for why I walked down the church aisle. It's not enough to say I was depressed about my brother's death and the fresh wound that it was, or my complicity in his "resurrection" with his wife, however long and tawdry it might have later been. Yes, I was troubled by those things, naturally. But as Mr. Wilhelm Friedrich Hegel said, the real is rational and the rational is real. There was something else altogether that made me seek out that church beyond the logic that if I did, I had a job.

The truth is, I was being stalked. When I had fulfilled all the obligations of the church, giving them my name and address and being assured that whatever prayer needs I had would be theirs, I was asked to stand while the congregation was told my name. Then I stood and once again shook hands with each person in a long line, who all promised they would help me in my new walk with God. I smiled and nodded and thanked them, each handshake growing more and more painful given that I was once again being asked to have contact with another person, and yet another, and still another. They all smiled, they didn't suspect a thing of me, other than that my profession was genuine and that I belonged among them. How could they understand? After all, they had been stalked too, but that was in the past. They had been overtaken, and somehow, they had all made their peace with it.

Of course, to be pursued, there must be a *Pursuer*. I didn't believe that then.

4

There is a rule that eighty percent of what is done in a church is done by twenty percent of the people who attend it. Most church goers repeat this without realizing the rule is true for the rest of the world as well. It didn't take very long for me to realize that Prescott, my boss, was one of the twenty percent.

When Prescott spoke to anyone, he had the habit of standing with his hands in his pockets, one leg thrust forward like an Egyptian temple idol. He would then rock back and forth on that leg, which gave him the impression of a pendulum swinging your way. It also gave one the feeling that whatever he was about to say was being communicated with a maniacal sense of absolute concern. In the whole time I knew him, I kept waiting for him to just blink. His stare had a way of transfixing you. And yet, I never felt as though he was actually looking at me the whole time. He had a curious way of avoiding eye contact without seeming to do so.

"Cameron," he said. He had by that first day discarded whatever informality we adopted during the interview. "Cameron, I've got a job for you." It didn't take long for me to realize that if I was to be a success at this job, I too would have to join the overworked twenty percent of both the foundation and the church. "Need you to jump in the bus and go deliver a shipment to the food pantry. Food's already loaded."

"Food pantry?"

"Community food bank. Donated food in bulk for the homeless and working poor." He said "working poor" like I'd heard politicians say the words.

"Where's that?" I asked.

He told me. "They may ask you to drive the food out to some shut ins. It's something we do pretty regularly around here."

"Is this foundation or church work?"

"Strictly speaking, it's both." The question seemed to make him uncomfortable.

"How long will it take?" I had the feeling I was being drafted to do a job that Prescott would normally have done himself.

"Could be all day. Something wrong?"

"Not at all. I just wondered about this..." I held up the papers he had given me to work on.

"Don't worry about that," he said. "I'll take care of the paperwork. One thing about this job is that you'll have to improvise a lot. We do a great deal of our work on the fly. Is that a problem? Do you like a lot of structure?"

"I suppose I expected this."

"Splendid," he said. "All part of serving that 'Jesus guy.'" He said the words and waited for a response from me. I smiled but didn't rise to his mocking challenge. I suspected that if there was a probationary period to the job, I was in the midst of it. Somehow I had the feeling that with Prescott, that period might be everlasting. "Mr. Forster likes people who can improvise."

Prescott smiled and wiped the corner of his right eye with his pinky. He then handed me a sheet of paper with printed instructions as to where I could pick up the bus he mentioned.

"Does he come around here often? Mr. Forster, I mean?"

"Hardly ever. Most of the people who work for him, I would

imagine, have never seen him. Or, I should say, aren't aware that they've seen him."

What did that mean? I wondered. "So you've seen him?"

"Oh, yes," Prescott said. "He's the one who hired me. Not too long ago, he came in here every day to make sure everything was done exactly as he wanted. Then one day, without warning, he came in, called a meeting, pointed to me and told everyone that if they spoke to me it was as good as speaking to him, and then he was gone. Hasn't been back since."

"Why is that?"

"I'm not supposed to say, really. Let me just put it this way — Mr. Forster is a man who appreciates what human contact can do to others, both good and bad."

Somehow Prescott's earlier statement was more revealing than this one. I had visions of Howard Hughes opening door knobs with Kleenex tucked between his fingers, panicked that he might brush up against a stray germ. "Is it some kind of compulsion?"

"Don't worry about that, Cameron. Just go about your business."

And so, I jumped in the bus — a nice, modern, air-conditioned thing with tinted windows, the sort that might shuttle passengers between airports in a big city — and found cartons and cases of food. I smelled fresh fruit and produce and heard coolers of meat knock against each other when I took sharp corners too fast. At the end of the directions was a warehouse with no signs to indicate it was the community food bank, save a few men standing outside, as though born to unload boxes from passing trucks. They looked like they had been expecting me. I stepped from the bus and the men muscled their way past me to get at the work.

"Mr. Prescott," said a man walking up to shake my hand. "I'm Gordon Marvell. Good to see you again." He was a black man with a large mouth and long, searching fingers. I took his offered hand without correcting him. "We thought you'd be here a little sooner."

"Sorry, I didn't quite know the way." That was a subtle opening, I felt, to let him know I wasn't Prescott without embarrassing him.

"Even though you've been here before?" He wasn't getting my

point.

I opened my mouth to speak up when Gordon grabbed the shoulders of a man who came ambling up. "Okay, Jimmy. You can go too." The man — Jimmy, I assumed — was shaking about the arms and kept his mouth open. In a glance I summed him up as mentally retarded in some way, and his only response was a series of low moans. "You know Mr. Prescott, don't you?" Gordon pointed to me.

I traded a glance with Jimmy just long enough to know that Jimmy understood at least that I was not Prescott, and I thought I perceived a smile on Jimmy's face, knowing and sly.

"Jimmy's alright. He rides with us now and then. He's real good with his hands." One of Jimmy's arms curled up against his chest, the fingers splayed in every direction. I tried not to look at it. Gordon reached a hand out toward me. "You got the sheet?" I assumed he meant the one Prescott had handed to me, so I gave it to him. He put it on a clipboard he was holding in his right hand and began checking off boxes on the sheet as boxes came out of the bus.

"You been alright, Mr. Prescott?" he asked.

"Yeah," I said. By this time, I had just accepted my new name, if only the moment.

"I'll tell you what. I don't know what we'd do if we didn't you looking out for us. It sure means a lot."

"Don't mention it. It's nothing," I said, which for me at least was the truth.

"May take us awhile today. We've got the deliveries to the nursing home and the shelter and we're supposed to run some by the shut-ins."

I tried to imagine what the day would hold.

"The shut-ins are always something. They mention Jesus like He just stopped by a few minutes before we got there." Gordon shook his head. "Could be a long day."

"That's alright," I said. "As long as it takes."

Gordon smiled, continued to check off his list, and I paused long enough to realize I was standing, just like Prescott, with both of my hands in my pockets, rocking back and forth. And for some reason, Jimmy looked as though he was laughing at me.

5

He probably was. An hour later, I was sponging off a man I'd never met at a nursing home so he could eat the food we had brought.

Perhaps I'd better back up and explain. We brought the food boxes inside the building, taking about half an hour to get everything in that had been scheduled for delivery. I had never been in a shelter before. People in clothes that were dirty yet faded from repeated washings met me at the door and gave me vivid, bucktoothed smiles for bringing the food. On a cheap, simulated wood paneled wall the face of Jesus stared back from a dime store tapestry. A man with matted hair and several days of beard nodded at me from a table where he was playing cards with another man in a ballcap. I shook several hands coming in and out, people assuming my suit meant some sort of importance. They shook my hand with the tatters of their own dignity showing, as though I might offer them some way out of their individual fixes.

I was conscious of the fact that I had never moved among these kinds of people before. I felt pity and a lingering fear of someone

BRILLIANT DISGUISES

stealing my wallet. I felt shame at the mixture of fascination and embarrassment at being among them. The gentleman with the cards asked me to referee a disagreement. I looked at my watch and politely declined.

Gordon directed me to drive the bus with its remaining supplies north of town to a nursing home I had heard of but never actually seen before. Actually, I wasn't sure how I had ever heard of it, but there it was, a little campus tucked in some towering thin pine trees, waiting for the food we were delivering through the courtesy of the mysterious Mr. Forster. The bus was filled with smells that I guessed were roast beef, gravy, and broccoli, or some similar species of eatable. The scent was overpowering and not at all appetizing. I didn't stop to consider that I was delivering food to people who had little choice but to eat it. If I had, I might have wondered just what kind of gift I was involved in giving, and whether they would have considered it a gift at all worth having. No, that day I wasn't thinking about any of those things as much as simply learning to do a job that had very little apparent logic.

I should point out that neither the good people of the Forster Foundation nor my accomplices in feeding that day were probably students of the Darwinian theory of evolution through natural selection. At least, not like myself. Now, it is not my intention to begin some sort of discussion about whether it's just a theory. I will only point out one very tiny portion of that theory — the field of mimicry.

A mimic is a species that evolves to appear similar to another species or to that species' environment. The mimic does this in order to deceive predators, or to lure prey in unawares. A mimic can do this through appearance, habitat, or behavior. Now, mimicry is different from camouflage. A mimic is not trying to blend in with the surroundings. It is trying to appear as something it is not.

I mention all of this in light of what happened when we arrived at our destination. When I brought the bus to a stop outside the home, Gordon and Jimmy and I began unloading the food, already prepared in trays and ready for serving. A nurse greeted me at the door once

32

again as Mr. Prescott, and began taking trays as we went back for more. In the space of a few minutes, we had dropped off more than fifty. The nurse then wordlessly escorted me down the hall and into a room, where I saw an elderly man, sitting fully naked in a tub of milky water, apparently insensible.

"Just stand here while I get his bath done," she said. She was a very large black woman with fat fingers and a commanding voice that would compel me to follow her every wish. I had no idea what she wanted me to do other than witness this man's most vulnerable moment. He seemed unaware of what was going on, barely moving as she strained a washcloth over his back.

He had a face of varying shades, pale around the cheeks but livid red in the ears, which fairly glowed. His hair, short and spiky, was white at the temples but darkening to an almost black shade further up the head. He was one of those men who looks as though he stays in a hard sweat even when he is clean and dry. The hair on his forehead was thinning and non-existent in some places. His eyes were cloudy under bushy, craggy eyebrows, pointed at some indeterminate point just above his head, like a saint poised in the middle of a vision. His mouth trembled open, quivering like a tuning fork. His hands lay, with palms splayed out from his body, useless on either side, the arms bunched up at awkward angles. The tips of his feet peeked out from beneath the water as though it was a short blanket covering his legs. There were liver spots, blemishes, marks of many kinds over him. He made no sound, but others in other rooms were making up for his silence. I heard screeches, coughs, calls for help and conversations straining over another's aging deafness. One man let out a strangled, two-second wordless cry that was repeated with the regularity of a clock. Every four seconds, the same sound, as though programmed. I wondered if some needle in his brain might be skipping, and what it was catching on. One room we had passed had a woman talking animatedly to one corner of her room, where no one at all was sitting. I wondered what conversation she was reliving, and in what departed era the interlocutor might be found.

Regardless of what was going on elsewhere, I was caught. I should have said very early on that my name was not Prescott, that it had never been, and that whatever Prescott was expected to do, I could not do it. But I was embarrassed. I hadn't said anything yet up to this point, so I wasn't sure if part of my job was simply being Prescott's surrogate.

The nurse began chatting on about something, and I wasn't quite sure if she was talking to me or her patient. If the tone was any judge, it was the patient, who made no movement unless she pushed him forward or back. I had no reason for thinking so, but I had the impression that the man was capable of more. He simply would not engage himself. It was as if he was storing up whatever energy still lay within his body, ravaged by time and, it seemed, disease. I thought perhaps that part of Prescott's job had been listening to this nurse.

"Gotta get you out of here," she said. "Your food is here. Mr. Prescott made sure of that." She smiled at me as though passing on a blessing, if improperly aimed. "Nothing like a nice meal after a bath."

"Wish I had one," I said. I must have realized that I had suddenly developed the habit of saying things I didn't mean to fill the air. I had no such wish to have a bath nor eat any of the food that still filled my nostrils with its unpalatable odor.

The nurse smiled and nodded. Did she understand that I wasn't saying anything worth listening to, or was she amused at how ridiculously awkward the whole thing was? If so, she had to enjoy the next instant, when the door opened behind me and a woman told the nurse there was a call for her. And then, she uttered two words I should have expected.

"Take over," she said, handing me the sponge on the way out the door. By the time the door shut behind her, I was aware of what she said.

The soap's aroma was overpowering, but I could still smell a persistent odor which I guessed was this man, who was now suddenly *my* patient. I supposed it was the smell of old age, but was more or less comparable to a strong cleanser masking a rotting smell. The man coughed and it startled me.

So, I supposed I was just to stand there, holding a dripping sponge as I did, holding it out and away from me like a match that was burning down to the nub. I was fully prepared to do so, until the nurse stuck her head back in. I felt her hand pushing against my shoulder blade. "Go ahead," she said. "He needs to get out to eat."

I was fully prepared to feed him, frankly, just not bathe him. It made me wonder if Prescott had done something to earn this dubious honor, and by stepping into his shoes, I was sharing in whatever punishment was being called down on him. I was aware that Forster was funding food pantries the world over, relief efforts in the Far East, reconciliation programs in the Middle East, missionaries the world over. I was willing to walk to Africa from my present spot, so long as I did not have to bathe this sick, pathetic man.

I heard the sound of water descending down the sponge, off his back and into the tub. Somehow that calmed me from various impulses of outrage, revulsion, and fear. Because by that time I realized I was standing behind this man, and I was giving him a bath.

I kept searching for some line of reasoning to keep my mind elsewhere. I was simply doing what someone, somewhere expected of me in this job. What I could not tell at that moment, what would bear scrutiny in years to come, was whether I was a Batesian mimic or a Vavilovian mimic.

Batesian mimics, named after Henry Walter Bates, resemble a successful species but do not share some of its attributes. For example, the False Cobra, which has the Indian Cobra's distinctive hood when threatened, but is only mildly venomous and essentially harmless. There is also the Ash Borer Moth, which resembles a wasp but does not sting. Female Congo Peafowls, strangely enough, can mimic venomous Bush Vipers by rattling their quills and hissing.

Now Vavilovian mimics, which are named after Nikolai Ivanovich Vavilov, are plants resembling a domesticated plant, and may over time, become domesticated themselves. There is a species of grass which looks like rice and its seeds are often hard to separate from rice. Weedings over successive generations only make it harder for this grass to be taken away. The solution, I came to learn, is to allow both to grow together until the harvest, as Someone once said.

"So how did we end up like this?" I asked him, not expecting an answer. Yet I heard one in my head. A voice I did not recognize, one I could have come up with on my own, the sort I might have imagined coming out of this man's face.

Sorry. I hadn't expected to wind up like this. I could imagine the voice being embarrassed, humbled, trying to preserve even a scrap of dignity through the apology.

"I'm sure," I found myself saying in reply. "Neither did I."

Nobody does. You never see any of this happening to yourself. It doesn't even feel like it's happening now. I just get to watch.

Wish I was as lucky, I thought.

I smiled. I could hear him laughing at me, the two of us sharing a joke without either moving our lips. I don't think I had ever felt anything like that before, not as real as I did in that moment. I felt the great kinship that one is supposed to feel at such times, when one recognizes the bond that exists within every human heart, when we are all part of the tyranny of heartbeats that are not perpetual, bloodstreams that do not flow with quicksilver, and bodies that are powerless before time.

And then, as I dipped the sponge deeply into the water, he let out a grunt and relaxed as the water around my hand turned dark and brown. The smell was so bad that I immediately covered my nose. With the hand that had been in the water.

Which was the moment when the nurse decided to rejoin us.

Whatever pretensions toward the great chain of being I had felt a moment before, they disappeared as I ran for the bathroom, and my erstwhile brother and connection to the human race was once again decidedly on his own. I did not stick around for whatever the nurse wanted to say to Mr. Prescott.

When I did see Prescott again, it was after the bus had pulled into the parking lot at the foundation offices. The smell of the food, I gathered from Gordon, was still very powerful, but that was not what still filled my nostrils. I had the feeling that Gordon and Jimmy were sharing a very muted laugh at my expense, though there was no way they could have known what had happened. Instead, I kept rubbing my nose with the hand I had washed a good twenty times, and still wiping that hand on my clothes, which I was sure I would never wear again.

I stepped out of the bus and Prescott was there to greet me, with the same preposterous smile he wore at the beginning of the day.

"See you tomorrow?" he asked.

He did see me the next day. I put in a full day of work with not a nursing home or food bank in sight. Whether Prescott took pity on me or decided to send me as his surrogate in some other direction, I comforted myself with the idea — that I had no reason to believe — that things could never be worse than that first day. At the end of that first week, I left the office exhausted with Prescott calling after me, "See you in church."

So he had probably seen through me on that little gambit. I had in mind the idea that he had merely wanted me to join the church, and then, if he never saw me again, he would at least know I was on the roll. Perhaps he might see me at Christmas or Easter if I felt the need, but he would at least leave that up to me. But then again, I suppose I was determined to do the job as fully as I was able.

Yeah, I know it doesn't make any sense.

My alarm rang on Sunday morning as though it was another work day. I showered, shaved, and raced through a quick breakfast, as I normally did on any other day. My suit was indistinguishable from the others I wore during the week. I expected to see Prescott when I went through the door. He was not there this time. He hadn't mentioned a trip or anything at the office, but I assumed the agency of the enigmatic Mr. Forster in Prescott's absence.

Strangely enough, when I walked into church, they recognized me. More importantly, they recognized *me* — I was not mistaken for Prescott, but a host of people whose names I had not even an educated guess for called me by name and shook my hand. Within fifteen minutes, my right hand was swollen and I felt as though my name was on a ballot somewhere. A man named Thomas Hagler siddled up to explain to me that I was needed to take up the offering.

"We're a little short," he said, pointing to a squad of men in suits standing nearby. They were either ushers or deacons, and for the day, I was one of their number. They smiled and I shook their hands without thinking, wondering how I would be able to hold a collection plate with throbbing fingers. There seemed enough well-dressed men to get up a well-dressed game of football with a few substitutions.

Hagler was a man shorter than myself with a nice tan and a thinning hairline he disguised with a combover that was noticeable without being appalling. He wore bifocals and had a gold tooth among his molars that gleamed when he smiled, which was often and broadly. He stood during the hymns and swayed on the balls of his feet, fingering a gaudy class ring that looked service academy but easily could have been an artifact of a championship team somewhere.

"Normally, we wouldn't let somebody do this so soon after joining, but you've got people who will vouch for you," Hagler told me.

I gave a modest nod and looked away. A second later a woman walked up to Hagler. He put his arm around her while taking her aside. She appeared to be a woman in her fifties with swirls of gray worked into the blond streaks of her hair. She wore a sleeveless dress and by the way Hagler's finger swirled on her bare shoulder, I assumed they were married. She glanced over long enough for me to realize I was staring at her, and I quickly looked elsewhere.

Hagler got my attention. "This is Rebecca, my better half," he said. She smiled perfunctorily and shifted her hips to appraise me for a moment before returning to the conversation with her husband. I heard enough of the words between them to understand that Rebecca wanted her husband to write a check for her to place in the offering plate. Hagler breathed out an audible, hard sigh, pulled a checkbook from his jacket, and wrote out one in loud pen strokes audible across the church hallway. He tore the check out and handed it to her with a look on his face that pleaded for her to be satisfied. She clattered off atop a pair of stiletto heels. I found myself admiring her legs just as she shot another glance at me. I was once again staring, and felt once again that I had been wordlessly chastised for it. I looked back at Hagler to see him wiping his forehead, mindful of his hair, and relaxing just for a moment. And then, the moment was gone, and he was again tense.

I waited until the music director was supposed to give a signal. I never saw one, and I wouldn't have known it if I had. Instead, I waited for the others to begin walking to the altar and followed them a few paces back, just in case I had gotten it all wrong. During this, Hagler kept arching his shoulders up and down jerkily, like a boxer getting ready for a fight. He drummed his fingers on the plate, and during the prayer as I kept my eyes open, I saw him spinning the plate between his two hands.

I kept my eyes on him for some reason as we made the rounds from pew to pew. I should have been paying attention to the plates, never having done this before. I glanced over the crowd of worshippers, probably eight to nine hundred, but Prescott was nowhere to be seen. I saw Hagler, who stood near me, take up the plate with his wife's check. Unlike others, it was not folded but lay face up, as though inviting the eyes of those who might be wrestling with their own uneasy personal budgets.

It turned out to be easier than I would have assumed. I was conscious not to hot finger the plate and drop the bills, coins, checks and envelopes all over the floor. But I was not the one who eventually did that — it was Hagler. Just as we were coming through the doors back into the receiving hall, Hagler tripped and fell, spilling the contents of his plate all over the floor. I handed mine to one of the other men and began gathering up what I could to help him. While the other men bundled their collections into a bank bag, I saw Hagler take one of the checks and shove it into his jacket pocket. He happened to glance up suspiciously, as if he expected to be caught in the act. Our eyes met and I saw the barest smile pass over his lips. He winked at me, and I gave him what money I had managed to gather up.

I was getting ready to sit down back in the sanctuary, when I felt a hand at my elbow. It was Hagler, who motioned me outside, keeping the same slight smile I had seen a second earlier. I followed him, wondering if we were stepping outside with the expectation that we were beyond the scrutiny of the Almighty.

Hagler looked around, his eyes not meeting mine. "Can I trust you?" he said, never looking at me, his lips barely moving, like a ventriloquist's. The effect was jarring. I almost asked him to repeat himself.

I nodded. "Of course."

"I did that for her sake. Rebecca, I mean."

I nodded again, as though his admission made perfect sense.

"She browbeat me into writing a check without realizing we don't have enough money to cover it. I thought I'd look out for her. You know how it is."

"Sure," I said. I shrugged my shoulders, expecting that to be the end of it. I had even looked back to the doors without taking a step.

"You see," he began, wishing to stop me, "I'm actually, um, very deeply in debt." He coughed. "There's no way Rebecca knows. She shouldn't have to know or care, really, the way I see it. It's my fault, totally." Hagler would have been content with just this explanation, but then I could see the gears of his mind working, trying to anticipate what my reaction would be.

Then, he cleared his throat and his voice took on a correcting tone. "It's nothing like gambling or anything like that, you understand. Just not being very smart with my money. Rebecca's very touchy about it. I think she expects other people to see us by what we give here." I could see that he had assumed I would not understand, or that

I would make some kind of guess about how he had racked up debts. Gambling? Prostitution? Drugs? A second business? Mistress?

"What does..."

"Right. What does it matter? I keep telling her that. Nobody knows what we give anyway, I think I've told her...oh, about five thousand times." He rubbed the back of his neck vigorously, still not looking at me.

"Hey," I said, "it's okay. You don't owe me an explanation. I'm new here."

"I just didn't want you thinking I was stealing or anything like that. You won't say anything?"

"What can I say?" I coughed and rubbed the back of my neck. "You tripped. That's all. Honest accident."

Hagler smiled, his eyes still studiously avoiding mine. I perceived this satisfied him enough that I could move toward the door.

But he sounded as though he needed to add one last thing. "Actually, you know, it hurts me to come to church."

"What do you mean?"

"I don't belong here," he said. "I'm not good enough for this place. Pray for me. *Please*." He turned and went back into the auditorium without looking back at me. The words were so choked and desperate that, without thinking about the fact that I did not pray, I assured him I would. I doubt he even heard me.

Z

My first day on the job aside, I settled quickly into a routine. An office routine allows you to comfort yourself with the lie that nobody will notice you, since you're all doing the same thing. It reminds me of the story of Mr. Kim Philby, the British intelligence officer who worked in deep cover for the Soviets for thirty years, compromised the secrets of America's atomic stockpile, frustrated attempts to take back Albania from the communists, may have indirectly brought about the Berlin blockade, and sold out any number of agents before disappearing behind the Iron Curtain into a haze of vodka and loneliness. His unfaithfulness to his country was mirrored in his private life as he leaped into beds with the spouses of his betrayed friends. By his checkered career, he inspired any number of spy thrillers, usually as the man who does his job too well for too long and finally gets caught.

He said to betray, you must first belong.

Each day, before any paper or activity was dispatched, we had prayer. Each of the staff members folded themselves into a conference room just big enough to accommodate a table which could barely accommodate all of us. There were about twelve most mornings, which made me snicker. I expected that Forster himself would have made us the equivalent of the Last Supper, but he was always absent. We sat at the table and held hands. I was uncomfortable with this at first because I have sweaty palms. As I came to discover, practically everyone else in the office did as well so it was no incriminating mark. The whole thing reminded me of a spiritualist séance. It was a few days before I realized the room did not have a window, so once the door shut, we were all unconscious of what might be going on far from our prayers. One day, as my mind wandered, I was seized by the absurd fear that our prayers might somehow be stuck inside the room, with no way out until we opened the door. Did that mean they might evaporate?

This might tell you how little acquainted I was with the notion of prayer, beyond the dusting one receives from watching television or knowing that somewhere, someone is still praying, just as somewhere in the world, someone is still unaware that there are electric lights. That is who I was, even this late in the game. When I heard that we began every morning with prayer, my first thought was something akin to what they do in Middle Eastern countries, with whatever refinements Prescott might conjure up. We would be brought into a room and judged on how deeply we bowed or if we bent low and kissed the ground or some similar public act of devotion. But no — these morning supplications were practically twelve-step material: We were bringing it "all out into the open," sharing what was on our mind with each other, and presumably, with God.

I noticed a few things after awhile. Prescott would begin these prayers by asking everyone to take up hands and bow their heads. He would say it every morning as though we had forgotten the routine in the intervening hours. Then, he would always begin the prayer by addressing the Almighty as *"Dear Lord"* in a rasp before clearing his throat. At first, it struck me that it sounded like the greeting one writes at the beginning of a letter. It took perhaps two weeks of listening to this before I realized that each time he said it, I had the same thought. I began feeling a sting of guilt. The man was praying, I told myself. What right did I have to make fun of him?

I'm not making fun of him, I assured myself. It's merely an observation.

Yes, but why so much glee in that observation?

There were other things as well. Dean Pinker, the guy in charge of the foundation's counseling section, would always ask, in a noticeably loud voice, that God watch out for "our leadership, and the skills you have given Mr. Prescott." He would go on to ask that "you wrap your enfolding arms around him, to comfort and strengthen him." It was a nice phrase I thought, the first time I heard it. By the fifteenth day when I heard it repeated for the fifteenth time, I was convinced it was too good a phrase for him to have taken up on his own, and therefore he must have heard it in someone else's prayer and taken it for himself. Did the phrase really mean anything, or did Melissa Garvey's "we give you praise and honor?" Perhaps she too had done the same thing, her comforting line stolen from some other source. I wondered if stolen was too harsh a word for something like that. Appropriated, perhaps? Did she get that from her ex-husband, whose divorce kept her from coming into work some days until Prescott personally went out to make sure she was okay? I doubted it, but I wondered how she could praise God at that time in her life. Dean had his own phrases that he kept returning to, so that at a moment's notice, he could string together a prayer with the right rhythms which made no sense, or left an unintended meaning, such as the time he said, in a clear, crisp voice, "We thank you Lord for our many sins." I assumed he meant to thank God for forgiving those sins instead of somehow savoring them.

Then, there was Carl Lucas. He was one of the department heads in charge of transportation for needy families. It took me awhile before I understood that I could open at least one eye during the prayer and see who was saying what. In Carl's case, his voice was more forceful during his prayers. His face would sometimes get red, and I noticed him grasping the hands of those on either side of him with almost vindictive strength, as though he would get God's attention if he pulled hard enough. A couple of times, I noticed Connie Lovell, one of those who sometimes sat next to him, wincing as his voice shot up. He was crushing her hand without realizing it. At first I thought it happened randomly, then I understood. It came each time he said one word: *Jesus.*

It took me awhile to understand that Carl was breaking some kind of etiquette. Each of those who chose to pray would usually do it quickly, in a low voice, and like Pinker, using a few familiar phrases to speed things along. They would also couch their phrases in some kind of polite language, such as Connie's practice of addressing the Almighty as "Father God," and saying the phrase over and over when she was obviously stuck and couldn't think of what else to say. One might liken it to a form of stage fright — she, and the others, were aware that they were talking to God but that others were listening.

But Lucas seemed to be flouting those conventions. He said the word *Jesus* as though there was some scandal attached to the name. And he lingered over the word, drawing the first vowel out until the vibrations snaked down your spine. I wondered if he was trying to wake them up, get them to make up their own prayers, or merely drawing attention to himself by the quality of his words or the volume of his voice.

As with Prescott's salutation, I felt bad noticing these things. They sounded ungenerous, and hypercritical. And there was my own silence in these matters. I wasn't the only one. Si Gelb was one of Forster's long-time friends and the only higher up excused from the prayer sessions because of their unquestionably Christian nature. Si, being the loveably deadpan scamp that he was, would usually make some comment before departing about putting a good word in with "the Lord" for him. The invisible quotation marks were palpable in his speech. He had a thinning hairline and large hands that swallowed others whole when he reached out to shake them. He ran triathlons and his suit barely concealed a body that would have looked at home in either Olympus or Eden, had he believed in either. Si's presence among us was a source of wonder to me, for what it said about our unseen benefactor. I wondered why I had been coerced into a profession of faith, and not him. It at least provided a side to Forster that intrigued me, given Gelb's polite yet forceful humanism.

Prescott had told me before that there was no mandate that one had to pray at these sessions, and I didn't have the usual things to ask for. Besides, I was afraid that this was one way they'd smoke me out — discover that my presence among them was alien and unacceptable. In some ways, I expected that I was not alone — that others were probably posing as much as I. But I hadn't yet found any evidence. And I could not address a prayer to a presence I still did not believe in. It would have felt silly for a number of reasons.

Chief among them was the intimate nature of the whole enterprise. Before long, I knew more about these people from their prayers than I ever gleaned from any conversation I had with them. Gordon Marvell, for example, had a teenage boy with a learning disability. I got the impression that it somehow was a blow to his pride that his son was having trouble reading — and that he interpreted this as his own fault, as though the boy had inherited something from his father that was holding him back. And when Melissa prayed for her husband, it led me to believe that there was more than a hint or two of trouble in their marriage. I wondered if I might be reading too much into these simple requests. If I ever brought anything more than my own borrowed, shopworn phrases, others might be tempted to get between *my* ears.

By this time, though, Prescott realized that I was not contributing.

"Something wrong?" he asked me one morning, taking me aside before we went in. "You don't feel comfortable praying yet?"

I bobbed my head slightly as though he was taking a swing at me. "I'm not a very good speaker."

"Don't worry. The Lord knows what your needs are before you ask Him. Jesus said that."

"Yeah," I said, feigning that I already knew this.

"Just let it come out," he said. "Nobody's taking notes."

Sure, I thought.

What troubled me about this observation, more than anything, was Prescott's fatherly tone, proud as a griffin, which seemed to speak from experience. I could not remember any real prayer request of his touching anything of a personal nature. This was an aspect of Prescott's character in keeping with the other elements I had noticed, like his calculated use of the word "splendid" and the way he would pass sentence on something I said, saying "exactly" like a proctor awarding a point at a test. Prescott wanted you at a safe distance that was manageable and could be observed from far off, should you drift into an unsatisfactory course. Perhaps I transferred some of my hostility from him to the idea of God, because I saw him as a supercilious proxy for the power I was supposed to be petitioning.

So when I heard him speak of the absence of *my* supplications, I understood that was a prompt to say something that very day. I had already begun to periodically adjust the amount of money taken out on my credit card for the offering plate, increasing it as I felt was needed to improve my profile in the Foundation. The credit card bills that quickly accumulated did not concern me as much as they should have. I gladly paid the monthly minimum without worrying about where the rest of my contributions would be coming from in the future. I told myself this was what passed for faith with me. I knew that the amounts I was giving would be seen by someone, just as the silence of my prayers had been observed. Inspector Prescott was evidently on the case. I could no longer advance to the altar anonymously and retreat in like manner. So I waited until Lucas had finished wrenching Melissa's knuckles before I cleared my throat. I kept my eyes shut but I perceived a few heads turning my way, the room hushing up in preparation for what I might say. I opened my mouth, which was suddenly as dry as an exhausted oil well, and if I had prayed to myself, I would have prayed for the words to come that would help me get through the moment.

That, I realized, was what everyone was more or less praying for anyway, and they probably weren't faced with the absolutely blank slate of a mind that suddenly confronted me when I cleared my throat.

"Dear Lord," I began with a surprisingly familiar rasp.

PROFESSION OF FAITH

8

The ethnographer Donald E. Brown compiled a list of "surface" universals of behavior that all human beings have. He was trying to prove that there are inherent characteristics that we all share, not for cultural reasons but biological. In addition to age status, the concept of shelter, a sense of identity, and the fear of death, he recognized manipulation of self-image as one of these. In other words, we all come out of the womb ... *spinning*.

One night, I was called to help Chuck Fuentes, the church's Spanish-language minister, find someone who had attended a few weeks earlier. Chuck was a Puerto Rican with gleaming teeth and a dashing taste in clothes who gave up life as an immigration lawyer to preach. I was called at a moment's notice around nine thirty to pick up Chuck outside his house. Our mission was to find a Mexican by the name of Emiliano. We would find him in a thick forest of trailers in a park on the north edge of town. There had been a time only three years before when the same trailer park had been called Green Estates and it had been known as the regular haven of meth and pot dealers and newly divorced factory workers trying to accumulate enough money to move on to an apartment. Now, it was home to mostly Mexican immigrants, legal and illegal, who worked on farms and in chicken plants and went out of the way not to attract attention from police. Locals now called it "Gringo Estates" for a silly laugh.

As far I was concerned, I was simply driving Chuck in hopes we might find Emiliano. Chuck told me on the way that he had gotten a call from a woman who knew another person saying that Emiliano needed to know his father was dead of cancer in Monterrey and his sister Elena would be needing money soon.

"What's Emiliano's last name?"

Chuck gave a rueful smile. "I, ah, don't know. I've heard two different names but they call him T-Bone."

"T-Bone?"

"He evidently wanted an American nickname."

"Does he speak American?" Within a split second, I rolled my eyes at the mistake. "I mean, English?"

"I don't think so."

"Do we know if the guy's legal?"

"I don't think he is."

"Do you know what he looks like?"

"I think I do," Chuck said. He then shrugged his shoulders. "I know it's not much to go on. But we at least need to try and find him."

There was one thing I didn't quite know. "Why do you need me? Couldn't you just come over yourself..."

"I'm going to need you to..."

"I don't know any Spanish."

"You don't have to. Just go asking around."

"Asking around?"

"Yeah. We'll knock on some doors and ask about him. It shouldn't take very long."

"Are you sure about this Chuck? I mean, somebody who doesn't speak Spanish looking for..."

"It'll be alright, it'll be alright," he said, his voice a little too loud, as though he shared my misgivings but didn't want to admit it. I heard him sigh a little, then he cleared his throat and looked in my direction as I drove. "I know." He grinned. "But you're all I've got, Cam. They said you'd be just what I needed."

"They?" I really didn't need to know the answer to that one, and he didn't offer. It was Prescott and Forster, and probably news of what I had done, and the silent vouching of Thomas Hagler. They had nothing else to judge me on other than the way I had done the jobs provided for me — jobs that supposedly no one else would do. I was available. Being single and not really caring about what was on television, it seemed I had little choice.

"Well, what does this Emiliano look like? You have to know *something*."

"The last time I saw him, he was wearing a kind of blue soccer T-shirt and what could have been work jeans. He didn't have any gray hair, but I wouldn't call him young. He may have had a mustache. I think I remember him being short, but he may have been a little taller."

Emiliano did not sound easily found nor especially distinguished. His identity was so thinly drawn as to be transparent. And to think I had not even tried to find him yet.

"Don't worry," he repeated. "This sort of thing happens. You just have to be patient."

"You sure?"

Then the strangest thing happened. Chuck got my eye for just a second and said, "You do what you have to do."

Chuck and I arrived at the trailer park and split up, him taking the first three rows of fifteen trailers while I took the next fifteen. If we hadn't found him by then, we still had another three-quarters of the park to navigate as the sun was going down. Before we parted, perhaps to set my mind at ease, Chuck wrote out on a piece of paper that I should ask any man I met who remotely fit the description — *"Su nombre es Emiliano?"* If they answered "si," I was to hand them another piece of paper which had instructions and words to the effect that we would help him and his family and get them anything they needed.

At the first trailer I came to a man answered the door. In a second

I realized he roughly resembled Chuck's description. "Su nombre es Emiliano?" I asked.

He nodded. I handed him the piece of paper, which he began reading. Before his eyes had crossed over half the page, he began shaking his head. "No me."

"It's not you?"

He shook his head. "No me. No hermana. No sister."

"You don't have a sister?" My voice got louder and slower for no logical reason, other than I assumed he might understand me better that way.

"No."

I thanked him, and he nodded and shut the door. I wanted to ask if there were any other men in there who might be named Emiliano, but I assumed he would have known.

And so it went, for the next fourteen trailers. I encountered more than a dozen men who all answered to the name Emiliano, until I handed them the sheet of paper. Then they would shake their head. They either had no sister, no father in Monterrey, no father still alive, or something else. By the seventh Emiliano I met, I was ready to ask if his middle name might be Spartacus. Each of the men, in turn, had a strange smile over his face, as though I had told them the punch line of a long-forgotten joke they suddenly recalled from the deep recesses of memory. One man rushed over to another man standing nearby who had gray hair and answered to the name Emiliano until I handed him the sheet of paper. They all seemed to step forward at the moment I asked the question, as though I had uttered a proud name to conjure with, like someone upon the announcement that a promising bottle of wine was about to be opened. One of the unshakeable rules of logic is that a thing cannot both be and not be the same thing at the same time. I wasn't sure if this applied to my situation with my increasingly good friend Emiliano, but it made me feel at least better that I might be moving toward some diagnosis of this quickly proliferating name. I had the feeling by the time I left the area that my own name might be Emiliano.

After the fifteenth trailer, which contained five men who

momentarily answered to the increasingly ubiquitous name of
Emiliano, I finally saw Chuck, waiting for me.

"Let's go," he said.

"You find him?" I asked, laughing at myself.

"No. We won't find him here," he said. I guessed from the look
on his face that he had also encountered an entire nest of Emilianos,
seemingly ready to be discovered.

"What's going on?" I asked.

"It's the name," Chuck said. "All the men here work as
pickers. They belong to a society that meets out here. A political
organization."

"Let me guess. They're called the Emilianos."

Chuck shook his head in the negative. "It took me about four
times before I figured it out. They think we're here to take him away.
They're all saying they're Emiliano because they think he's a brother
in this society. They're trying to protect him."

"Don't they realize we're trying to help him?"

"Doesn't matter. It'll get back to the real Emiliano. They'll get the
message to him. Sometimes it works that way."

"Why did they all say they were Emiliano then? Wouldn't it have
made more sense for them to deny it?"

Chuck tilted his head slightly, as though the horizon had
momentarily shifted. "They suppose we'll get tired of asking and
move on."

"Which is what we're doing," I said.

"Then it works, doesn't it?" I suppose I was frustrated and
didn't really want to leave. I had invested enough time to feel mad
about abandoning this quest. I probably thought I could find the
right Emiliano if given enough time. But I never paused to consider
what got me there in the first place, whether finding him was that
important, or whether it might satisfy me if I did find him.

If you want to know when things changed for me, when I began to
really see things differently, it might have been that moment. I was not
surprised a few days later when I found out that Emiliano had finally
shown up at the church to seek Chuck out, or that another five men
claiming to be Emiliano had come with him just in case. It was the

reason for us being in that trailer park, and the reaction of those we encountered, and how it had all worked out that finally drove me to a conclusion that had probably been long in the making:

The real is not rational.

9

I was at a restaurant with Prescott, who was telling me how I could learn to play the piano in just a few weeks. This was suggested so I could to better serve the elderly when we did twice-weekly visits at the nursing home. He sat across from me in a booth and made all these suggestions with a straight face.

"Do *you* know how to play the piano?" I asked him.

"No. Never had the patience for it. But it shouldn't take *you* too long." He waved at the air as we sat in a booth, his hand making the pantomime of playing the keys on a piano. He dashed off his imaginary notes as though I could take it up in about half an hour.

"Why do you say that?"

"Well, you pick up things very easily, Cameron. You've shown that on the job. And I have a feeling you're very musically inclined. You seem to know a lot of things."

"*Seem* is the right word there. What makes you think I can succeed where you haven't even tried?"

He wouldn't have any of this line of questioning. "You're perfect.

I'll get you hooked up with someone to learn."

"But..."

"You should see those people when there's music. They clap and skip and jump. It's thrilling."

"Is being tone deaf a potential liability?"

"Most of them can't hear anyway."

"So what you're saying is you need a warm body?"

"No, of course not. I can't understand why you're putting up a struggle on this issue. You've performed brilliantly these past few weeks. Delivering food, assisting with preschools and phonics teaching, grass cutting. It's thrilling to see someone attack the work with such zeal. The Lord has His hand on you."

"And it's down full throttle," I muttered.

The food arrived. Prescott asked me if I wished to say the blessing. It was a ridiculous question. He didn't order anything. I asked him to do it. I didn't feel like it, but I should have known Prescott's voice would carry as we bowed our heads. I could feel the eyes gravitate toward me, which is why my hands went reflexively up to cover my face, guilty thing that it was. I'm sure I looked devout instead of in agony.

When I opened my eyes, he resumed talking as though there hadn't been an interruption. "I don't think you realize how rare it is to see someone..."

Just behind Prescott, I saw her.

My breath caught and I tripped over the table getting up in one motion, with him still talking. Cecelia was headed out the restaurant's front door when I got her attention. I don't know how I expected her to look. Perhaps I wanted her distracted, dark rings around her eyes, hair askew, the appearance of someone whose mind was somewhere else. I might have wanted this for my brother's sake, as some misguided test of her loyalty to his memory. It was a ridiculous notion. If I should have been convinced of *anything*, it was that Cecelia missed Peter.

No, she was beautiful. Perfect. Cecelia had a skin tone slightly lighter than olive, which made her look healthy and exotic. Her dark eyes stood out not against bloodshot irises but behind her full lashes. Her hair was swept to one side and she looked not like a woman on the make, but more as one daring someone to approach her. She didn't outwardly seem to need companionship. Her clothes called attention to her body without displaying it. She wore a pin above her left breast that resembled a New Orleans Mardi Gras mask.

When she saw me, she paused in the act of pushing the door open. There was a split second of recognition, and even the outlines of a smile of greeting, and then just as suddenly the beginning of the expression disappeared and hardened, and I saw her move again as though she was determined to leave. And then, just as quickly, I saw her stop. It was as if she was restraining herself from a natural reaction. If I could guess what her thoughts were in those two seconds, it went from *There's Cam, my brother in law. I haven't seen him in awhile. When was it? Oh, God, the funeral. But then I like seeing him, except for that, oh God, no...* I reminded her of everything good and bad in her life that she wanted to cling to and flee from, at every single step.

I almost called her name, but I saw there was no need. I stopped walking in her direction.

She nodded, as much as she wanted to acknowledge, then she looked around as if to see if anyone was heading inside, then she nodded again, bit her bottom lip, and walked out. I didn't move to stop her.

Prescott was watching all this. "Who was that? Your girlfriend?"

"No. My ex-sister-in-law." I heard myself say the words. "I mean, my sister-in-law."

"Your brother's divorced?" I think he perceived some embarrassment from me.

"No. Her husband died about two months ago. I suppose that still makes her my sister-in-law."

"You mean your brother died?"

"Yeah, that's what I mean. I'm sorry. It's still hard to believe."

"I'm sorry." Prescott was quiet for a second. "Let me make sure I understand you..."

I cleared my throat without looking at him. "My brother Peter was killed in a car accident. Cecelia was...is...his wife. They were..."

"I see. I see. I'm sorry."

"No, I should be able to talk about this."

"Your brother older or younger?"

"Older."

"How's she holding up? How are *you* holding up?'

"We're ...doing. Not a lot you can say beyond that." I took a bite of my lunch. "You probably understand why I wanted the job now."

"Needed a change?"

"I guess. Needed something."

"Probably had something to do with your *decision* too. You needed this job more than you realized."

It took a second before I realized he meant the decision I made in joining the church. I nodded and looked for something else to talk about. He seemed willing to invest it with all the mysticism and portent of smoke from the sacred altar, but I barely remembered it, as I barely remembered the meal that followed the service or the way I passed that afternoon.

Before I could open my mouth, he spoke. "You know Cameron, I'm quite impressed with you. You're thorough, you observe very closely, you're quick to perceive problems and their solutions, and you have a certain quiet assurance that's endearing. It sets people at ease."

"I do?"

"No need to be humble."

"I wasn't aware I was being humble, just as I wasn't aware I was ... all that."

"No, you are. There's a lot about you that's fascinating. Like those books you're always quoting. I can tell you've actually taken the time to read them instead of merely memorizing the right quotes to drop in front of the boss."

"I just like to read."

"I understand that. I know it isn't a case of you looking for ways to impress me. You do that enough. Effortlessly."

"The greatest effort goes into that which is effortless."

"Who said that?"

"Not sure, really. Just seemed right."

"How much recall do you have about what you read?"

"Not as much as I'd like."

"The fact that you've been doing all this through a haze of grief to me is, actually, quite astounding. Further proof that you're coming here was providential." He didn't look up as he said this. There had been a knife, fork and spoon wrapped in a napkin that he took out and began arranging, switching out, arranging again.

I laughed at his observation. "Hadn't quite thought of it that way." Actually, I had, as just another pose — *actions that a man might play, but I have that within which passes show; these but the trappings and the suits of woe.*

"That's not surprising. You're still new to the faith. In the end, we all see the falling sparrow and which column it goes into in the divine ledger. It just takes awhile to get there." I took a bite and repeated what he'd said in my mind, probably dozens of times, unable to discern just what — literally, in God's name — he was on about. "Does your sister-in-law's grief bother you?"

Lord, but he was thorough. "What makes you say that?"

"I'm a counselor. I can pick up on things. Just the sight of your sister-in-law seems to attract *and* repel you."

Doesn't do much for her either. "Reminder."

"Remainder, actually. At a time like this, you are both drawn to your lives before the other intruded. You remember your brother as he was in his childhood and yours, before he became someone else's husband. She only knows your brother as her husband, and both of you are unpleasant remainders of attachments that no longer exist."

I picked at the meal and slid it away. "You're probably right," I said, and it did make sense, as long as he was talking about two people who were not me or Cecelia. I saw him drawing on a career of counseling and working with people who were fine and in need of counseling but not to be confused with the twisted, infernal things that I was carrying around inside me. As I sat there half-listening to what he was saying, my mind kept replaying the half-second glance I got at Cecelia's cleavage as she turned toward me, then away. I would see the way her feet glided and the parting of her lips when I called her name. I was sure that on some level I was burnishing these images, remaking them as through a soft-focus lens.

Now you know why I stayed home nights.

That was Peter's voice, playing in my head. It wasn't the sort of thing he would have said on his own. It was more the sort of stock, vaudeville cliché phrase he would have enjoyed repeating to see my reaction. It occurred to me that the imitation of my brother that I was carrying in my head was doing an imitation.

Hearing his voice repelled me. My brother would never have talked about his wife that way to me, and the idea of him enjoying my ogling her made me feel ... *unclean.*

I heard him laughing. *You're killing me, man. You're just killing me.* The laughter continued.

What was I to do? Telling my brother to shut up was second nature; I had done it all of my life. Was telling this dybbuk that had crawled into my skull to shut up a way of killing my brother again? Or was that what I was doing already with this imitation that had begun as a way of getting his wife off the phone? Did I really not want to hear my brother again?

Another thought: Had I done it for *her*, or because *I* wanted so badly to hear his voice again?

Maybe I'm doing an impersonation of you? the fake Peter said.

"While we're talking about your job, I need to let you know about something," Prescott said. "You're doing well. Mr. Forster was very pleased with you."

"Tell him thanks," I said, shifting in the booth. "I was unaware that we'd met."

"He keeps tabs on us. He has his ways." Prescott cleared his throat. "When the boss takes note of you, you can only go up."

As with many things Prescott said, I wasn't sure if he meant a promotion or some transmigration of the soul to a higher level of being. I assumed the later because I couldn't see him telling me I was getting a raise. It had to be something intangible, like the overestimated value of a "job well done" and other related old saws.

"The further up you go in the foundation, the more pressure

there is to make certain life choices. Appearance is how people form their opinions, right or wrong, and we have to be conscious of that. A direction that we take may lead others along similar paths, carrying civilization forward through the balance of time." Prescott's tone resembled that of a man reciting the Gettysburg Address — a text of truths whose context had been removed by time, leaving behind words that had a certain music but a missing meter. Lincoln's words, at least, had the benefit of being spoken and written by a genius in the service of history, instead of a flak looking for a raise and some denied recognition.

"Enough with the after-dinner speech. I thought I already made that kind of decision," I said, glancing at what I thought was the nub of his meaning.

His hands took in the whole picture of me sitting before him. "You're a young man, of a certain age, with a professional position. You're making a good, steady paycheck. You're active in your church and community. A man like that is very attractive and should have no trouble finding a wife."

"A wife," I repeated.

"The right kind of wife, I should say. Someone who complements you rather than mirrors you, a sensible contrast to your own flaws, a buttress against the buffets of life, a comforter and restorer."

"I think they sell that in drug stores for..."

Prescott shook his head.

"You want me to get married?" I asked.

"Not immediately, to be sure. Just keep in mind that you're doing everything right. I just wouldn't want someone so promising to run into a road block, needlessly."

"Perception," I said.

"Just making sure you're mindful of how you appear."

"And how do I appear?"

"I just told you. Very impressive. That's the sudden rush of a young man who makes a splendid impression on short notice. Such an impression is always bound to fade with time, just as the expectations surrounding such a man soon become routine as well. Nobody expects you to dip below the horizon after you've scaled the clouds. At the moment, you're a star. There are always those who want to know if you're a shooting star."

"And what about the future Mrs. Leon?"

"I think you take my meaning, Cameron. When others see you, will they see your wife in you? Will others see Jesus in you?"

So *there* was the meaning, sort of. At least as close as he would allow himself to come to the point. He wanted me to get married to some as yet unidentified woman after convincing me to tie the knot with the Lord. Though not exactly shotgun weddings, they seemed more adequately described as paycheck affairs. I wondered briefly if there was a bonus in it for me if I had the ceremony by a certain date.

"What about love?" I asked.

"That goes without saying."

"Does it?"

"Well, I'll say it if you want me to. Yes, in a marriage, it's a very good idea to marry someone you love." His tone was just serious enough to make me believe for a second he wasn't joking.

"For how long?"

"Cameron, I'm sure you'll do the right thing."

"Just so I'll know, what is the right thing?"

He cleared his throat again, and the tone of recitation returned, his voice refined and crystalline. "A loving, God-centered marriage with fidelity and honesty." Hidden within that explanation were compromises and interpretations and impressions on my life, and presumably the life of another woman whom I did not know but would be connected to. And whose particular definition did each of these have to meet? Would Prescott measure the depth of our love, or Forster calculate the latitude and longitude of this marriage in relation to the Almighty?

"How many children?"

"Cameron..."

"How many? One? Two?"

"However many God blesses you with."

"What if she can't have any? What if I can't have any?"

"Then, we'll pray for you. For you both."

"How long should I stay married?"

"As long as you both shall live, I think is the phrase."

"This is insane. I have to get married to keep my job?"

"I didn't say that..."

"What about Melissa Garvey? At the office. She's divorced. Is she going to lose her job?"

"If you must know, even though it's none of your business, her divorce is not her fault. Besides, there are laws about that sort of thing."

"But in my case?"

At the time, I suppose I thought I was asking these questions in a sarcastic haze, hoping to provoke Prescott into some further, ridiculous Talmudic interpretation of the height, breadth, and depth of my presumed devotion to God, family, and employer. But I suppose I was really asking for the plumb line and marking it down, deep down, inside me.

Prescott, as usual, would have none of it. "I would give you one piece of advice. Marry a woman who's allergic to flowers. You'll save a ton in the long run. That's what I did." He gave me a ridiculous, nauseating smile.

Prescott got up from the booth. "Keep up the good work," he said, touching me on the shoulder. He picked up the check and walked to the cash register.

After he walked out, I got the waitress' attention and ordered coffee. I was determined to order and consume something he hadn't paid for. I hadn't been sleeping well still, and I'd gotten into the habit of drinking coffee throughout the day, in order to keep going. Besides, with my mind racing, I could properly obsess over my latest instruction from Prescott.

I happen to know somebody who's available, Peter's voice said.

"Shut up," I said, just as Cecelia walked back into the restaurant and headed straight for my booth.

10

"Hi," she said, with a relaxed smile, surprising in how it combined both coolness and warmth.

"I thought you left."

"I came back." She rolled her eyes and smiled. "I felt kind of silly just leaving like that. I didn't want you to think I was running from you."

"Were you?"

She shrugged her shoulders. "Of course."

"No big deal. I didn't stop you, did I?" There was silence between us for a few minutes before I gave up first. "How are you?"

"Fine."

"Uh-huh."

"No, really."

"Really."

"No, I mean it."

What didn't I believe? Was it the way she said my name, which does not begin with a "p" sound but nearly did from her lips, by my count, about four times? She would stop herself before forming the word, close her eyes to hold herself together, the cool disappearing from her wraithlike frame, before forging ahead as though nothing had happened.

"Are you sleeping any?" I asked.

"No. I mean, I do sleep, but I don't expect to be sleepy for some time. I guess I'm going on sheer nerve. "

"You look great. What do you do instead of sleep?"

"My house is immaculate. I clean because I can't lie in bed. I'll think about him and hours will drag on. Only they seem to go fast and slow at the same time, you know?" Her face took on an anguished *"don't you just hate it?"* attitude.

"I know."

She closed her eyes and spoke. "It's like someone's doing an autopsy on you without ever opening your skin." When her eyes popped open, it had the effect of making her face look different. More frail, I thought.

"And it's you that's doing the autopsy."

"Yeah. Shows you what you're made of."

"What *are* you made of?" I asked.

She frowned. She reached into her purse and pulled out a makeup case and began dabbing her cheeks after giving each side a quick look in the tiny mirror. She never took her eyes off the reflection as she talked. "I don't know, but there's less of me now. He took some of me with him. So I not only miss him, I miss me with him. I miss *me*." Her voice was even and observational, as though this was happening to someone else.

I was quiet for a minute. "Maybe he didn't take that with him, so much as you're trying to get rid of it."

"I wouldn't say that," she said. She rubbed her left cheek for a solid minute, like someone polishing silver. "I guess I'm just stuck."

"Stuck," I repeated.

She moved on to the other cheek, moving her mouth in an exaggerated grimace to stretch her nose out. The way her face contorted, it was almost as though she expected to still be talking as she applied the makeup. Then, she looked at me. "I don't know quite what to say around you, Cameron."

"I'm still Cam. And I'm still the same. And I'm sorry that I listened to you." I made sure there were appropriate pauses in between each of my sentences.

"I'm not. I needed you to do that for me."

"I feel like..."

"Like what?"

"I was in church and I looked it up. Necromancy. That's what they called it in the Dark Ages. Speaking with the voice of the dead. They used to stone people for it."

"You? In church? Explain."

"I sold out. It's a long story. I needed a job. That has nothing to do with what I did for you."

"You make it sound worse than what it actually was."

"Then why do I feel so horrible?"

"Perhaps that has more to do with Peter than with me. It's so hard to know. His not being here has a way of bleeding into everything I touch." She gave the impression in her tone that she was already growing bored with grief, like a restless theatergoer checking her watch for intermission.

Yet what she said was so obvious to be ridiculous.

"Well, yeah? I wouldn't be sad about imitating my brother if he wasn't dead. And doing it for you..."

"I didn't think you'd do it, to be honest. But I needed that." She snapped the makeup case loudly. "Cam, you say you were looking in the Bible? I know a little something about that. You know what the husband's brother used to do to the wives when the husband died?"

"Kill them?"

"They were expected to take their sister-in-law as a wife, to provide their dead brother with an heir."

"You don't say." I cleared my throat and swallowed hard. *Wouldn't that have had an unhealthy effect on the murder rate?* I wondered. "Actually I wouldn't know if that thing about necromancy was in the Bible. It's..."

"I'm not suggesting anything. I'm just trying to tell you that I needed Peter and I needed someone to tell me he wasn't coming home. Not that night. And I heard *him* say that to me. I think that's all I needed." She took up the makeup pad and began the ritual again, as though attempting to wipe away any natural color left in her cheeks.

"So it seems more real to you? You think it helped?"

"It helped that night." I nodded, and I looked down. She sounded convincing, at least. "But that night is over, Cam."

"Are you sure?"

She nodded her head, then reached up with her left hand to play with her hair.

I wondered if I was asking her this question, or myself. Looking into my sister-in-law's eyes, her trying so desperately to reassure me that everything was still manageable, I had the terrible feeling that everything as it appeared that moment was an utter sham. Cecelia with her perfectly polished fingernails and immaculate makup, a picture of the silent widow bravely besting waves of grief, and me loudly protesting my revulsion at appropriating the silent voice of my late brother, using it to keep more than his memory alive for an evening.

I suspected the truth was that Cecelia was desperate with grief, and she dabbed her face with that makeup pad in fear, and that my guilt was because I wanted more than just my brother's voice and it scared me to have his widow sitting so close to me when I could smell her.

But then she reassured me, and I reassured myself, and we parted company. We gave each other an awkward hug, not getting close enough for any real physical bond to assert itself. She gave another apology for not lingering to speak to me earlier, and I swatted it away as though I understood, and tried to ignore the anger I still had lingering over it inside. She left and I sat there for a few minutes, drinking my coffee, trying to convince myself that all was well with both of us.

When I got home later, I restlessly flitted around the apartment, unable to concentrate on television and once again unable to sleep when I crawled into bed. For some reason, I was expecting something. It was only a little while before I admitted it to myself — I expected

Cecelia to call. I expected her to be frantic with grief, calling to tell me that no, she wasn't holding up well and that seeing me had reminded her of Peter and *Oh my God how horrible it is now that he's gone...* When she didn't call, I felt disappointment when I recalled her fingers and the freckles I had seen on her chest when she leaned over to touch my wrist as she got up from the table. Then I told myself that all I needed was some sleep and all would be well.

I suppose at that moment I crossed some other bridge of consciousness. While I didn't yet believe in God, I suppose I started at that instant to believe fervently in the existence of Satan. I felt tempted, and by a presence that was not Cecelia nor my ghostly voice of Peter.

Mr. Franz Kafka wrote that the afterthoughts with which we justify our accommodations to the Evil One are in fact not ours, but the Evil One's. I closed my eyes in the darkness and was conscious of a mocking malignancy bearing its faded yellowing teeth, taunting me with a full-throated laugh when I told myself I was a good man. Suddenly I believed in him, and yet I couldn't figure out which of the internal voices I heard was his.

Would Satan accuse me, or reassure me?

Jim Janssen was helping me one night with the phone ministry. Jim was about five years older than I was, and probably equally perplexed at why we were there. The phone ministry was the church's switchboard room which stayed manned 24 hours a day for what were called "prayer emergencies." The idea was that, given the size of our church and the scope of its ministries, there had to be something akin to a mini-emergency dispatch system if someone needed prayer or counseling at a moment's notice.

We had been sitting in the room for hours, my eyes passing over the pages of my book and occasionally looking up to check if the phone was still working. There wasn't a single ring in more than four hours, and I still had two more to go on the shift. It was probably 9:45 in the evening and I had carried with me a copy of "Das Kapital."

Yeah.

I remember looking over my book shelves for something to read as I went out the door. I felt a conspiratorial, self-satisfied smile break over me when my eye saw Mr. Karl Marx's work. There was something pugnacious about it. It struck me as funny that I was going out to participate in prayer counseling carrying Marx, though I wasn't sure whether I was rubbing Marx's nose in it or the Almighty's. As I recall, I still didn't believe in God at that time. That is what I told myself. But if that is so, I have no clue who I thought I was jesting.

Still, I was embarrassed to be reading it, so I slipped it in a magazine as I walked in and read it on one side of the room while Jim sat listening to his iPod on the other. Jim had been there for only two hours, but I saw him stretch his arms behind his head, fiddle with the controls and ear buds, tap both feet, one hand, bop his head and move in time with the music, and get up several times to stretch his legs. Every few minutes I saw him run his fingers through his spiky black hair and nervously brush the tuft of hair under his bottom lip with his index finger, like a man brushing his teeth. At one point, he leaned forward with his hands clasped before him, his head down, looking like a man in very intense prayer, but sounding like a man with an intense snoring problem.

I had just read Mr. Karl Marx's observation that it is not the consciousness of men that determines their existence, but their social existence that determines their consciousness when I saw Jim get up again.

"I'm leaving," he said.

"Leaving? You just got here."

"Seems like it, doesn't it? No, there's nothing going to happen. No reason to stay."

"But your shift's not over yet."

"I can't take it here any more. There's just nothing to do. And *nobody's* going to call. You know that. You've been here longer than I have and nobody's called since you got here. They never do."

"I got a hang-up a few weeks ago."

"See? That's no reason to stay. Anybody who wants help bad enough knows who to call."

Though the service was catered toward helping church members, I didn't need to remind Jim that a whole network of signs around

town advertised the 24-hour prayer switchboard. The church kept
checking the line to make sure there were no problems with it. There
was just nobody calling.

"Jim, come on. Man up. I'm sticking around."

"Cam, what is it with you? How do you keep going? You're at this
enough with the foundation, aren't you? I mean, you work for Forster
too, right?"

I nodded.

"Lord knows you're barely able to take a spare breath. I mean,
what is it with you?"

I blinked, unsure how to take what he was saying. "You do what
you have to do," I offered, without thinking where I had heard this.

Jim was a little older than me, a man in his thirties. He had a
young family and, unlike me, he worked a regular job running a
construction company outside the Foundation, which meant whatever
he did with the church was volunteer work. I didn't think all that
much about being there because I wasn't sleeping anyway, so sitting
with a book in front of a phone that wasn't ringing didn't sound all
that unappetizing. Jim, on the other hand, had the impatience of a
man who fears his free time is evaporating before his eyes and there is
little he can do to stop it. It took him a second or two, I guess, to grasp
what I said. He shook his head, gave me a salute worthy of a returning
war hero, and casually strode out the door. I could picture him within
minutes stretched out a sofa somewhere while children played in
a nearby room. The way he simply walked out registered a certain
amount of awe in me.

Leave? I thought. *I didn't know you could do that...*

And I should have done the same thing, for several reasons, not
the least of which was that with Jim gone, I was alone and forced to
do the counseling. But I didn't leave. There was no reason to believe
there would be any counseling. One of the unbreakable rules of the
counseling hotline was that it was necessary for two to do it — not
because of the volume of calls but because of the necessity that if
a call came through, the person taking the call might need to pay a
counseling visit, and it was essential that two people go. Witnesses,

moral support, even in case someone later sued. It was the sort of thing Prescott went bonkers about. I can hear him saying that two men going to a woman's house precluded the possibility of something "untoward" happening.

Such as what next occurred.

The phone rang and I answered it. A woman on the other end of the phone said she needed help. Immediately, she said. Her voice was girlish and overwrought, breaking at times when she strained to get out certain words. She said her boyfriend had beaten her in a jealous fit. She said she had told him she wanted nothing more to do with him. Those were her exact words — nothing more to do with him. She repeated them with pride and I nodded, trying not to lose my place in the book.

"I knew he wasn't good enough for me, and he hated hearing me say that," she said. "Now he's gone."

Then she began telling me everything about the moments leading up to it, about how he had come into her home, licking his lips and snapping his fingers, anxious about something. He had seen her out somewhere with what he called "a strange man." She said he was wrong, that this man he had seen her with was simply a man she had talked to while standing in line for a bus. *Don't you lie to me!* he had told her. She had managed to stay away from him for awhile, running from room to room until he caught her under her left eye with his fist. She was sure he had left the imprint of his class ring in her face. He was so proud of that thing, she said. You'd think they would have taught him in law school that you're not supposed to beat women, she said.

I listened, conscious of the fact that as I listened part of my brain went down a checklist, making a mark each time I heard something that I expected or recognized. Selfish, prideful professional man. A mistaken social setting. Inability to listen to reason. I heard the tone of her voice and the way she paused for breath and understood that she was talking herself down from the press of adrenaline.

I asked her if she shouldn't call the police to make sure her boyfriend didn't come back.

"Oh, but I did. I just need some help right now."

I looked down at the sheet I'd been handed to consult when I did my first session of prayer counseling. I was so caught up in what she was saying that I momentarily forgot that this was my first call. The paper told me I was to ask the caller if he or she needed prayer. It even provided a short suggested prayer with blanks provided for whatever travail might be on the caller's mind. The mental distance encompassed by those blanks amused me. The power of God, available to those with credit card problems or a flood wall moving toward their front door.

But I didn't ask if she needed prayer. "What can I do for you?"

"Come over until they get here. I'll feel better."

"But I don't even know where you live," I said. "I may not get there before the police do." *Or your boyfriend*, I thought.

"Oh, I only live one block away from your church."

I, of all people, should know what it's like to try to picture how someone looks, judging only by their voice. I pictured a woman clutching a phone with both hands, her hair matted by blood, looking frantically out her windows through a swollen eye. I was surprised at how well she held it together, getting out what she needed to tell me. It was obvious she didn't wish to be alone, but I wondered what it said about her that she was willing to invite any stranger into her house after being beaten by someone she must have trusted some time in the past.

"Are you a church member?" I wondered if I knew this woman, or perhaps had seen her.

"No," she said. "Does that matter? I've just seen your signs everywhere."

"Tell me where you live."

12

Her name was Cynthia Jester. When I knocked on her door, I
announced my name and where I was from. She opened the door
just far enough to see me, thanked me, and asked me in. I could hear
the inner voice of Prescott warning me not to enter the house of
an unmarried woman alone on a counseling visit. But Prescott was
nowhere around and he didn't have to deal with this situation.

What was more, Prescott did not have this woman's china doll
pale skin and the vivid dark eyes of a child. Cynthia looked like a
school girl just learning to dress up. In fact, what she wore looked
much like a school uniform — mildly dressy but not stiff. She wore a
mid-thigh skirt with a white blouse and a cardigan. She had on a pair
of tasteful heels. If I had stopped to consider everything, I might have
thought she was overdressed for a battery victim. Not much polish to
her, a certain roughness around the edges, but that would be expected
from a woman who had just presumably fought for her life. She was
rushed and flushed; a platinum blonde with pink cheeks like someone
who had just come in from a dash through the snow. Under her

left eye, puffy and red, was a darkening mark like a football player's. When I walked in, I understood that enough time had passed for the remaining energy left from her boyfriend to have dissipated. The room was quiet and dark as she shut the door.

I waited a second. "You'd better lock it," I suggested, while she stood at the door. She looked at me and smiled.

"I'm sorry," she said. "I'm not myself lately." She gave the dead bolt an embarrassed tug.

"Are you okay?"

"I'm fine," she said, her hand going up to shield the eye. "It doesn't hurt too much."

"How long ago did you call the police?"

She coughed. "I don't think he's coming back. I really appreciate you coming. Can I get you something?" Even though she was outwardly calm, she flitted from one sentence to the other, as though speaking all of them at once.

"Don't worry about me. What I can do for you?"

"Really, I'm fine. I don't think he's coming back."

"Why's that?"

"He's just been gone so long."

"How long ago did it happen?"

She started to tell me the story again, in much more detail this time. I coaxed her into sitting down while I walked over to the window, looking out. She recounted again how he came in, and I looked at passing cars, waiting for one to pull into the driveway and an angry man to jump out. She kept fiddling with her hair as she said the words, looking over at me.

"'Don't you lie to me!' he said. 'He kept saying that, the whole time he was chasing me around the house.'"

I supposed it had been long enough since she had called the police, or me, that she had had time to straighten up the place.

"You shouldn't have put things back in their place," I said. "That would have helped when you told the police."

"What?"

"The house." I pointed around the room. She evidently had money because it was a well-furnished house for a single woman in her twenties, which I guessed she was. "You were running around. You must have knocked over chairs or things. He probably did the same. The place looks great now."

"Oh, thanks," she said. Her response startled me. A moment passed. "You mean, you think the police won't believe me?"

"Oh, no. I didn't mean that. All they have to do is look at your eye. Just make sure they understand that *I'm* not your boyfriend." As I said the words, I felt that strange sensation of Prescott over my shoulder, somewhat magnified. I could momentarily see myself being hauled off to jail, a news photographer snapping my picture as I was pushed head first into a squad car, the next day's paper thrust in my face as Forster himself finally appeared to usher me out the Foundation's door.

"Don't worry," she said. "I really appreciate you coming. I really needed someone to be here. I'm just glad it was you. You seem...very nice. You never can tell over the phone."

I was reminded of Cecelia. "Thanks," I choked.

"Listen, really, you've come all this way. Can I get you something?"

"No, I probably need to do something for *you*. Do you want me to call the police and see what's keeping them?"

"That's okay. He's not coming."

"You mean your boyfriend."

"Yeah. My boyfriend. He's not coming."

"But about the police..."

"I wouldn't expect them either."

"Why? You called them, right?"

"Yeah, but they said they were kind of busy. That's why I called you."

"Busy? What..."

"I guess a lot of other important stuff is going on," she said. She rose from the sofa and smoothed out her skirt and brushed her hair back again. She gave a fragile smile. "Would you like some tea? I'm not sure I have any, but..."

"What did they say was going on?"

"Just... stuff," she said. "I could probably get the tea ready by the time they get here. If I have some."

"So you think they'll be here?" I looked back in her direction, but she had gotten up and moved into what I guessed was the kitchen. I heard her saying things but I couldn't make out the words. Whatever she was saying had something to do with tea, though. That much I understood.

I milled around the room and heard her making noises which I assumed was running water into a pot and turning on a gas stove. I looked at the reproductions of French impressionists on the walls and sat down for a moment on the imitation leather sofa and heard a siren. I got up long enough to look out the window and see a police car pass by on its way somewhere else.

"Sorry," she said, finally coming back into the room. "I got you over here for nothing." Her hands, suddenly limp, smacked against her hips as they went dead, as though all the lifeblood fled from them.

I looked over at her. She was covering her eye, her head down. Her tone was embarrassed, mortified.

"The police aren't coming."

"You didn't call them. You were too scared," I said.

"No," she said. "The truth is I didn't call the police because I don't have a boyfriend."

"Somebody else beat you?"

"No. Nobody beat me. The truth is I don't have a boyfriend and nobody beat me up." Her voice broke on the word *nobody*.

"Listen, if you're trying to, ah, cover for somebody, I understand."

"Oh, God, you are so *nice*! You're trying to understand and there's nothing to really understand here. It doesn't make any sense."

"What…"

"What I mean is that I was here alone and I fell and hit my face on that table over there." She pointed at an end table. I said nothing. "I hit the table and I got this black eye and I felt so bad."

A respectable amount of time passed. "And you were ashamed?"

She shrugged. "I was alone. You see." Again, she was quiet, and a moment passed, as I suspected she had to realize that I simply needed to hear the whole story. Finally, she rolled her eyes, gave another embarrassed shrug, and slapped her hips again. "I was dressed up and thought I wanted to go out and here I've got this enormous black eye and nobody to help me. Nobody was here. I didn't know what to do.

I wanted to call somebody but I can't because I don't know anybody to call. The only person I could think of calling was that number at your church. I ride by the billboard everyday on the way to work. So I knew it, and I figured I would call. But I thought it would sound really foolish, just to call because you're lonely, so I called and said I'd been beat up. That was the only way I thought I could get somebody over here."

"You sure that's the truth?"

"You mean you don't believe that? A crazy story like that? Well, who could blame you? Doesn't make any sense does it? Of course not. Crazy lonely girl calls up the church and fakes getting beat up just so she can get somebody to come by? Why, who wouldn't believe that?"

I let out a low laugh while my hands went up to restrain her wildly gesturing arms.

"I'm so, so sorry." Then she covered her face. "If you really want the truth, I called a church because I wanted to meet a nice guy. They could have sent over somebody's grandfather."

Her hands stopped dancing and I held them.

She spoke in short bursts, sighing heavily between the sentences. "Like I said, I'm lonely. I've been lonely. You spend enough nights in bars looking for a nice guy, you realize you're not going to find him there. So I wondered. Where do nice guys hang out?"

"And you thought — church?"

"Is that so strange?"

Her question startled me, perhaps because it made me realize that I *had* been surprised by her deduction.

"I'm sorry. I spend a *lot* of time in church."

"And you think I was wrong?"

Again, I paused, groping for something to say. "Unfortunately, I'm the one that showed up."

"I know, I know," she said. "I'm so sorry I dragged *you* up here."

By the way she said *you* I wasn't sure if I should feel insulted. "It's okay..."

"No, I mean it."

"It's okay, really."

"You can hate me, really hate me, I wouldn't blame you in the least. I wouldn't blame you if you took a crack at my other eye. Just, I know you're from a church, just forgive me, please? If you can?"

"Calm down." Her head focused on the floor, so I nudged her chin up until her eyes met mine. The swelling was bad but I doubted it would last long. In a day or two you'd wouldn't be able to tell it had happened. "Don't beat yourself up," I said. It was probably the worst choice of words in my life.

We both laughed, looking at each other.

"Tell you what. Why don't you make me some of that tea?"

"You sure? You don't hate me? I mean, I'm not keeping you from actually talking to somebody *sane* up there, am I?"

"No," I said. "Nobody's been calling. Besides, I was just about ready for my shift to end. When the next person gets there, they'll just go on."

"Thanks," she said. "I would really appreciate it."

"So would I."

She smiled at me, perhaps for the first time, like a woman who had called a strange man to her house. And for a second, I thought I felt something stir inside of me.

I don't want to think that Prescott's advice about taking a wife was on my mind, but it probably was.

13

Mrs. Edith Wharton observed that beauty is a gift that justifies every success and excuses a certain number of failings. Perhaps that was why I was willing to overlook the fact that my first meeting with Cynthia was due to a lie. I've found that most people will impute a certain amount of intelligence, or polish, or bearing to a person if his or her looks are good enough. In Cynthia's case, assuming such things wasn't a stretch. She had the silent confidence of a card sharp and the daring of a burglar, all hiding behind those innocent eyes that bade me believe every word about her fictional boyfriend. Even much later, I thought to myself that there *was* such a man to be found in the trappings of her house. I looked at the end table with its black imitation mahogany legs that resembled a beast's and assumed it was a *male* table, an unforgiving manly spirit that had tripped her and lashed out like a hardened man full of drink and violence. I could see her laying on the floor, looking up at the table as though it was a man with muscles clinging to the outlines of a sleeveless T-shirt, one hand a fist and the other clutching a bat. She would look up bravely, full of the quiet dignity of a woman enduring the worst of a short-sighted man. I felt proud of her, and I wanted to rescue her. It was a story worth believing, especially since I would be its hero. I resolved I would sell the table once we married, as I knew we would, or I would have it disassembled and feminized somehow — painted pink or converted to some womanly purpose.

It was Cynthia and the way she smothered me with herself, made me want to believe anything that I could to make her over into this innocent girl I had perceived the minute I walked through her door. Cynthia Jester, in face, form and feature, was perfect for me. I couldn't look at her without silently calculating within myself what Prescott might think of her, and Forster, and all the people who knew me from church. All the ministries, once they saw my wife, would somehow credit the innocence I perceived in her back upon me. She was as good as a voucher for a steady stream of promotions, were I to marry her.

Even there, in her little kitchen, drinking her tea from a chipped cup — she served it with a saucer — I could tell she was in some measure high maintenance, but then, so was I.

"Do you do this sort of thing often?" she asked.

"What? You mean, come to strange women's houses on phony assault reports?"

Thankfully, she laughed, and when she did, she covered her mouth like a child. "No, I mean, help people."

"Am I helping?"

"Yes," she said, nodding her head as though convincing herself. "I feel much better than I did earlier."

"The swelling's gone down in your eye."

"It has?" she asked. She had carried a hand mirror into the kitchen at some point in the past. I had seen it when I sat down at her kitchen table. She got up at my words to run to check. She seemed happier, relieved.

"I do a lot in my church." I don't think I had ever called it *my* church before, implying as much a sense of ownership as membership. "It's part of my job with the Forster Foundation. They're involved in just about every kind of outreach. If there were homeless people on the moon, Forster would be firing rockets at them with tents and freeze dried soup. He really cares about other people."

"What about you?" she asked.

"Yeah sure."

"I guess you're too busy to do anything else. No time to give anyone else."

"Well, I'm not married, if that's what you mean."

"No, I..." she began, confirming that I had correctly guessed at her question's target.

"You see these people, and they really need help. All of them. But it can get kind of lonely. They're not really focused on you all that much. They appreciate what you do. They'll even ask if they can help, but how can they? That's the whole point, I guess. What you're doing can never be repaid. That's why it has to be done."

"And you're doing it."

"Not me. It's just a job. The guy writing the checks is the one doing it."

"No, no," she said. "I mean, what you're doing here. This doesn't have anything to do with the Foundation, does it?"

"Not directly," I said. "I guess I just do it because it's expected of me."

"Yeah, I can see why that *would* be lonely." She held her tea cup to her lips without drinking, chewing on her observation silently. "Must be hard to keep going."

"What I can't understand is why a girl like you would ever be lonely."

"Me either!" she said, in mock exasperation. I laughed, as she expected. "The truth is, I guess, I'm hard to deal with. I don't trust other people to want to stay with me. That they would want me around. God, I don't know why I'm telling you this! I don't even know you really."

"Oh, you know me. You know me enough to tell the truth. That's something."

"I guess I can talk to you, at least. You'll probably never think any less of me than you do right now."

"Oh, that's wrong," I said, with a beat to think about it. "Let me rephrase that..."

She laughed again, covering her mouth a second time. "I think my mother told me once that I couldn't help it. I was too much like her. She didn't have any confidence in herself. And I always admired her."

I nodded my head.

"What about you? Who did you want to be like?"

"My brother," I said.

And so, on we went. By the time I left, I had wrung from her a commitment to a date. I promised to take her to a bar, as a joke, since she'd said she couldn't meet good men there. And I was probably anxious to trade the Foundation and its moral wrappings for a night of light licentiousness. She walked me to the door and gripped my hand as I left.

Yes, it was very much on my mind, marriage, even that early on. The effect she had on me is easy to recount. I didn't sleep that night. That in itself was not unusual. I hadn't slept more than three hours a night since I had taken the job, but that had more to do with my conversation with Cecelia months before, on the night before the interview. But after meeting Cynthia that night, I closed my eyes and summoned up the memory of her face, like I was rubbing a lamp in order to make the genie appear. I summoned her in my closed eyes to see her smile back, reassuring me that she did, in fact, exist. And so the very next day during the morning staff meeting, I said a prayer for her. To be clear, I didn't feel confident enough to say it plainly. I gave that most tantalizing of all petitions for my fellow penitent listeners in the room to chew upon. "I have an unspoken request," I said, leaving it at that. I could hear their ears perk up all over the room. A job offer? Private stress? Premonition of getting fired? Counseling? They all could audibly telegraph their questions through their silence.

The fact that I said a prayer for her, to this God I supposedly didn't believe in, and hadn't given my life to, somehow didn't have the effect on me that it should have. I guess I was still kidding myself about not believing, or believing that a prayer would be enough to appease God, should He listen and choose to defy me by existing.

But no, I did pray for her, though I'm not sure what my motives were. I suppose I thought marrying Cynthia would please my bosses, and so, be enough to satisfy their God. I would have a wife and a reputation for good work on my job. People would think I was *saved*, and so I would be.

And besides, she called the church expecting a good man to arrive. So I had to give that to her. It was God, I assumed, who had made the mistake in sending me.

So I wonder now, did I pray because I knew she would not be spending her life with me, but with the person I suspected at this point that everyone assumed I was? Did I pray for her because I knew that regardless of what lies she told me when I first saw her, virtually everything that came out of my mouth to her, every caress, every kiss, every waking and sleeping moment, would more or less be a lie?

Of course, that was also the night that Cecelia decided to call me again.

14

I picked up the phone expecting some salesperson wanting me to renew my car warranty. "Is Peter there?" The voice was shaky and high, like an old woman who had trouble clearing her throat.

"Peter? No. He's not." I didn't want to say anymore. Did I have to explain it all again?

"Cam. It's me. Again." Cecelia cleared her throat and her voice asserted itself, as though it had been held captive by some other power. Suddenly, I knew in an instant what she meant. *It's me. Again. The lonely widow. I'd like to talk to my dead husband. You are the only one who can oblige me.*

"Cecelia."

"I'm sorry. I know it's late."

"No. No."

"I woke you up, didn't I?"

"No. I don't sleep much anymore." I didn't like the way that sounded. The finality. "Not lately, I mean."

There was a deep sigh on the other end. "Cam, I need to talk to

Peter again."

"Cecelia, I thought you..."

"I know what I said. I was wrong. I need to hear him."

"I need him too, Cecelia." Just then, I got a beep that told me another call was waiting on the line. I wanted to break away. Perhaps she could tell in my voice. But I knew I would have to let the other call slip away. I didn't have the guts to hang up on her.

"But that's not fair. You have him. Whenever you need him. All you have to do is open your mouth and speak."

"He was more...is more... than just a voice," I said. "You have him too! All you have to..."

"Oh, don't give me that 'he'll always be a part of you' crap! Everybody keeps telling me that. Does it feel to you like he's still here?" The deep throated rasp in her voice bespoke an animal's anger, something instinctive and unnamable, like the imperatives of hunger and survival.

"No. No it doesn't."

"Of course it doesn't! You think it feels like he's here in this house? I talk and I can hear my voice echoing off the walls! The other night, I walked into his closet and put my head in his shirts just because I thought I could still smell him! I know how pathetic that sounds, and I don't care!"

"But that's not Peter, Cecelia. You're talking about what's left of his memory. What he left behind. You've still got what he gave you inside."

"Is that enough for you?"

"Cecelia, I know it's different. But what you're asking me to do is wrong. You know it. I know it. It's not him. It's...it's *obscene*. It's wrong to him!"

"Why?" Her voice suddenly shifted here, taking on a strange, girlish, even playful character that unsettled me even more. "Couldn't we just, well, pretend that he's there? You just put him on and I'll talk to him for a second."

Put him on. Like a coat, meaning that he can later be "taken off" just as easily.

I didn't say anything to this, which was enough.

She exploded. "He'll never know! He's long gone, Cam. I'm stuck here. I *need* him." There was a pause. I thought maybe the anger of her grief had startled her, as it had me. I thought maybe the words had brought her back — the realization of hearing herself admit he was gone. Then her voice got louder. "I need you Peter! Come back to me! Speak to me!" On some base, instinctive level, she was calling the husband she somehow sensed inside of me to get out.

Peter was stuck inside Cameron. Cameron was preventing him from getting out. But Peter was somehow stronger. He had to be, for her sake.

But he wasn't. "Cecelia, I'm Cameron. I'm not my brother. *My brother is dead.*"

"I don't care! I want to talk to him! Let me talk to him!"

"I'm Cameron, Cecelia."

"I don't care about Cameron! I want Peter! Give him to me!"

"Cecelia," I said, but the voice wasn't mine. It was Peter's.

It was the same voice Peter gave me when I had tried, unsuccessfully, to talk him out of marrying Cecelia. It was the night before he popped the question. He had taken me along to buy the ring, wanted my feedback on whether I thought it was good enough (too good for her, I said) and rolled his eyes appropriately at my responses. I could tell I was getting under his skin, and I could tell he was trying to figure out just why I wanted to talk him out of it. The reasons I gave him — that Cecelia was a nutcase who would smother him, be jealous of his family, and hypercritical of us all — didn't seem to move him. He just thought that was me being his brother, and I suppose I was giving him what he expected.

The real truth was that I really coveted him finding somebody, and especially Cecelia. There was a part of me that was hoping it wouldn't work out between them. I was never able to admit that to myself at the time, and probably wasn't sure about the feelings until I admitted to myself that he was dead. The guilt, daily and in generous portions, was as overwhelming as the grief.

Listen here, I remember him saying. He was driving and he pulled over and gripped the steering wheel with both hands, like it might fly off if he let go. He fixed his eyes on me and squinted like Superman training his heat vision to seal up the crack in a failing dam. *This is what I'm going to do. I don't care if you like it. I didn't ask to spend my life with you. I'll spend it with whoever I want to. And if you want to see me, you'll accept it and like it. And if you don't, you can get out right now and never speak to me again and I'll be just as happy as I am right now.*

I think the anger surprised him as much as it did me. I don't even think he really meant it, though it probably felt good for him to say it to me. I said nothing until he turned away. I think he half expected me to get out. Then, from some place I can't really explain, I said, "Well, if you ask me, you don't sound all that happy right now."

He laughed, and I never heard that voice again, until I opened my mouth to speak to his widowed wife.

"Listen here, Cecelia," I said. Though I couldn't hear anything except a gasp, I envisioned in my head something like her spine straightening, the same as a private being inspected on the parade grounds.

Great, I thought. *What do we say now, Big Boy?*

I cleared Peter's throat. In my mind I could picture him grabbing his belt buckle and adjusting his pants. "I asked to spend my life with you. But my life is over. You have to accept it."

I thought I could picture her nodding her head, but then she spoke. "But I can't, baby. I just can't."

"Beauty," Peter said, "you told Cam yourself just now. I'm not coming back. I'm long gone."

"I'm sorry, Peter! Oh God forgive me! I'm so sorry. I didn't mean it like that..." I had no idea what she was doing, or if she really meant to talk to me like I was Peter. Was she humoring me or herself?

"I know, I know. You just want me back."

"I just want you. Can you see me?"

"What?" This voice was not Peter's. It was mine.

"Please? Ask Cam to let you come over here."

"Cecelia, Cecelia, wait! That's too much. I can't..."

"No! I want Peter back."

"You're talking to Cameron now. You want me to come over."

"No. I want you to come over and be Peter. I want you to put on his clothes and talk to me like him. I'll turn the lights low."

"Cecelia, you're insane."

"Doesn't part of you want to come over?"

The part of me that's my brother? "What about Ricky?"

"He's at my mother's. He won't be back until late tomorrow afternoon."

"No."

"Cameron."

"No!"

"This is not fair, Cameron! *You* did this to me!"

"Go to bed, Cecelia. If you need me to, I'll call somebody to come over. But I am not coming over there, and I'm not coming as Peter."

"If you don't come over here, I'll kill myself, Cam. I swear I will. You come over here and give me back my husband."

"No."

"I know you want to, Cameron? How many times have you thought about it? I've seen you looking at me. Don't you want to come over here? It's not like it would even be you! Just once!"

"How many times, Cecelia? How many times is it going to take? You want me to move in? You want me to change my name? Put on about fifty pounds? Make it really stick? How would you like your son to call me Dad? Is that what you want?"

"No. I'll only need it once. I promise."

"I don't believe you, Cecelia. If I come over there..."

"Please, Cameron. Please do this for me. Peter loved me so much."

"Yes he did," I said, after a moment.

She sniffled and waited. "Are you coming over then, baby?"

15

I took Cynthia to a karaoke bar a few days later. Strange, how I kept looking over my shoulder as I spirited her in. I had started doing this a few weeks before, not really sure who I was looking for but positive that I would recognize them if and when I saw them. Even stranger was how I felt like I had to conceal my identity. I didn't, but I suppose I kept thinking Prescott was hiding in some parked car, waiting to spring out and tell me not to come back to work. I don't know why I thought that. After all, I hadn't seen him in church in months. Why should I see him anywhere? It was almost like he only existed in Forster's world. And besides, Prescott seemed more than happy with everything I was doing.

No, it was Cynthia. I was afraid of someone discovering how we had met. And it was Cecelia. I wondered what might happen if I saw her, and if she saw me.

Cynthia was the only one who seemed intent on concealing her identity. When I showed up at her doorstep, her hair was black, a luminous jet black that shined like the matter between stars. It was the sort of shade you could lose yourself in. I blinked when I saw her, she stunned me so.

"Sorry, this is the real color," she said. She grabbed a few locks with her fingertips, as though examining it. "Hope you don't reconsider."

"No," I said, walking in. "It's lovely." I meant it. It took the edginess off her looks, made her appear more like the innocent I had understood her to be. Strange how something small like that can make such a difference. She had been hiding something from the whole world underneath that dye.

"I'd been coloring it blonde and got tired of it. You sure you like it?"

"Positive," I said. "It's your hair, anyway."

She gave a girlish, satisfied smile. There was relief in it, I suppose, that I was there to see *her*, not simply to minister to some beating victim I didn't know. I had reassured her without meaning to, and she had done the same.

It was the sort of smile that had nothing in common with the one Cecelia greeted me with the night I came to her home.

Peter's home.

Her home.

I knocked on the door and I thought I saw some relief in Cecelia's features too. But she wasn't relieved to see me. There was only the expectation that she might, just for a small second or two, be reunited with Peter. She pulled me into the house — literally, with both hands — and laid on the couch, in the murky light coming through the window, was one of Peter's suits. I could smell it from across the room. She told me not to turn on any lights, which prevented me from seeing her once she shut the door.

"What do you want me to do?" I asked.

That was the question I asked Cynthia for some reason, just as I walked into her place. It startled her, since it was a pointless question *for her*. She had no way of knowing I was saying the first thing that came out when I walked into Cecelia's house.

"What?" Cynthia asked.

"I mean, where do you want to go?"

"I don't know. What did you have in mind?"

"Nothing. I'm used to my day being planned for me."

"They do that a lot at your job."

"Tell me what to do, where to go." I paused. "Who to be..." I added, chuckling.

"So who are you tonight?"

"Let's not get into that. Where do you want to go?"

If I had asked Cecelia that question, I would have had to take her to a place in time perhaps a year or two earlier, when she and Peter had celebrated a quiet anniversary at home. From the moment I walked into the house, she spoke to me as if I was Peter, telling me that once I got on the clothes she would put the music on. And then we would have dinner. She had been preparing it all night. I recognized from the situation that this was something that had actually happened. Peter had even told me about it, about how he had come home expecting to take Cecelia out and she had prepared the entire evening around *taking care of him*. I allowed this euphemism to stand, and so drew a curtain on my brother's marriage that respected their privacy and kept me from forming any intrusive images in my mind.

The great art forger, Elmyr de Hory, used to evade detection from art critics and museum directors by painting, not a copy of an old master, but an original painting in the style of the master he wished to forge. Then he could pass it off as a newly discovered, previously unknown work and get even more money for it. But I could see that Cecelia was picking at the embers of a memory she wished to revisit, to reclaim, perhaps even to retouch and burnish for all time. All she needed was a reasonable facsimile of her husband. Unfortunately for her, all she had was me.

"I appreciate you doing this," Cynthia said.

"Like it's a favor to you. I'm seen out with a gorgeous woman and I'm doing *you* a favor."

"You're very sweet," she said. I perceived that she was trying me out. I was trying to say all the right things to put her mind at ease.

Still I winced when she called me *sweet*. Something I would never have told her was that I was quietly frantic that perhaps she would get the wrong impression about me from the way we had met. She called a church and happened to get me, the most unchurched man she could have gotten. I had shared with her my weekly schedule of charity runs, food bank visits, the odd missions to lepers, etc., and she had been impressed, as I figured she would be. But the power of being perceived as *nice* has an emasculating effect on men. I didn't want her to look on the facts of my life and decide that for all my activity, I was just another boring, faceless nice guy she didn't want to spend any more of her time with. And so, despairing of my role in bettering the lives of my fellow man, I took her to a bar and hoped she might draw a conclusion that I was dangerous enough to keep.

"You're not through with me yet, Mister," Cecelia had told me, or Peter, rather, as I sat down in the room after I had put my brother's ill-fitting clothes on me. It was a tailored suit, tailored for him. I had to draw the belt tightly around the pants just to keep them from falling down. I believe the tie was red, but the light was uncertain. Cecelia was dressed in something that would have been revealing if I could have seen it. I assume the lights were drawn to keep her illusion alive, where she could only see the dim outlines of my face and hear the voice. She stayed at a safe distance, a teasing distance, not close enough to touch me, but just beyond my fingertips should I suddenly decide to do anything. I understood these were the rules — I was to be Peter up to a certain point, just as I had been in our first conversation. There were rules, but I wondered how long those rules would last.

You're not through with me yet, she said. Did she believe Peter had wanted to go? Was she afraid that I...I mean, he... had decided she no longer interested him, and so he had left her?

"Beauty, what do you want me to do?"

"You mean, what do *you* desire?" I understood she was correcting me. This is what Peter *would* have said.

I chuckled, as Peter would have. "I'm sorry. I'm not feeling myself."

That was what Cynthia had said to me the first date, wasn't it? Cynthia seemed pleased with the bar I selected. It had good food but from what I gathered, it also had a slight reputation. She seemed impressed, and a little startled that I knew of the place.

I asked her if the music was too loud.

"No, it's perfect," she said. The music was the karaoke machine, but nobody yet had the guts to get up on the stage yet. It was still early evening.

"Can you sing?" I asked her.

"A little," she said. "You probably wouldn't think I could. What about you?"

"Eh, a little," I said. "Just good enough probably to think too highly of myself."

"We'll test that out later," she said. "Whatever you want to do."

When Cecelia had said that — *Whatever you want to do* — I understood that she didn't really mean it. She was saying what she would have said to Peter. Once she had me stationed on the couch, she worked the stereo. Then with me sitting there, she began dancing for him, and me. The light coming through the windows illuminated her, and the sheer material of her gown seemed invisible. I had obviously never seen her like this before — but I understood this was totally in keeping with her character. The Cecelia that I had seen in the restaurant, and every time on the arm of my brother, was a woman who was confident in herself and enjoyed that confidence. And I was seeing that on display before me, the way she glided through the room as though she knew exactly how to arouse her husband. She was listening for me, and she seemed satisfied when she heard the rise and fall of my breathing change its rhythm to the dictates of her movements.

"How about this one?" Cynthia had said, looking through the titles on the machine. "This is my favorite. It's so...dark."

I knew the song, but I didn't know she expected us to sing a duet.

We looked at the lyrics, and off we went. It took a few bars before I could get the harmony straight, but it was fine, and we sounded by the end as though we had rehearsed the thing. I looked into Cynthia's eyes, which were as confident as her voice, and I knew that she actually took great pride in her singing but was modest enough about it to let it be discovered on its own.

When Cecelia's music was over, she went out of the room, gently telling Peter to keep his seat, that she would be right back. She said it like a teacher leaving a room full of anxious kindergartners. When she returned, she had a plate of food and she kneeled down in front of me and began feeding me little morsels. It was something sweet but I had no idea what it was. All I could recognize was her bearing — the straight back and the way she seemed to condescend to me. *I don't have to do this, but I want to.* It was the sort of thing a self-assertive wife would silently pass to her husband in whatever guise he may appear in on a dark night. It only illustrated the vastness of the space left by my brother. I understood that he wouldn't have left by choice, not if this grand, devastated woman was the monument left in his wake. I knew this version of Cecelia, strong and strange, would disappear the moment she again recognized Peter's unchanging absence.

She put the plate down, and surprised me. She placed a hand on my cheek, rubbing it. Her fingers seemed to savor the movement across my whiskers, and she drew her face close to mine. I closed my eyes.

"It's not right," she finally said. "You'll have to go, Cameron."

My eyes bolted open and the breaking of the spell. "I tried to tell you."

"No, no," she said. "Your face. It's not right. Peter never would have had whiskers. It was something he was sensitive about."

I shifted in the baggy suit.

"You'll have to do better next time," she said.

That wasn't quite what Cynthia said to me when the song was over. It was more like, "Did you disguise your voice?"

"No. Did it sound like it?"

"No. It sounded great. What happened?" I almost answered back until she broke out into her girlish smile again. That was good enough. We enjoyed a nice meal, sang a few more songs, and filled the silences by looking at each other with hopeful eyes. I suppose I felt that I had given her glimpses of the best parts of myself mixed with enough of what I might call genuine affection to leave her curious and wanting another meeting.

We were just coming out of the bar when I felt someone tap on my shoulder. For a split second I thought it might be Prescott. Perhaps it was, in some form or another.

"Excuse me brother, do you know Jesus Christ as your personal savior?" The voice belonged to a kid, probably eighteen or twenty. He had on a T-shirt and jeans and I realized he had been standing outside the bar when we walked in, only he had been talking to somebody else. He had been standing outside, accosting as many people as he could as they came into the bar.

"What?" I asked. I supposed if he indeed had a brother, it would have been an older brother. He was one of those boys on the verge of manhood who somehow look younger because of it.

The boy smiled. I realized I had made a mistake by giving him an opportunity to talk to me. I should have kept on going. "I wanted to know about your salvation? Do you know Jesus Christ?"

"Do you?" I asked. Though I wasn't conscious of it, I suppose the idea that Cynthia was with me had silently fallen away from my perception. It was just me and the missionary, staking out our positions.

"Yes, I do," he said confidently. "And because of that, I want to make sure as many people know about Him as I can."

"And what happens to them?"

"To them?" he repeated, as though unsure of himself. "Why, they become one with Christ."

"No," I said. "What happens to *them*? If they become one with Christ, they lose themselves, don't they?"

"Lose themselves?" The kid asked the question as though he had never considered such a thing before.

"Yeah. You're not the same person you were *before* you met Christ right?"

"No. And that's good."

"But what about who you *were*? Don't you miss that person? Don't you miss yourself?"

"But..." he said, groping for words, "how can I miss what I'm happy is gone?"

"Happy?"

"Yes," he said. "When Jesus showed me who I really was, I didn't want to be that person anymore. I wanted to be like Him."

"And now you want me to be like Him too?" I said.

The boy smiled again. "Only if you want to be. That's totally up to you."

Mr. Friedrich Nietzsche said that Christianity was mainly a religion of resentment, that it constructed a worldview that castigated those who were strong and uplifted the weak, turning the whole world upside down and convincing those on the bottom that they were, in fact, on top. This was necessary, he said, since it was the weak who had made this way of looking at the world. That way, they felt a certain amount of pride every time they were pushed around.

So I smiled at the boy with the offer of Christ and hit him squarely on the jaw, watching him fall with his arms splayed in every direction, his eyes emanating a shocked spaciness. If Prescott had indeed been watching, he would have seen me jump on the boy's prone figure and begin pounding his midsection until he convulsed in coughs, unable to speak. Cynthia, who had been watching the whole thing, fell on top of me and began pulling at my arms, probably after a moment of dumbfounded fascination.

"Stop! Stop! What in God's name are you doing?" she demanded.

It would have been a good question, if I had been able to answer. And if I had, the answer probably would have been something like this: *Why should He want me? Doesn't He know what I am? He's got me doing everything He wants right now. Isn't that enough? Must He demand everything?*

I kept wailing away at him, feeling him decrease a little with each punch, until the punches themselves started to fade away as I realized what I was doing. The boy had no idea what he had done.

"Who sent you to do this?" I demanded of him. It's always good to blame your own conduct, as well as someone else's, on an unseen adversary. It removes all the guilt from both of you. Of course I knew who had sent him, but I've always thought it was unseemly when celebrities, politicians, or relatives getting out of prison blame things on God.

"He sent me!"

"Who? Prescott?"

"The Lord sent me," he said.

"Well tell the Lord to leave me alone. You hang around here long enough and you'll get to tell Him yourself!"

"Cam!" Cynthia said, holding down one of my arms.

"What's his deal?" the boy asked.

"He already goes to church," she said to the boy, who wasn't smart enough to run away. "He's in a ministry."

"He must need it," the boy said. "I'll pray for him."

"I said leave me alone!" I shouted. "I need silence!"

The boy, who probably knew nothing of Nietzsche but everything of the better part of valor, ran away looking for more willing converts. Cynthia spent the next twenty minutes or so, kneeling with me, patting my back, rubbing my shoulders, speaking in the seasoned voice of a comforter, promising me she would not leave until she was sure I was alright. Strangely enough, her voice reminded me of Cecelia's — the gentle, strong woman who knows the secret desires and turmoils in her man's heart and wishes to navigate them as best she can.

When we were once again alone, I could tell she needed some reassuring. And so, I rendered a perfect duplication of the boy witness' voice, right down to the pimply break when his voice reached the upper reaches of its register.

"Stop it!" she said, in mock horror, amazed that I was able to recall it so completely. It allowed us both to laugh at the boy, who had foolishly thought my soul worth saving. "How do you do that?"

"A gift," I said, and relished the look of pleasure I saw working its way through her features.

By the end of the evening, she had resolved she would see me the following night. I suppose if I had wanted to implant in her a sense that I was dangerous, I couldn't have done any better.

Because on that score, I wasn't pretending to be anybody.

16

I woke up the next morning at four-thirty, or more accurately, I got out of bed. In truth, I only dozed for a few hours and had been laying there, eyes wide open, for more than an hour. For a few weeks, I had let some duties with the church and the foundation pile up, and as I sat there, I began silently ticking them off, arranging and rearranging them in my head, torturing myself, running myself ragged in dreamtime, until I realized that I could get them all done in one day provided I was willing to get to it. So I did. I put my clothes on, splashed water on my face, and I was out the door just as the first dim, red light began seeping into the sky. Not a scrap to eat. In a minute, I was at the church and getting the ladder out to change the marquee out front, replacing last week's intended thought-provoking message for passing drivers with a new one. I found the new message scrawled out by one of the church secretaries on a sheet of paper. She had left it in the shed where the letters were kept. I had no idea who came up with these bon mots but I was willing to place them.

I was replacing "Live once — die twice — Live twice — die

once." I climbed the ladder and spelled out, in big, black letters, "God knows." A few car horns honked at me. I assumed they either approved of the message or disapproved, showing either sign with their horns and convinced I would be able to tell the difference. I stood there for a few moments, slightly panic stricken that I might have misspelled one of the words. It was the Word of God, on some level, wasn't it? I didn't want to get it wrong. But what was I afraid of, since I didn't believe? By the time the sun was over the treetops, I had worked up a considerable sweat. The vague panic left me for the real kind when I checked my watch and saw that I was late for the community kitchen's daily breakfast serving.

I ladled out great mounds of scrambled eggs mixed with bacon and cheese for the lines of people who showed up. It was my first time to do this, and I don't know why I had visions of Depression-era derelicts wandering in, shadowy, vaguely bearded men with saggy-brimmed hats clutching at threadbare jackets that had once been purchased from Wall Street tailors. The image was even more ridiculous, as it was summer. They were mostly young black and white men with T-shirts that had seen better days. I could tell how old some of the shirts were since they celebrated the long-gone championship seasons of some professional sports teams. All of the men looked to be in their twenties or thirties, but for some reason, older, whether by the conditions of poverty, pride, or drug use. There was an unnamable smile among some of the men, a certain laughing scorn for the food, while the others looked concerned they might be recognized by someone else. The women who came were usually accompanied by toddlers who picked at the eggs, gobbled up the bacon and washed it down with orange juice.

Once that was over, most of the volunteers left to go to their own individual jobs, which meant I got to finish cleaning up and washing the dishes. I laid into the pots and trays and forks with missionary zeal, smiling while the kitchen staff piled pan after pan before me, occasionally plopping them directly into the water and spraying me with suds. It took more than an hour to finish, by which time I received the grateful thanks of the regulars in the kitchen and nods of recognition from those who were already busy preparing lunch for the next crowd.

I ran by the office where they had about 2,000 fliers for me to pass out and attach to windshield wipers at the shopping mall parking lot. I loaded the bundles into my SUV and got to the mall just as its doors opened. I reasoned that more people would have a chance to get the pages if I moved from entrance to entrance every fifteen minutes, which was what I did. That allowed me about two hours to hand them out as I watched the parking lot fill up and my nose turn red from the sun. I shook hands, handed out the papers, and moved fast enough to avoid being tagged as a solicitor from the mall security staff. I received a few "God bless you"s and "Have a blessed day"s, then I moved on to putting the fliers on cars. I went through all my stacks before I ever looked at the paper. It was asking for donations of cash, blankets and old clothes for victims of a hurricane on the Atlantic coast. When I returned to drop off the handful of fliers I had left, I made a donation, and a mental note to look through my closet.

Then there was the Japanese guy. Prescott had told me that a group of Japanese men had just moved into the community and were leasing houses about three blocks from where I lived. They were in the country for five-year stints as engineers at a nearby automobile plant. The way he understood it, they had come to America and left their wives and children back in Japan because it would be too disruptive removing the children from school. Prescott had recommended going to see them, dropping off church pamphlets, and asking them if they needed anything.

On the way over to their house though, I saw some prisoners from the county jail picking up trash by the side of the road. There were about two dozen, some carrying clear plastic bags that flapped in the breeze, others with sticks to pick up the trash. Each wore their white coveralls and walked at a slow pace on the road shoulder in full view of rifle-carrying deputies. A van idled nearby waiting to carry them to the next highway when this job was over. I drove on to a gas station and picked up about thirty soft drinks to give them. I walked up to one of the deputies with the bags and dropped them in front of him.

PROFESSION OF FAITH

At first, I think he was suspicious that this might be some elaborate escape gambit for the men. It took a second or two to make him relax, and when I drove off, I saw the prisoners wave to me and lift the drinks in thanks. It was the sort of thing I guessed that Forster might approve of.

Resuming my way to the Japanese worker's house, I cut off someone by accident while changing lanes. I had assumed no one was in my blind spot, but when I moved left I heard a sudden screech of tires and the smell of burned rubber, followed by a series of horns. But no crash. A quick glance in my rearview mirror showed that a truck had been just behind me and it had narrowly avoided two crashes — one with me and one with a car in the oncoming lane that had swerved to miss him when he veered over because of me. I pulled over until the driver of the truck caught up with me. I rolled down my window and began apologizing so profusely that within a few seconds the most I could get from him was a mild chastising to watch where I was going.

I reasoned that I had read somewhere that it was customary in Japan when meeting someone to bring a small gift. I thought food might be a good touch. I also remembered reading sweets were highly prized there, so I stopped and got a box of chocolate candy. Nothing beyond what you might give a new neighbor. The address Prescott had provided me with was right, and I rang the doorbell three times. Evidently, according to his information, the guy was a hard worker. He must have been, since I woke him up. He answered the door in a bathrobe, his eyes barely open and his jet black hair shooting skyward like stalactites deep within the earth groping for the absent sun.

I handed him the box of candy. It took a moment for him to perceive what was going on. I realized the information Prescott had given me was wrong on one key point — the guy didn't speak a syllable of English. When he looked at the pictures on the box, he bowed his head and said *please* to me several times, in a grateful sounding voice. I asked if there was anything I could do, to which he smiled pleasantly but impassively. Then I repeated the words, louder. Then I bowed, turned and walked away, with him repeating his pleases several more times before shutting the door.

BRILLIANT DISGUISES

By now, it was closing in on dinner time, but I was supposed to take part in the week of prayer at the church. We had all signed up for specific hours where we would go to the sanctuary, pick up a stack of papers on which people had filled out their prayer requests, then go about making individual prayers for these people, before passing them to our fellow penitents in the room. Most of the requests were unsigned. I should also mention that by this time, my lack of sleep had caught up with me. I grabbed a stack of about fifty of these requests and found a dark, quiet corner of the sanctuary, sitting down in a pew where I could rest my head and gently fall asleep. If I had a prayer, it was that I might not snore.

But I couldn't quite get there. The prayers kept me awake. There were a mass of men, probably six or seven, gathered at the altar with their heads down, their arms locked around each other, their heads bowed, their voices just above the level of a murmur, going over the prayers and each taking a turn begging God's attention to the lives of these people. Something about the insistence of their voices made me look at the slips of paper I sat down beside me like scraps collected from the aftermath of a parade. There was something shaming me about them, perhaps the mere fact that scrawled on these irregular sheets of what would normally be scratch paper were probably the most important, deepest desperate desires of these people I moved among and saw every week.

There on the pages next to me were people asking God to help them get a job, or take away their mother's cancer, or take away the pain they felt over someone abusing them decades earlier. A child's anonymous scrawl prayed that Daddy would quit shouting Mommy. A woman's spidery words prayed that her child wouldn't turn out like she had.

Why was I doing all this? Why did these people's concerns prick at my conscience? Did they really? What in God's name possessed me to buy drinks for a bunch of petty criminals and juvenile offenders who were picking up trash? Why was I bone tired over these people? Was I simply trying to make up for hitting somebody?

PROFESSION OF FAITH

In a fit of madness induced by the goddess Hera, Hercules murdered his own wife and children and then went into the wilderness to live alone. After a time, he went to the oracle at Delphi and was told he must, as penance, execute twelve tasks for King Eurystheus, the man he most hated among all others. When he was finished, his deeds were appropriately called Herculean.

And yet what did I feel as I ran from task to task "doing something?" The entire time my brain refused to turn off, so on and on I went, in search of the next thing, as though some destination approached with terrible finality. Why? Was I trying, somehow, to even the score after decking someone interested in the destination of my eternal soul? What kind of ridiculous penance did I seek?

I felt like a man waking up in the pew, instead of someone falling asleep. I really had lost track of myself. And yet I hadn't made any leap of faith. I wasn't born again. This Jesus these people were praying to was exerting His will over me. After waiting an hour with my head resting on the pew, I took my stack of prayers and walked out.

Let me back up. I should say, just for the sake of my own image, that I did say a prayer, if you might call it that. I was ready to get up and leave, but something in the weight of those pages made me stop and kneel. I didn't say anything. Whatever was communicated came from how I gripped those requests in my hand, and how much I fought the urge to say something on their behalf. That was all I was going to muster. And then I left.

By that time, the sun had gone down. I was so tired I didn't stop for food anywhere. I wanted to come home. I thought I would just crash on my bed and get something to eat the next morning. But my cell phone rang. I fumbled it out of my pants' pocket and answered. Somehow, even through the six or seven rings it took to get it out, I never considered not answering it.

It was Prescott's secretary, Rachel, who wanted me to know that Elliot Dalrymple's wife Charlotte was in critical condition at the hospital and not expected to live. He was there alone because all of their children were still flying in. Charlotte had come to the hospital in the grip of pneumonia and suddenly had a heart attack just a day

105

in. She had been in a coma for several hours, kept alive only by the ventilator. Rachel assured me that all I had to do was mention Forster's name and I would get in to see them, since the intensive care unit bore Forster's name. Without so much as a grumble, I got out of my bed and drove to the hospital.

Eliot Dalrymple sat next to Charlotte in the ward as I walked in. He recognized me and wordlessly choreographed me to a chair on the other side of the bed. His wife lay between us. He was holding her hand, and once he saw that I had sat down, he turned his face to her as she continue to breathe, forced to by the ruthless efficiency of the ventilator. A heart monitor beat out the pace of her barely remaining life.

I was so tired, I just sat there. I didn't attempt to make any conversation. I kept my head down and leaned forward, resting my head in my hands. Within a few seconds, I had closed my eyes. The music of the heart monitor and the regularity of the breathing machine put me instantly to sleep. I didn't hear him utter a sound the whole of the time I was there.

I have no idea how much time passed.

But the next thing I was aware of was Peter. He had come into the room, and somehow he had taken Dalrymple's place there in the chair next to bed. And instead of Dalrymple's insensible wife lying there on the bed, I was there. I was looking at myself, hooked up to a heart monitor and breathing on a ventilator. Peter, with a devilish, conspiratorial look on his face, winked at me, and I convulsed into laughter. Somehow, I knew what he had suggested without so much as a syllable. I reached down to the body lying on the table, my own, and wrenched off my left foot. There wasn't so much as a twitch from the body lying there. The foot was heavier somehow than I expected, like a brick ready to be thrown through a window. Instead of flinging it, I handed the foot to Peter. Next to him was a scale hanging from the ceiling, much like one might see in an old grocery store for produce. He grabbed the foot by the big toe, shaking it like a fish fresh from the ocean, and placed it on the scale. He gave a silly, self-amused laugh. He then flicked the foot off into the floor with his fingers, as if shooing away a fly. Peter was dressed like an Englishman on a hunt, with a tweed coat and sweater vest and a bow tie, and breeches and brown shoes. I had never in my life seen him like this. He walked over to the edge of the bed and took the other foot, and one by one, we giggled and disassembled me as I lay there, the ventilator still going and heart monitor still rapping out a beat after there was no longer a chest left to register one.

Somehow, my mind focused on that sound of the heart monitor, and the sound of her breath, and the sound of my breath, and the sound of my dead brother's voice.

Are you going to wake up anytime soon?

I snapped up, and all was as it had been. Dalrymple was there with his wife still, his head down, his index finger circling over her limp hand, her chest rising and falling with all-too-mechanical precision. I looked up at the clock. It was midnight. I hadn't moved from the spot in probably four hours. My knees were raw from where my elbows had lodged on them. My arms tingled from inactivity.

I quickly rose, and Eliot stirred back to consciousness himself. He hadn't been asleep, but he hadn't moved probably in the whole time I had been there.

"Thank you so much," he said.

I nodded, and left before any other words could be said. I realized as I left that he had assumed I had been praying the whole time. I drove home and fell back into bed.

So why didn't I go to sleep, still? Perhaps because I thought back on the day and I couldn't recall a single feature on any of the faces of the people I had encountered the whole day through. If I had meant for all of my activity to somehow atone for the day before, then all that these people had done or cared for or needed had just been a means to my end.

And why did this bother me, as I lay sleepless, the whole night? There was nothing to do but look for something to read. It was hours until sun up.

ii. THE WITNESS

17.

I was speaking to Christine Thrower. She was a woman in her fifties who had been a member of the church for about thirty-seven years. She looked like somebody's grandmother, provided that Grandma was having a nervous breakdown.

"All these things I thought I understood ... I'm not sure of anymore," she said. Her voice was weary from sobbing. We had been talking for hours.

"Why aren't you sure?"

"I don't know. I don't know why I don't know."

"Is that why you came here?"

She nodded. I had my arm around her shoulder without realizing I had put it there.

Why was I talking to her? It was my turn. As with my meeting Cynthia several years before, I had my shift as a counselor, only this session was in person at the church. As before, I was alone to dispense my supposed wisdom.

I knew Christine, as did most people in church. She was a fixture. She worked in the kitchen during socials, taught Sunday School for preschoolers, played the organ when the regular organist was on vacation. Every child growing up in the church had passed through her class, and every family losing a member had returned a casserole dish after she sent something over during their week of mourning. She attended morning and evening on Sunday, Wednesdays, and any special events. The preacher, whomever he might be, sometimes joked that Christine was at church more than he was. Where some people might choose to stay away, whether from illness or obligation or simply early morning laziness, Christine would be there. She planned her family vacations to avoid missing church.

When she walked in, I thought perhaps her husband had died. Her face seemed to speak of some kind of death, of desperation. She was weeping uncontrollably, and that seemed inconceivable to me. I don't think I had ever seen Christine sad, or even with a neutral face. Anything less than geniality, a pleased posture in the world, was radically different in my experience with her.

What had brought her to me was a creeping, sinister feeling she couldn't quite name that had convinced her she was not what everyone assumed she was — a Christian. She doubted her faith for some reason, and I had to not only find out why but reassure her.

"It happened when I woke up this morning."

"Anything in particular about this morning that made you think that?" I asked the question with a kind of droll amusement — not mocking, but trying to set her at ease. I knew that while some Christians had crises of faith, almost all of them felt they were the very first to ever do so. The main thing was to set them at ease.

"I ... I guess that's not true. This is something I've been struggling with for awhile." That too was normal. She didn't want to admit that whatever doubts she had were probably wrapped up in her own feelings about herself. *How can God love me when I don't love myself?* That sort of thing. It actually made sense. Christine going to church every time the doors opened, possibly because she needed assurance every day that God still cared, that God *could* still care, about her.

"What have you been struggling with?"

"No...I can't..."

"Christine, you'll feel better if you tell me."

"No. I can't even make myself say it. I shouldn't even think it."

"What?"

She fiddled with her hands, still sitting down, not looking at me. My mind wandered over the possibilities. It never failed, all the ways that people found to keep secrets that suddenly came tumbling out when they no longer felt safe keeping them.

"I wonder if there's any truth to it all."

"Truth to what?"

"You know. The Bible." She whispered the words, as though someone else might be listening.

"Oh," I said, once again, slightly droll, as though I'd heard this one before. Which I had.

"I mean, I don't doubt it. I just wonder about some things."

"Like what?"

"Oh, you know. The stuff people usually talk about. The creation story."

I nodded.

"The story of Jonah and the whale."

"The big fish, you mean."

"Right. I know that!" She gave an irritated growl. "I don't know how many times I've been over that with the kids."

"Well, surely you know, Christine, that..."

"I know. We're dealing with stories about God, and if God exists, He can do anyth... listen to that. *If* God exists. That's what I mean. I don't think on any other day I would have said such a thing."

"Do you think God exists?"

"Well, yes." She said the words as though *I* had been the one coming in with doubts. "I know He does."

"Good. So what's the problem?"

"Well, what about Jesus? Him rising from the grave. I mean, if you don't believe that..."

"And you don't?"

"Cameron, do you?"

My eyes shifted and then I turned the question back on her. "Tell me about you first."

"Well, I ask myself, what would I do? I mean, if I thought somebody was God, and I had seen Him do all these wonderful things, and then He died. Well, wouldn't I *want* Him to come back from the dead? Wouldn't I want more than anything to see Him?"

Though my head stayed perfectly still, I'm sure she thought I was nodding in agreement.

"And then, what's to keep me from coming up with a story that He's not really dead? He's not around to contradict me. They couldn't have known how far this would go."

"Christine, I understand what you're saying. But I'm not sure *you* understand what you're saying. You're saying you think there is a God, right? And you're saying you *do* think Jesus was capable of working miracles?"

"Now, I do believe that. Yes." She put her finger down as though making a bet on a strong hand of cards.

"But you're saying you have a hard time believing, then, in the Resurrection?"

"Well, wouldn't you find it easy to make up that story? Wouldn't you miss someone so much you'd want to keep them alive in any way you could?"

"No," I said. "I don't accept that."

"You don't?"

"No. You think it would have been easy to keep on listening to Jesus? Think about what His being around did just to Peter. He was never the same man. Following Jesus was a very taxing, grueling thing for him. Jesus challenged him every day and in every way conceivable."

"But they loved Him."

"Yes."

"And love can make people do regrettable things."

I cleared my throat and looked away. "Christine, I don't think you're having trouble believing. You're just having questions. That's normal. We walk by faith."

"I know that. But can Jesus still love me even when I question

Him?"

"You know the answer to that."

"But Cameron..." she dissolved into sobs again.

I patted her shoulder. "Maybe grief could make you do that for a little while, but even grief only lasts so long. You can miss somebody, but life *makes* you move on after awhile. The world *hasn't* moved on from Jesus. We're still dealing with Him."

"Oh, yes. Yes, that's very good." She brightened at the thought.

"And you can't keep somebody alive, not even with a story. You can't pretend...you can't make them...what about Lazarus, you still believe in that story?"

"Yes," she said, dogged.

"He came back from the dead. Why?"

"Jesus brought him back."

"You think that was because He cried so much over Lazarus, that He simply told people Lazarus was still alive, even though he wasn't, and they bought it?"

"No, no, Jesus really brought him back."

"Well wouldn't it be the same? Jesus making up a story that Lazarus was still alive. He was a good friend. Didn't want to see him go."

"No, no. I believe that. But you know how it is. You lose somebody. You ever lost anybody?"

"My brother. He died in a car crash about five years ago."

"Have a hard time dealing with it?"

"Oh, yes." I shook my head and cleared my suddenly parched throat. "I don't think my sister-in-law has ever excepted the fact. I know for a fact she hasn't."

"Then you know."

"Christine, what's bothering you? You say you believe all this, but..."

"Oh, the truth is that I just don't think I'm saved."

"Why not? If anybody..."

"That's just it. *Everybody* thinks I am. When I don't *feel* it. I've never *felt* it."

"You sure you've never felt it? What should it *feel* like?"

"I don't know. But that's the whole point. I don't think that I've ever..."

"You doubt your salvation because you have doubts."

"Yes, that's it!"

I nodded this time. "Everyone has doubts, Christine. You're only human. It happens. The point is that you still believe, in spite of the doubts. Wasn't that what the man prayed when he brought his son to Jesus to cast out a demon?"

"But what can I do?"

Not too many people understand, really, the terrifying quality of the Almighty, the crushing, devouring characteristics of His will. When most people read God's promise in Leviticus that "you shall be holy," they read it either as an admonition, or as a call to better living. But I think I hear it correctly when I hear it as a blood vow, as God warning His people that one day, we absolutely will be holy. Because He will *make* it happen.

And yet, it's us He has to work with. Which is why I wasn't feigning amusement when I spoke to this woman about her very real crisis. She had no way of knowing that I was convincing her of a faith that I still did not belong to five years later. What could I tell her, other than what I had been trained to say, and what I thought was appropriate?

Oh, by that time, I *did* believe. I most certainly believed. But I did not belong. By this time, it was a point of honor to me. I was outside, yet I was inside.

Well, He's used worse people than me, I told myself.

I told her that Jesus promised He would be faithful to us, and if we prayed together, it would take away any doubt she had about herself. It might not clear up every doubt in particular, but I felt her own doubts might become manageable, if they remained.

She nodded gratefully, and I prayed for her. It was quite a good prayer, I thought. My voice matched Prescott for cadence and diction. I used some of his favorite phrases to arrive at what I thought was a forceful, reassuring Amen.

"Did you feel it?" I asked, smiling.

She thought for a second, then shook her head mournfully. "No," she croaked. "No, I didn't."

"Alright, I said, let's do it again." She shut her eyes immediately, and I said the exact words I had before, only this time, while holding her hand, I gave a barely perceptible but definite squeeze.

"Did you feel it that time?"

"Yes!" she exclaimed, unaware of what I had done. "Oh, thank you! I feel so much better!"

18.

On that sleepless night five years in the past, one of many sleepless nights, only distinguished by my daylong search for absolution after hitting a man who witnessed to me, the book I finally picked up was a Bible. It was the first time since I had started working for Forster, and Forster's church, that I did this. I suppose *my hour* had come. A lifetime of reading books had more or less prepared me for what I found in the Bible.

My reading habits before I ever joined the Forster Foundation had a purpose. When I was a child, during the long hours of summer when parents must work and children are at loose ends, I was usually deposited at 9 a.m. at the doors of the city library and picked up shortly before noon for a quick lunch. Within half an hour, I was back and left by myself for another five hours until whichever parent could make it picked me up. There was necessity in this: my parents did not have enough money for a sitter, and they believed my education could only benefit from being surrounded by books. They never told me which books to read, and only occasionally asked. Over the silent summers of eyestrain and ennui, I eventually groped my way toward the classics, history, science, and philosophy, and never quite left those shelves. Or as Mr. Walker Percy put it, during those years I stood outside the universe and sought to understand it. I lived in my room as an Anyone living Anywhere and read fundamental books.

As an adult, I trooped off some days to my previous jobs — those before the Foundation — with a volume of Gogol or Camus or Thurber or Capote or Beckett, letting it rest on my desk until a free moment presented itself. Sometimes, these books would be visible. Sometimes, I would hide them, embarrassed that someone might be getting more of a look at me than I might have wanted through my reading choices. Other times, I wanted someone to pay attention, feeling on some unspoken level that I was different.

Ah, to be *different*.

If anyone noticed, they accused me of simply putting the books on my desk and moving the bookmark through "The Foundations of the Metaphysics of Morals" and whatever else, just to impress somebody. I wasn't playing a part then. I started doing it to differentiate myself from Peter. My brother was a very physical person when he was younger. I don't mean the overweight version that moped off into the last years of his life before it was violently cut short. When I was younger, my brother played tennis with elan, golf with aplomb, could call a good game behind the plate, and was known for the quality of his sky hook. He did all of this with the same disgusting ease with which he sailed through school.

What I wanted was not to be like my brother, merely a copy, but to be his equal in some other way. By dipping my nose into thick books and coming back with quotations to summon and recite on command, I could speak back to him in a foreign language and yet I knew he would recognize and understand. I wanted his respect. By the time he died, my habit of crawling into books was yet another part of my life that continued on without him. Another part that seemed meaningless without its inspiration.

Yet when I finally approached the Bible, it didn't seem as foreign as I had thought it would be. I couldn't help but recognize the ideas, the phrases, the cadences from all the other reading I had done over the course of my life. You could see that these ideas had been peeking out behind the other ideas I had crammed into my head. The book was familiar and new at the same time.

I would take my lunch hour in those first days and find a restaurant where I could sit in a corner and read. What does it say about me that I bought a cheap, paperback copy of the Bible, ripped the cover off, and read it so as not to draw attention? This was after spending years in coffee shops with my book of the moment propped up just so high so as to advertise the title. I do remember once feeling a pang of embarrassment in a previous job when someone asked me what I was reading, and I didn't wish to say Mr. Evelyn Waugh, because I wasn't sure how to pronounce the name. Nobody asked me how to pronounce Mephibosheth or Eleazer, and I wouldn't have known.

Cynthia was aware of what I was doing, and though we never talked about it, I had the impression I had her endorsement. God knows what she thought, considering what she knew about me — that I was some kind of church counselor with an extremely sensitive streak who at least once got violently offended by a benevolent stranger. Not exactly the sort you would want to take home to mother. But then, I thought, a man who reads the Bible obsessively can't be all bad to a potential spouse. I figured out that it would take multiple readings for me to digest it and be able to call out the appropriate quotations in the right moments. This meant that for a solid year I read virtually nothing else in my spare time. I read it clinically, memorizing the words while dashing between the letters to keep from digesting its substance. As I had with my brother, I wanted to speak the appropriate language. But for a different reason. This time, I didn't want to stand out. I was now Cynthia's husband, and I could recite chapter and verse.

And even after my wife went to bed, I moved into the living room of our thirty-five hundred square foot house and continued to read and reread the Bible by the light of a small lamp. What surprised me the most was what I didn't find there.

THE WITNESS

I had previously learned of the Hero's journey — the aspects that Mr. Joseph Campbell, among others, had identified in all the great tales of antiquity. The hero who must confront his old nemesis, Death, man's greatest, ultimate villain. Through the wisdom of a wise old teacher, the hero encounters great tests along the way, sometimes failing, but in the end, conquering the foe and thereby learning the great truths of being human.

But I looked in vain for this blue print in the Bible. It simply wasn't there. The heroes, if you could call them that, kept making ridiculous mistakes, learning nothing from their teachers or fathers, constantly getting (and earning) the righteous ire of God, and emerging broken. Their only foe was not death, but themselves. Death, when they were gathered back unto their fathers, only gave way to another generation of similar cluelessness, and yet God would somehow be able to use all these pigheaded spokesmen and women He assembled toward a great purpose — gathering all the clueless under His banner. Indeed, the only hero of the Bible was ...God.

But there was much that was at home with me as well. God was just like me. He was never just one person. I think I understood almost immediately the mystery of the Trinity because people needed God for so much more, and how could one being be more than ...everything? He wasn't just the God of Abraham, but also of Isaac and Jacob. He was the Ancient of Days. He was prophet, and priest, and king. Whatever the times needed. He would not tell Moses a name other than one that stated his simple existence. *You will have no power over me by invoking my name,* he was saying. After all, as Mr. William Shakespeare said, what's in a name?

And He had plenty of them. In my church hymnal alone, he was A Mighty Fortress, the King of Glory, King Eternal, King of Love, Great Redeemer, My Redeemer, Blessed Redeemer, Shepherd, Our Help In Ages Past, Savior, Blessed Savior, Gentle Savior, Man of Sorrows, Man of Nazareth, the Strong, Righteous Man of Galilee, Strong Salvation, Joy of Loving Hearts, Dayspring, Friend of Thronging Pilgrims, The Great Physician, Sacred Head, The One Who Was Crowned, Rock of Ages, Lover of My Soul, Balm of Gilead, Lord of the Harvest, Lord My God, Dear Lord and Father of Mankind, Lord of All, World's

True Light, The Mighty Word, The Christ of God, God of Mercy, God of Grace, The Solid Rock, The Reed of Life, Majestic Sweetness, Hope of the World, Sunshine of My Soul, Lily of the Valley and God of Our Fathers, amongst many, many other things.

And what of His children? Didn't Abraham and Isaac both assume a different identity in Egypt, in order to preserve their lives? What about Jacob, who pretended to be his brother in order to hoodwink his blind father out of his older brother's inheritance? Moses, who lived most of his early life as a prince in the palace when he belonged with the rest of his people in slavery? Didn't Daniel and his friends in the fiery furnace all have Babylonian aliases? And Saul, who was Paul?

And what of Jesus? Wasn't that the ultimate secret identity, worthy of a Clark Kent or Peter Parker? Living as the son of a carpenter in a little backwater town, when all the while, He is the promised King? Eternal Word? Lord of All? And didn't He heal people sometimes and demand they keep His identity a secret? And wasn't He executed for an act of impersonation — as the Almighty? Weren't His disciples unable, for some unclear reason, at times after the Resurrection, simply to recognize Him? Who else could be both the Great Shepherd and the Lamb?

I remember talking about this in the office once with Si Gelb. He had just had a conversation with Prescott about Biblical prophecies on the end of the world. Prescott sometimes brought these up because one school of End Times interpretation believed that Jews would take the word of Christ to the rest of the world just before the Second Coming. I always felt Prescott was using conversations like this as a way to perhaps slowly usher Gelb into the fold. It was his way of saying, Why wait around for something like that to happen? Why not join the party right now? Gelb would listen benignly with an expression of silently patient scorn, a thanks but no thanks never quite said aloud, followed by a few hasty steps in any available direction.

But this time, Gelb said something about how secret identities held a special allure in Jewish culture, that most superheroes have secret identities because they were created by Jewish writers. Jews have needed secret identities to flourish in hostile cultures all over the world, so the idea of Jews suddenly emerging from underground, as it were, to spread any message, however unlikely, wasn't quite out of the question. After all, wasn't he there, among us Bible thumpers doing the work of the Savior?

"Hey, I'm here for a reason," he said, with the same patient, slightly strained voice, as though he was having to convince himself as much as us. "Maybe *I'm* really in disguise."

I held a hand to the side of my mouth, giving him a conspiratorial gesture, as though getting a confidence out of him. "Seriously," I said, "how did you wind up here?"

He nodded, as if to say *no big deal*. "What are you gonna do? I've known Ben Forster for a long time, and I wanted to help him out. I suppose if there is a God, He expects you to do good regardless of where it is. Some places are more of a challenge than others."

It was a testament to Gelb that he was the only man in the entire office who could have gotten away with saying the words "if there is a God." In his case, everyone more or less accepted that was his way and perhaps even smiled. I felt a subversive shock flood warmly through my body. "So how big a challenge is it here?"

"Ah, this place is a piece of cake," he said, waving his hand derisively.

"Doesn't it get on your nerves though? Conversations like that with Prescott?"

"I tell him he's going to be shocked when he gets to Heaven and I'm there to greet him. 'Not exactly the Jew you were expecting, eh?'" I laughed and he seemed appreciative. "What are *you* doing here?"

"I needed a job."

"There are other jobs out there."

I suppose I could have quoted Mr. Emmanuel Levinas' position that we cannot know who we are unless we understand the Other -unless we accept responsibility for that which is not ourselves. You can't know God unless you know your fellow man. But this would have involved a much longer discussion — such as why I *would* care about such a thing. That would mean that I was rejecting God by serving Him, or something like that. And I didn't want to sound pretentious, which is what it sounds like when you drop names and spout ideas that aren't your own, like I'm doing now with you. At least, when you imitate someone, you can hide behind the conjuring of their voice.

So I answered Gelb by imitating him. "What are you gonna do?" I said, even delivering back his head shrug and hands out, palms up gesture. Mr. Levinas also said it is of the highest importance to know whether we are not duped by morality. Wouldn't that involve the kind of deception involved in mimicry?

Gelb's head bobbed backward at the summoning of his own voice, and he smiled. There was a moment or two of awkward silence, and then he continued on. "But like I was saying. The secret identity. The Jews have integrated into virtually every culture on the planet. In Europe there were Jews who converted to Islam, some to Christianity, only they did it outwardly and kept the faith to themselves."

"Is it hard to be two things at once?" I asked.

"Who wants to be only two things?" he said. "After all, don't you people believe God is best understood in threes?"

How true he was. And how is the whole story supposed to end? Isn't the end of the world supposed to be heralded by someone *pretending* to be Christ? And isn't the one standing next to him called the *False* Prophet?

So I kept my nose in a book as usual, even if it was only one Book, and tried to make sure that no one, when they looked my way, was for any reason suspicious.

Oh, and there was another reason, still clear to me five years on. Later that night, when I had picked up my Bible for the first time, I got a phone call from Eliot Dalrymple. He was calling to thank me. His wife had stirred for the first time in days only a few minutes after I had walked out of the intensive care ward. She still had most of her motor skills. "They say it's a miracle!" he told me. "It probably never would have happened if you hadn't been there that whole time, praying for her." So the Dalrymples probably never understood why,

THE WITNESS

even years later, I would disappear when they came walking through the church in my direction, with grateful steps to give thanks for something which I had no wish to take credit.

19.

Cynthia and I were married shortly after we met. It was academic that Forster had a job for me on my wedding night, which he had to know in advance since I sent him an invitation. It was a provocative gesture for me to send him one, and you can imagine my shock when his wife telephoned Cynthia with an RSVP saying they would be delighted to be there. Prescott and his wife were also on board, and I realized that my side of the church would need more representation from people I actually might enjoy seeing.

And yet, I was not there for the ceremony. Forster had sent me off on a mission just two days before to meet a man in the exploratory phases of a presidential campaign. My mission was to observe the possible candidate for some length of time — that was all I was told — and determine whether his stated "moral and religious" goals were born out in his personal life. Forster told me, through Prescott naturally, that he wanted to endorse this man, which was something he never did. I understood how important this was, but I wanted them to understand how important my own wedding was to me. Prescott assured me it would only take a day, and I would be back in time for the rehearsal.

I won't use any names because the man never made it past the primaries. That had nothing to do with Forster, who didn't endorse him. I spent a day waiting to see the man, and my impression was that he was acting. It gave me a kind of grudging appreciation, like a con man playing another con man, to see this wonderful fraud spouting some of the same things I had said myself, but with the sure knowledge he meant none of them. I had the feeling that if getting the job called for the man to speak Esperanto, shave his head and paint it like a billiard ball, he would have performed the tasks flawlessly.

By the time I had gathered enough information, I had missed my plane, and a connecting flight was also delayed. And so, by telephone, I married my wife by proxy in the church where I had earlier stood in for someone who actually believed. *My* stand-in for the ceremony, naturally, was Dr. Benjamin Forster, a man I had never met. He did everything but kiss the bride and cut the groom's cake. In the years after, Cynthia assured me he did exist, and was the nicest man she had ever met. By the time I pulled into the church, the reception was in full swing and we were able to get pictures of a ceremony that never quite took place. Forster, by then, was long gone.

It was like that. Forster presided mysteriously over the first years of my marriage like a cross between Billy Graham and Jay Gatsby. It was a brooding evangelistic presence that kept me active and eventually pulled Cynthia into its orbit. The fact that I had never met the man had little to do with life, since he seemed to control every facet of mine without my knowing what he looked like. He had already sent a mountain of gifts through Prescott for my wife's bridal shower and contributed mightily to my ability to find a good condo for our honeymoon at the beach.

As the years began to accumulate, I marked how Cynthia cultivated her own enthusiasms apart from me. I observed these things from a distance like an anthropologist tracking the development of an infant civilization.

Cynthia began going to the gym with a single-mindedness that frightened me. She mercilessly attacked herself on the machines until she judged herself sufficiently sculpted. She took up cake decorating with a missionary zeal, loaning out her services to weddings and birthday parties. Through her I knew the great works that could be rendered with frosting, fondant, and a little patience. Cynthia began collecting decorative pewter chess pieces, enough for an entire bracket of tournament games. Neither she nor I played the game, yet in display cases in our house were Civil War generals blue and gray, comic books heroes and villains, rock stars, classical composers, Greek gods and goddesses, all rendered in miniature and waiting for the right moment to execute a checkmate. Her daily routine included an assault on the day's crossword puzzle, and she rarely had to ask what a seven-letter word for the author of "The Imitation of Christ" was, because she already knew it. That man, Mr. Thomas a'Kempis, told us that we should watch for good times to retreat into ourselves.

Somehow though, it surprised me a few months after we were married when she joined the church. She didn't do it as I had. Strangely enough, she was actually *looking* for salvation.

I stood during the invitation, holding her hand, thinking about where we might eat lunch afterwards, when I felt her grip convulsively tighten and I looked over to see her eyes bathed in tears. Her left hand went up to hide them, and she stepped out of the pew before I had a chance to say anything. But instead of dashing off to the bathroom like I expected her to, she turned toward the altar and began walking at a desperate pace until she literally keeled over in the pastor's arms. I walked down and stood next to her while she prayed that Jesus would save her soul, and I put an uncertain hand to her back as she did this, not knowing if I could comfort her or whether I had been the cause of her anguish. Did she suspect something about what was really going on inside my head?

We stood afterward to shake the hands of the congregation as they passed out the door, and she embraced me. "Thank you," she said.

"What?"

She wiped her eyes. "I never would have done this without you. I never would have even *thought* of it if I hadn't met you."

"*Me?*"

She smiled with a certain amount of annoyance. "Don't do that. It's just the way you are. You make me *want* to be better."

I suppose I thought that she understood our presence in the pews was just part of the job. We were there to satisfy the all-seeing eye of Forster and his minion Prescott, who somehow could see without being seen. I never dreamed that what I was doing would have that kind of effect on her. Somehow, I had fooled her, just as I had the rest of them. And I breathed a sigh of relief, because I supposed her soul would satisfy God. Maybe He would leave me alone.

But even after that day, for some reason, I suspected that she might be fooling me. Hadn't I met this woman under false pretenses anyway? As she volunteered around the church and participated in Bible studies and sang out her answers to spiritual questions in the same clear voice, I wondered if she did all this because she wanted to, felt she needed to, or was it because she thought it was expected of her? After all, hadn't that been my operating principle, the factor that kept me calculating out the full ten percent of our earnings before taxes in order to tithe properly? Wasn't it because I knew someone, probably Forster or Prescott, was watching?

We did not sleep together. The only reason for this was that I did not sleep. Cynthia fell asleep each night in our big bed and I sat next to her until I was sure she was out. I would then slip out and wander the house or read or watch television or do some work, sure that I wouldn't get tired enough to finally drop off until perhaps two or three in the morning. The sun usually found me stretched out on the couch to avoid disturbing her. She occasionally would say something to me about this, telling me that it wasn't necessary to stay away, she would much rather have me next to her. I thought that even though we were married, she would rather not have me around. Knowing this, you may not be surprised to learn that five years later, we had no children. I knew this bothered her, and it bothered me too. But I couldn't see myself attempting the role of father when I was playing so many other parts at the same time.

One thing about Cynthia, she had a way of bringing up topics suddenly that made you realize she had been deep in thought about such things long before she ever mentioned them. A seemingly innocuous suggestion might be a subject of Olympian proportions, and her silence on it only magnified its importance. This kept me silent much of the time, because I didn't wish to pass judgment on anything and inadvertently offend her. Which is why I had trouble answering one night when she asked me if I would mind us finding a surrogate mother.

We were lying in bed together after dinner. I was fully dressed, as was she, our shoes scuffing against the quilt. We had both fallen into bed tired, too tired to take off anything. We would have looked like an exhausted couple from one of those infamous all-night dances of the Depression except that we were too composed.

I was holding her hand but did not squeeze.

After a second or two, she said, "We don't have to, you know."

I scratched my ear.

"I mean, it wouldn't be hard, finding a surrogate mother. We would have to find somebody willing to do it. My sister probably could." Sarah lived two states away and had already given birth to three children of her own. I had no doubt that she would if Cynthia asked.

I said nothing and crossed my legs.

"I haven't asked Sarah, but I don't think she'd turn me down. She's always asking about how we are, asking if we're ever going to have children." The mention of Sarah was telling. I wondered how much of this was simply one sister wanting what the other already had, the continuation of a rivalry that had eaten up both of their lives, love and animosity walking hand-in-hand.

I rubbed my nose with the back of my left hand and took a deep breath. I had not looked at her since she had said any of this.

"I mean, what if we had a child? What do you think about that? What would we do with it?"

The words hung long enough before she snickered at the way they sounded. I smiled but still kept looking at the ceiling.

"What would we do with *it*? Listen to me. I make *it* sound like a TV or a stereo or something. We'll put it over there next to the microwave." She laughed again.

I smiled silently.

"What do you think, Cam? Please tell me."

What *was* I thinking? I remembered that the concept of the surrogate mother goes all the way back to Genesis, when Hagar, the maidservant of Abraham's wife, lies with him and gives birth to Ishmael. I remembered that Cynthia's sister had buck teeth that got worse with each pregnancy, for some reason.

I cleared my throat and made a sound that seemed to come from someone else. Then I found the right voice.

"I think if that's what you want, then we should," I said.

"But what do *you* want, Cam? It doesn't matter if I want a child. We're talking about a living being. We're talking..."

"You're talking about something that will change our lives forever. Something that will make us two totally different people."

"You don't..."

I finally looked at her. It was the same look she gave me years before when she tried to convince me that she had a boyfriend who had hit her.

"Maybe I need to be a totally different person," I said.

"You? Look at all you do. All that stuff you do on your job, away from it."

"That's part of the job."

"No it isn't. You do that because of who you are. I know who you are. I don't just love you. I'm proud of you. I'm proud to be your wife. I mean that." I couldn't believe that she was serious, but she certainly seemed that way.

The truth that I didn't want to admit to her was that I didn't want a child because I didn't want another version of myself in the world. Mr. Thomas a Kempis also reminds us that if you can't make yourself into what you wish for, you can't expect to mold another into something that conforms to your will. I could see myself standing silently over a young intelligence, a will just forming itself, and the flaws written on my soul imprinted in the same way on someone who never asked for such a thing.

Mr. Thomas a Kempis wrote a lot of things, I told myself, and he probably wasn't married.

"How can you say that?" I asked.

She laughed again. "I know plenty of women who would never say anything like that. Rebecca Hagler. You know."

"Yeah."

"Did you know her husband Thomas' mother had Parkinson's Disease for, I don't know, six or seven years. He visited her every day in the nursing home? Can you imagine what that does to a man?"

I nodded.

"And she killed herself one day after he left. She just couldn't take it anymore. She wasn't getting any better. Do you know what Rebecca said to him about it? She called him a Mama's boy! She said it was no wonder that she killed herself having a son like him."

"How did you hear about this?"

"Rebecca bragged about it! She'll tell anyone about it. She said she told him things like that to keep him in his place! A man who would treat his mother like that, and she said he was nothing but a spineless weakling. I won't use the language she did."

I gave a quick stab of a laugh.

"She said she told him that suicide runs in people's families, and she fully expected him to follow her any time. Can you believe that!" Cynthia was mimicking Rebecca's braying voice, and I could hear the contempt in her voice — both the echo of Rebecca's original malice and that growing in Cynthia against her. "Why do people say things like that to each other?"

"You never know what's going on in somebody's mind."

"No, you don't. I think about things like that and I figure it's better off not to bring somebody into the world when it's got people like that in it."

I knew what this was. Cynthia has listened to my reaction, gauged what she perceived were my thoughts about having a surrogate mother, and had already begun justifying to herself to shelve the idea.

I squeezed Cynthia's hand, and looked at her. "I think it would be a shame for someone who cares so much for others not to have a child of her own."

"But what about you?"

"Don't you think I want to make you happy?"

"No, Cam, that's not what I mean. Listen to yourself. Everything you're saying has to do with *me*. It's not just that I want to have a baby. It's that you have to want to have a baby too. I want *you* to want this."

"What makes you think I don't?"

She didn't reply immediately. She looked in my eyes as though she might find the answer there.

"Sometimes I'm not so sure what you want."

"Even if I say so?"

"You're a very accommodating person, Cam. You're selfless. Like I said. I don't want to take advantage of you. Make you miserable."

"We're talking about a baby, right? Like I said, what makes you think I don't want to be a father?"

"It's just..."

"What?"

"It's just...I never want us to end up like Thomas and Rebecca Hagler. Two people who are married who hate each other."

"You think having a child could do that?"

"No. Like you said, you never know what's going on in somebody's mind. We're happy now. At least, I think we are. I know I am."

"So am I," I said, in a tone of voice that I realized sounded implausible for happiness.

We embraced, we even kissed, and I held her for a long time like that. And we both fell asleep, fully clothed, right there on the bed.

I could understand how she felt. People get married sometimes by concealing who they are from their spouse until they feel safe enough within the marriage to truly emerge. An act can only last so long. But I was proud that I hadn't let my mask yet slip with her.

I had the feeling that Cynthia wanted a child, and because she didn't have one, wondered if her life had any meaning. Or worse. The logic might be inescapable for her. If God's will is absolute, then maybe her not having a child was His punishment. Not even science could comfort her, since the whole evolutionary purpose is to reproduce.

It was a question I often asked myself. Isn't it all life — everything — a bit maddening if it all comes to nothing?

Where would you go to complain?

20.

The job kept giving me things to do. For several evenings a week before Halloween, I shepherded a group of teenagers through Heaven and Hell.

It was the church's answer to haunted houses, those seasonal fundraisers for local charities. Instead, the church put on a staged tour through the afterlife. Some churches called it Judgment House. I was not yet midway through life's journey, or at least, I didn't think I was, but I was old enough to be a guide.

Forster bankrolled the whole affair, and it took about a month for the staff he paid to put together a light and sound show inside a warehouse that had enough parking for all the city's high schools. We had people outside to direct traffic, people to entertain those waiting to get in, people taking donations that were given back to the church, and people inside to work the props and direct drama teams inside. Some nights I directed cars to parking places and checked $20 bills to spot counterfeits. We didn't have an ultraviolet light to shine on the bills, so I learned to look for the color-shifting ink that makes the money look one way in the light and then another if you move it up or down. Most of the time though, I served as a guide, simply escorting people through the show.

The Judgment House show began with a bunch of teenage kids who could be heard in darkness discussing an evening trip out to a lake. This was a nice touch — it had the stuff of slasher films and a veneer of timelessness to it. Then the voices were drowned out by the sound of squealing tires and crunching metal, and the darkness erupted in red light. It was a police car's flashing lights, and I escorted the teenage visitors past a realistic wreck scene, with bodies being pulled from the car.

The whole idea of the tour was to follow these characters through their journey into the afterlife. We escorted them into a white room made to approximate the idea of Heaven — ethereal lights, smoke along the floor, beings in white robes, and a silent, stately figure meant to stand in for the enthroned Christ. Some of the teenagers were told they would stay, but others were instead pointed out a door. It was my job to take them past that door.

I never did this without my guts throbbing to escape from my belly. I felt the unmistakable terror of my charges contemplating even a momentary trip to Hell. They spoke flippantly about the traffic scene, hushed in the presence of our Christly stand-in, but the trip to Hell — with its screams of torment, otherworldly heat, generated flames and laughing, sneering play evil made their temples throb, as it did mine. Somehow, sin had carried us all there, and we all had better get used to the surroundings. I knew some of these condemned souls — the actors, I mean, who were church members *volunteering* — seemed to be enjoying themselves too much down in that pseudo-pandemonium.

Mr. C.S. Lewis, when he wrote his famous dialogue of the fictional demon Screwtape, called it "diabolical ventriloquism," and said the whole exercise was too hard to quit. If there is something in the human nature that truly is utterly depraved, then perhaps we risk more than we know by indulging this side of ourselves, even in playacting. Each time I took my young charges into our simulated

Styx, I heard the screams and mockings and beatings grow in volume and in their bloodcurdling quotient. The faces behind the masks worn by our would-be demons might have been just as terrifying in their imagined evil.

Perhaps the teenagers understood. Just as suddenly as our trip began, it was over. At the end, I could see relief in the kids, and more than a few who got back in line to take another trip through the whole thing.

I wondered what I was supposed to be in this pageant. Virgil? The Archangel Michael? A gate crasher? After a few trips, I discovered that whenever the actor playing Jesus entered the room, I would intentionally look at the floor, or look away, and silently fear that He would somehow contrive to get my attention.

Those times in Heaven, we would be surrounded by other actors being paid to walk in what were supposed to be sublime steps along golden streets. Though none of their faces were to matter, I understood that these were departed souls that were supposed to know us, indeed welcome us if we were worthy. And I found myself wondering if I might see my brother there. Would we embrace or would he hit me? Would he *be* there?

Of course, I tried to comfort myself with the whole notion that this representation was simply made to scare children into some kind of confession and salvation. I tried to tell myself that the whole anthropomorphic exercise — presenting dead souls as living, breathing, robed creatures of light was absurd, ludicrous, childish. What comfort I found was in the repeated reminders that it was all simply a play, a put-on, something that we had no way of knowing.

All of that was good, but I kept staring at the door Jesus walked through to enter the Heavenly room, and I wondered what was on the other side? And what might be through the other doors, infinite and mysterious? For some reason that no one could explain, someone had left a clock on the wall of the Heavenly set. Tell me, I could hear one soul asking another, what time did you arrive here? What was the day, the hour and the year? And how long will we be here? How many billions of millennia will we share? What time is lunch?

BRILLIANT DISGUISES

The longer I thought about these things, the more short of breath I became, trying to find the end of eternity, the limits of God. I understood that our stand-ins at this Judgment House were only there to allow our minds to grapple with the endless infinities in these ideas.

As Mr. E.L. Doctorow noted, if the universe is expanding, then we are left to contemplate nothing but profound, disastrous, hopeless infinitude, and if so, then God is so fearsome as to be beyond any human entreaty for our solace, or comfort, or the redemption that would come of our being brought into His secret.

But of course, there is another possibility, equally as disastrous. What if God is that, so totally staggeringly beyond our comprehension as to be unreachable, and yet He still cares about what we are, what we do, and our ultimate destination? What if this ridiculous playacting at eternity, was in fact, the Truth?

Why?

Why couldn't somebody pray to Buddha and the words get through to Jesus? Why was that so hard to believe?

For some reason, I heard Peter's voice: *Do you feel the same way about my wife calling you, expecting to talk to me?*

If indeed He does care, I thought, if he is involved in the most intimate details of our lives, if He does number the fall of sparrows, the hairs on heads, grains of sand, then how impatient must He grow with the easy comforts of mediocrity, the foolish, meaningless banalities, the narrow, flabby, fleshly false security that we assemble around us, consuming the bulk of our wandering lives? My life?

After a few nights of this, I took a break and went up on the roof of the converted warehouse, where I found another volunteer. He was smoking a cigarette, looking up at the stars, glancing over his shoulder for anyone's sudden appearance. He had the look of someone with long hours ahead of them and little hope of sleep. I supposed I looked just like him.

"Let me have one," I said, drawing nearer. For the record, I do not smoke, but I needed something to overtake my mind. The smoke, I reasoned, would obscure the everlasting, onlooking stars.

21.

One of the aspects of my job was that I was constantly being told to go to unlikely places to meet unexpected people. Once I had to drop everything to drive to a deserted gas station in an equally deserted small town in order to pick up a donation from someone who wished to remain anonymous. Occasionally a drug addict might show up at the church and I would have to get him to a counselor, as well as a place to stay for a time. Some nights I ferried prostitutes off their curbs and on to shelters after they had called the Foundation for help. Perhaps I was known around town by the company I kept.

Prescott told me I was to meet someone at an art gallery shortly after work one Thursday. He said it was a request of Dr. Forster and that was all he knew. He made no comment to betray whether he did indeed know more, or whether he suspected anything of it. It was merely an item among my usual list of things and if it did arouse any suspicion in him, he was his usual circumspect self.

I got to the gallery when no one else was there, save the owner, who eyed me semi-suspiciously through his de rigeur black frame eyeglasses. Exhibits hung on the avocado green walls in frames taller than a standing professional basketball player, with the appropriate lighting on each to add the appropriate intellectual heft. In the minutes before my meeting, I strolled looking at them. An artist had taken the front pages of newspapers from non-English speaking countries and silk-screened them onto canvas, adding the appropriate color and texture for whatever she was trying to achieve.

All of the front pages has the same thing in common — they depicted disasters, natural and man-made. A paper from the Philippines depicted flooding in the wake of a volcano. A Thai paper showed bodies floating in broken forests of debris from the 2004 tsunami. A blood red 2006 front page from India from the Mumbai train bombings. A 1994 African paper showing the bodies of Rwandan genocide. Russian school shootings. Japanese sarin gas attacks in the subway. Italian papers from the great earthquake of 1980. Faces in anguish. Dead bodies. Rubble. The corpse of civilization. A card at the front said the artist was interested in showing tragedies occurring outside the United States, in different languages, since she felt Americans were largely immune and apathetic to world tragedy. I recognized these scenes because I understood that many of Benjamin Forster's millions were floating in the wake of these tragedies, going to relief efforts, cleanup projects, foundations upon foundations. I knew Prescott had been to more than a few of these places himself to help in administering Forster's money. And I knew from people who had eventually made their way to America and our church — former Rwandans and Indonesians and Russians and others, fleeing from these and perhaps smaller disasters.

I looked over the pages for several minutes, thinking I might be able to recognize a few words for their English counterparts. I thought it was strange that the artist had picked out newspapers, since most people watched television and viewed Internet pages. Front pages probably lent themselves more to art, I reasoned.

In one panel, there was a group of masked men with AK-47s gesturing toward a camera for an image that looked taken from a videotape. All of their faces were concealed, except for their eyes. They had apparently killed someone for a camera and were exulting in the aftermath. Perhaps they did this to keep from taking their masks off. I thought of Gelb's talk on secret identities, and how these faceless ones might have thought themselves heroes in the great tradition of the Scarlet Pimpernel, the Lone Ranger and Batman. If my face is covered, they seemed to be saying, if we all wear masks, then we all look alike, and may only be defined by the idea we represent. *An idea is all I am. That is all I am.*

A few minutes later, Thomas Hagler walked in. I hadn't realized I would be meeting him. He wore one of his normal Sunday suits and straightened his glasses as he walked forward to shake my hand. He had a nice, easy casual stride.

He had no leisurely greeting though. "Cam, can I talk to you for a moment?" He took me by the arm and turned me down the gallery's long main hall. He seemed different from that day when I spotted him nicking his check from the collection plate. That day he had appeared broken, ashamed of having to admit to anyone else his own problems. This time he gestured as he spoke, as a man confident in his own position. What he asked of me smacked of someone bestowing a prize on an underling.

"You've attracted the attention of a lot of people. Good people. You've done a good job at a lot of things."

"Thanks," I said. I never trust compliments, especially when they seem too friendly. I was also curious about how good these good people presumably were.

"A good job," he repeated, as though *good* would be the final word on my life. *Was the job I was doing as good as the good people who were watching me?* "And anytime you do a good job and get noticed, more jobs come your way. To whom much is given, much will be wrung out of."

"That's not quite the way it goes, right?"

He smiled. "Cam, I think I ought to tell you right now that I'm speaking for Dr. Benjamin Forster."

I registered the appropriate amount of gravity. I paused to let him continue, assuming that anything else would smack of sarcasm.

"I know you normally hear from him through Charlie Prescott, which is why Dr. Forster approached me with this task." He sighed heavily. "I wish he'd...honored... somebody else with this."

"You don't feel comfortable with it?"

"No, not really." He sighed again.

"Well, go ahead and tell me."

"How much do you know about Prescott?"

"Enough after working with him for five years. He does his job. Totally committed to it. Totally committed to the Foundation. Probably doesn't have too many thoughts that aren't related to it. Looks like he's lost some weight lately."

"About what Dr. Foster expected you to say. Very loyal."

"What's wrong?"

"Dr. Forster would like for you to keep an eye on Mr. Prescott. A very careful eye. Some information recently came to his attention that is rather troubling."

"You mean spy on him?"

His candor shocked me. "Yes, I think that's what Forster meant. Sometimes, it's hard to tell. Lately, especially."

"What am I looking for?"

He bit his lip. "I think what Forster means is that Mr. Prescott, lately at least, may be suffering from some lapses in judgment."

"Lapses? What do you mean?"

"What do you think I mean?"

"I don't know. That's why I'm asking. What does he suggest? He's cheating on his taxes? His wife?"

Hagler's face didn't change, his head remained motionless. "Nothing that I've ever seen. Dr. Forster suspects *something*."

"Something. That's all?"

"Something."

We stopped in front of a page with pictures following a Chinese typhoon. "Why?"

"I don't know."

"So what does he want me to look for?"

"Anything that might embarrass the Foundation. Those were his exact words."

"Anything, he means."

"It is my experience that Dr. Forster says exactly what he means. Every day of his life." He cleared his throat. "I think that he came to me because he wanted somebody outside of the Foundation to speak to you. Somebody he trusts. Somebody he thinks you would trust."

"But I barely know you."

"You can call me Frank."

I rolled my eyes. "Thanks. I still hardly know you."

"I'm aware of that. Listen, Cameron, as I said, he trusts you. He trusts you as someone would from afar. He doesn't know you personally."

"It's mutual."

"He only knows you by the quality of your work. Dr. Forster feels he has a very strong personality and sometimes he tends to keep his associations with people at a minimum."

"Sounds like he has smallpox or something."

Hagler gave a noncommittal laugh. "He told me one of the great joys of his life is keeping up with all that you do."

Like everything else in my association with the man, this little bit of news left me both elated and feeling slightly spooky. "You realize, he knows me through Prescott."

"That's right."

"But if he doesn't trust Prescott, how can he trust his judgment about me?"

"The two aren't related."

"But they must be, otherwise he wouldn't be concerned about these rumors, if that's all they are. He's known Prescott a lot longer than me, and he's got a much stronger relationship with him."

"I would say that Dr. Forster probably wants to stop these rumors if that's all they are. Are you sure you've never heard anything..."

"No. Of course not." This time I sighed. "But I don't know Prescott outside of work. I'm not sure anybody besides Dr. Forster would."

"So you can see that Dr. Forster trusts you with something this sensitive?"

"Anybody watching me?"

"What?"

"Prescott's given his life to the Forster Foundation. If I'm spying on Prescott, then who's spying on me? Is it you?"

"No," he said, smiling a little too easily for me.

"Well then who is? Who can he trust? Who can I trust?"

"Cameron, calm down. You're a young man. You may feel that Dr. Forster is betraying a trust, but you also know deep down that appearances are everything. Take the Internet. You know how many people are out there with cameras and digital voice recorders looking to post whatever they want to about anyone? My daughter and all of her friends have their own personal pages, where they have files that they post everyday. They scandalize me. Nothing is too personal to keep to yourself anymore. Everything must be shared. In a world like that, everyone is watching everyone else, and everyone is watching themselves watch everyone else. It's not too hard to find out a secret in that kind of world. Sin is persistent, as is its memory."

Mr. Robert Hanssen, a career FBI agent, a family man in his church, who ended up selling secrets to the Soviet Union, was found out when he began plying a stripper with gifts and posting fantasy sex passages about his wife on the Internet. It probably wasn't something he was proud of. I had the feeling reading about him, reading about how he confessed to his priest and to his wife a portion of what he had done, that he wavered between regret and arrogance. The arrogance was apparent in the messages he sent to his Russian handlers under the pseudonym Ramon Garcia. I remember thinking when I read them that they sounded not like the words of a spy talking to invisible handlers as much as a man speaking to God while struggling against his senses.

I have come about as close as I ever want to come to sacrificing myself to help you, and I get silence. I hate silence. One might propose that I am either insanely brave or quite insane. I'd say neither. I'd say, insanely loyal. Take your pick. There is insanity in all the answers...I hate uncertainty. So far, I have judged the edge correctly.

Of course, when the FBI wanted to take down Hanssen, they used his subordinate.

"Just what do you mean?" I asked.

"I mean, Cameron, that when we can all be very unforgiving where someone else is concerned. If Prescott has a problem, any problem, Dr. Forster doesn't want it to destroy the life of a very gifted man, nor an organization that both of them have devoted a great deal of time to creating and nurturing."

I wiped my forehead. "I'm sorry. I thought this was some kind of witch hunt."

"That's why Dr. Forster chose you. He trusts that it won't become that sort of thing. He wants to trust Prescott. He just hopes you keep his faith in the man secure."

"And if I don't?"

"Then Dr. Forster is prepared to act in the matter, however it becomes necessary."

22.

The first person I had to see after Hagler's ... commission was Cynthia. I thought to myself that if I could just tell her, then I could keep it to myself from everyone else and be able to do the job. That was, as always, my mantra: Do the job.

I might have, if I had thought about it long enough, settled on someone closer to the office. Si Gelb, for example, probably would have given some kind of sage advice. The guy solved problems by running — literally. He did marathons and 10K runs and biathlons and triathlons and looked hard enough to survive the day's weather, the night's cold, and the elbows of his fellow runners. A man's got a lot of time running to think about life and death and everything in between. But I understood that Forster probably wanted to keep his associate as far away from Prescott's alleged whatever as possible. Si probably wouldn't have seen this as a question of, for lack of a better word, loyalty, as Forster would have.

The reasons why I sought Cynthia out after my meeting with Hagler probably ran much deeper than I am able to explain. As Mr.

THE WITNESS

Salman Rushdie declared, a man who invents himself needs someone to believe in him, to prove he's managed it. While one could say that's playing God, one might also say that's just being a man.

That day she was at the church, helping with preschoolers. She had the gift of being able to confer on any child a generous amount of wild-eyed wonder at whatever tumbled from his lips, and the exact tone of voice needed to correct and nurture at the same time. I found myself caring for her most when I saw her with someone's child. That was one of the reasons it had been so hard to look at her when she wanted to talk about surrogate mothers.

When I walked in, Cynthia was standing near the bathrooms with a line of boys and girls. She was surprised to see me, and pleased.

"Everything alright?"

I didn't look her in the eyes. "Have you got a minute?"

"Sure," she said.

We were about to find some place to talk when I felt something tugging at my right leg. It was a child — a little girl probably no more than two years old, who had my leg in a hug. She looked up at me with a cheeky little smile as if to say, *I've got you.* I smiled back, a bit uneasy.

"Don't worry," she said. "That's Emily. She's just friendly."

"Very," I said. Her embrace was quite strong.

"She thinks you're her daddy."

"Me?"

"Her mom's single. She hugs every man that comes in here and gets close enough to her."

"Doesn't matter who then. They all get a warm reception."

"I wouldn't say that. She has taste," Cynthia smiled. A young woman who was a regular at the preschool walked up to coax Emily off my leg, and I walked into the church's unoccupied wedding chapel to tell Cynthia what had just happened. She took it differently than I expected. She seemed intrigued, as though this was a chance for me to advance in my job.

"Are you okay with this? Have you noticed anything about him?"

"Prescott? No, nothing more than you might expect. Same

invincible cheerfulness. Same job well done zeal. No hint that he's got something going on the side."

"Do you think that's what Hagler meant? An affair?"

"Well yeah. Could he have meant anything else?"

"I suppose if it were just an affair, Hagler would have said so plainly. As it is, it might be something else. What if Prescott's looking at another job?"

"Huh?"

"What were Hagler's exact words?"

"Anything that might embarrass the Foundation. Those were apparently Forster's exact words too. That's what I'm supposed to look out for."

"That covers a lot of ground. Drug problems. Drinking. Or maybe he just wants out."

"Do you think he'd have me looking into it if Prescott's simply shopping his resume around?"

"I don't know. It's possible Hagler didn't want to influence whatever you might find. Maybe there's something Forster doesn't want out that Prescott knows."

I grunted.

"You ever thought about that?"

"What? Getting another job?"

"Yeah," she said.

The question piqued my interest, wondering how receptive she might be to the idea of going somewhere else. After she joined the church, I guess I understood on some unconscious level that I was stuck there in the Foundation, since it was doing one of us some good.

"No," was all I would say to answer that question. "However it is, I couldn't picture Prescott getting out of the Foundation. He's as responsible for building it as Forster is."

"That's just it. Maybe he expects a certain amount of loyalty from his people. You know how it is. Or you should."

"No," I said. "I'm not sure."

"Well what bothers you about it?"

"It's Prescott. I don't now if I could do this to him. What if I *find* something?"

"Cam, you know who pays your check. If he asks you to do something, you ought to do it. Like you do everything else."

"This is Prescott though. I feel like I owe him at least a *little* loyalty. Why is Forster doing this?"

"Don't you think he has a good reason? Why don't you trust him?"

"Who said I don't?"

"Well, it's obvious you don't. You're worried about what might happen to Prescott. If he did something wrong, maybe Dr. Forster's the only one who can help him. If he hasn't done anything wrong, then he has nothing to worry about."

"How much do we know about the man?"

"Prescott's your boss..."

"I'm not talking about Prescott. I mean Forster."

"You're the one who works for him, honey."

"Yeah, but I don't know anything about him, other than what Prescott's told me. Which ain't much."

"So Prescott trusts him?"

"He idolizes him. It's not too much to say that."

"If he does, then he wouldn't do anything to jeopardize that. In that case, you wouldn't have anything to worry about."

"No. You never know what's going on in somebody's head."

"You don't have to worry about that," she said. "It's not his *thoughts* that are the issue." I looked at her, expected some sort of knowing glance. As always, I was worried that any moment she would see right through me.

"So what do I do?"

"You do the right thing."

"Well, what is that?"

She sighed. "What would Forster do?"

I couldn't help the snorting laugh that snuck out of me. When the words Cynthia spoke echoed in her own head, she began laughing too. Then I considered it again. "That's a good question, you know." I smiled at her.

"Look honey. I trust you do the right thing. Anyway, maybe it's not Hagler who's showing you he trusts you, or even Forster."

I paused for the next possibility, which I already knew.

"Maybe it's the Lord," she said.

How pure she is, I thought. And how oblivious.

I was ready to dismiss the question as I walked out, but something prevented me. It was the girl again, Emily. As I had paused at the door to give my wife a little goodbye kiss, Emily had grabbed hold of my leg again. I glanced down to see her, with the same mischievous grin as before.

"It's okay," I told her. "I'll be back some other time." I trusted she wouldn't know the difference when the next man came into the room, and he too would get the same treatment, since we were all the same men to her and potential candidates for this kind of adoration.

But she wouldn't let go. No matter how I tugged, her smile grew more fixed and her arms more powerful. I could hear a voice in my head, which I ascribed at first to her, like those movies where a baby talks with an adult voice.

You're not getting away from me so easily.

What's it going to take?

Why won't you pay attention?

I have, but now I have to go.

What's your hurry? We were only getting to know each other.

I smiled to hear myself conjuring up this voice. I was going to have to be something a little less than an animal tamer, I told myself. Like a snake charmer. Little children have the same reactions as animals, but they grow out of them. It's all about survival and basic recognition of threats. It was Mr. Thomas Aquinas who divided the world into the animate and the inanimate, those things with and without souls. I found myself wondering, as I gently tried to coax the child away from me, are we born with souls? And if not, at what point do they enter us? And what are they when they come? Did I believe in them? I had to. If there aren't any souls, then that would mean that the Gettysburg Address and the ceiling of the Sistine Chapel and the Ode to Joy and a cup of water to a small child could have nothing more to commend them than a dog swatting its tail to chase away a fly. It's sentimental to hold onto such things, I told myself, and science, like nature, has no room for sentiment.

Besides, even a child learns early on the difference between what is good and what is bad. We mimic our parents and we learn to make the same mistakes as they did, only we tell ourselves we will learn. Do we spend our life mimicking God, or the devil?

The child smiled at me again, a little deeper this time, and I knew who it was speaking to me. Cynthia was right. I was being called.

No, I said within myself, grabbing the girl's hands just a little too hard. I will not listen to You, in whatever form You come to me. Wrap Yourself in the guise of my wife or a child or whatever you like. You are merciless. But You will not remake me.

What are you worried about losing, Cameron?

Leave me alone, I said within myself. This was the Voice, I told myself. The voice that I tell myself maybe, or in fact is, God, but is really my own imagination. It's the internal Voice that is ourselves but we mistake for a higher power, created out of our own consciousness. Just a biochemical shadow that is not there. No more tangible than the blind spot in our vision.

Is it your soul you're scared of losing? Does it mean that much to you?

The bulk of the world's knowledge is an imaginary construction, building castles of information that will stand when we acquire more information. But it will not change the fact that this voice I'm hearing is really me, and not a higher being.

You addressed me first, and not in a very nice way. You can at least talk to me. Don't you owe me, after all, a little courtesy?

Is it possible to be rude to a being that does not exist? I asked myself. Can such a being be offended? And yet I felt a pang on my heart for this voice, like an aging mother who simply wants a telephone call every now and then. Mr. Sigmund Freud said that at the height of being in love, the boundary between ego and object threatens to melt away. Against whatever his senses may be telling him, a man who is in love will declare that I and you are one. I wondered if this explained the unconscious desire to resist the power of God, to declare yourself apart from Him?

That's the trouble with this religion, I told myself. You don't face a distant city across an ocean to pray. You have to face yourself.

Are you afraid of what you may find in Prescott's life, or your own?

It's none of your business.

You know you will eventually come to me. We were meant to be together forever.

I'm too screwed up for you.

I've got eternity to work on you, big boy.

You'll need every second.

The girl's face wrinkled with the beginnings of a grimace, and I could feel Cynthia looking down on me. I knew her earlier question — did I really want a child? — was probably playing in her mind. I was forgetting my lines.

As Mr. Horace once said, O imitators! You slavish herd!

I smiled at the child, and before she had time to divine that my smile was a sham, I pressed her close to me in an embrace. She returned it, a little unsure but ready to believe, and I stood up and felt her hug relax enough for me to escape. I gave my wife a quick peck on the lips and told her I would call her later.

And so I turned to face Monique Prescott, the wife of the man I had just been commissioned to undo. Her red hair stood out, as it always did, and her blue eyes held a question for the face she saw on me.

"Cam? What's wrong?"

"Oh, nothing," I said, leaving. "Say hi to your husband for me." As soon as the door slammed behind me I realized I had lied inside a church.

23.

For some reason, I *had* to call Cecelia. She had lost somebody — maybe that was the reason. Even though it hadn't yet happened, I felt like I had lost Prescott.

I dialed the number and realized I was clearing my throat. Deep within the recesses of my brain, the routine had become so engrained that when I dialed the familiar numbers, I knew immediately that I must prepare myself to assume my brother's voice.

That's why it was so surprising, I guess, when Peter answered the phone.

"Hello?" he said, in a voice so much more natural than anything I might have been able to approximate.

It was him, as though just awakened from a nap. The voice was a bit lower but more vital, and I was reminded of Peter when I was a little boy and he was my big brother, and his voice broke before mine. He would pick up the phone and his voice would suddenly assume a much deeper timbre than I was used to, and my father's friends would mistake him for Dad. He was so proud of himself, though for no reason other than the sudden conjuction of puberty and his newly-assertive vocal cords. I could hear him smirking behind the receiver.

I cleared my throat again, and got another, more impatient "Hello?" The huff of breath was him too. It was unmistakable that I was addressing the ghost of telephones past, come back to upbraid me for communing with his wife's morbid fantasies via the phone lines. He would take my voice away from me, banish me to some aural purgatory, and exchange my voice for something more excruciating. "*Serves you right, Big Boy,*" he might say.

"Uncle Cam, are you going to say something?"

It was Ricky, Peter's boy. The auditory area of my brain had recognized the voice as his father's, which tripped the memory areas where all the pent-up memories of my brother resided in their final repository. The careless way he clipped his fingernails, the overpowering cologne he wore in his teen years, the way he attached mountain bike handlebars to his 10-speed bike, the chipped tooth at the front of his smile — all of his individual parts in their power, terrible power. There was the sense that it had been a mistake to assume he was dead, and a sudden chalking on the board of human cluelessness, and then the unforgiving surge of loss, recoverability, and the ridiculousness of life. I knew instantly what it was like for Cecelia every time she had spoken, not to me, but to her dead husband.

"Ricky, oh, I'm sorry. You sounded like your dad. I didn't know quite what to do." The whole experience, which lasted perhaps all of fifteen seconds, made me long to be one of those people I had read about who suffers a head injury that leaves him unable to process the information reminding him why this voice is familiar, or that building is his house, or that the face he is staring at is his own reflection in a mirror.

"Yeah. Mom has me answer the phone to scare off anybody. We get lots of telemarketers."

"How did you know it was me?"

"Caller ID," he said, as though the invention predated the wheel. "What's up?"

"I was calling your Mom. How are you doing?"

"Okay, I guess. She's not here."

"She's not? Are you okay, by yourself?"

"Well, yeah," he said, as though the question was ridiculous. "I'm almost sixteen."

"Oh. I keep forgetting how old you are. Sorry, Ricky." It took my breath away to think that. *The boy will have spent more than half his life without his father in just a few years. Has it been that long?* I sounded like Cecelia. I tried to picture him in my mind's eye, and all I could gather together was a picture that looked much like the boy had at his father's funeral — a bit chunky, big cheeks, swollen eyes from crying, and an ill-fitting black suit that looked bought just the evening before. Now he was *almost* sixteen, the teenager's way of appropriating a whole year to add to the existing skinny number.

He grunted. "Yeah, could you call me Richard?"

I smirked. Just like his father. "Don't like the kiddie sounding name, huh?"

"Yeah," he said, as though I had been set straight.

"Your Dad was the same way. I called him Petey without realizing he didn't want to be called that anymore. He slugged me. Right in the eye."

"Nah." I could hear the excited wonder in his voice, as though I was telling a story about Paul Bunyan.

"Yeah. Your father was very conscious of how people perceived him."

Richard gave an uncertain "Uh-huh." I knew from his tone he didn't quite understand.

"I mean he wanted people to think he was a big man. And he was. He wanted to be seen as a big man."

"What'cha you mean big?" This was strange. The boy had adopted that peculiar kind of rapper's patois that white kids mimic when they appropriate black pop culture.

"As in he mattered. Some time I'd like to tell you what he was like. I don't think I've ever done that." Probably for reasons having to do with his mother, I had elected to stay away from Ricky and at probably the worst time, when he might need someone watching over him to deliver advice or simply watch him for signs of impending adulthood. But as I was already playing surrogate on one account in the family, I wasn't anxious to take up another position. In a flash it appeared to me that I had failed my brother all over again in a way I had not considered. "It's probably something he would have wanted me to do."

I waited a second for him to speak.

"Of course, that is, unless you don't want me to," I added.

"Yeah, yeah," he said. He almost sounded as though he *did* want me to.

"How are you doing? Everything okay in school?"

"It's summer."

"Oh, yeah. Well, I mean, was it going okay?"

"Guess." The boy was non-committal, and I realized the frustration I was feeling was because I expected him to talk to me like my brother. Get Peter started and you had to hold on until all the conversational avenues were exhausted. But by that time, he had already found about four other topics to embrace.

The boy's monosyllabic nature was to be expected, I guessed. He was a teenager, a experience beyond articulation that only frustrated the inarticulate powers of its victims. And it was hard to tell how the absence of a father had affected him. Perhaps too much for an absent uncle to suddenly take up the standard a few years too late.

"What do you like?"

"About what?"

"School," I said, my voice taking on a joshing edge, hoping to draw something out of the kid.

He gave a huffy laugh. "I don't know. I'm not sure what I like. Probably math."

"Really?"

"Yeah. You do the problem, you get the answer, that's it. It's pretty simple, and it's over." Interesting, I thought. Is this his idea of looking for certainty in a world where it's mostly been denied him? I wondered.

Stop analyzing my son. Especially when you're not competent to do it.

I recognized *that* voice.

"I'm sorry. I probably woke you up or disturbed you..."

"No, that's okay. I'll tell Mom you called."

"Thanks for talking to me."

"You mean nobody else wants to?" he asked, giving that same dry, huffy stuttering laugh as before. So there was a little of his father in him, after all.

24.

For some reason one afternoon I found myself paired with Gelb coaching elementary school girls in the vagaries of soccer. Pony tails bounced and shin guard encased legs scurried around us for almost two hours while we tried to teach our young charges to advance the ball instead of immediately defending after a well attempted kick. I did fair — it was an hour into practice before Gelb realized I knew nothing about the sport and had been impressed into labor because I had been the only one in the office. One of these days, I told myself, I'm going to go home early. And then they'll call me, if they can find me.

And they *will* find me. They always do.

Gelb at least had been doing this for awhile. He was the regular coach, but had called asking for help when his regular assistant bailed out on him. This particular league was being subsidized by Forster, who insisted that all of the teams have Biblically-themed names, even though the league was, in theory, secular. This particular team we watched over were known as the Doves.

"Which team is the Philistines?" I asked, half-joking.

"Over there," Gelb said, pointing to the far corner of the field. I detected no attempt at extending my lame joke — he was serious. "Hey! That's not how you do it! Do what she's doing over there. *She* knows how to play this game!" He was pointing at a sassy little Dove running at half-speed with her wrists out in a prance. The girl smiled at him, like an old Southern belle acknowledging a would-be suitor, and continued on.

"How long have you been doing this?" I asked, as the girls made their conditioning run around the field.

"Probably three or four years," he said. "It's good for them. We never win, but that's not the point. At least, that's what I tell myself so I don't lose any sleep over this."

"Do you?"

"I'm kidding, Cameron. I mean, it's not something important, like baseball."

I laughed and told one of the girls to pick up her pace.

Gelb shook his head ruefully. "That's my game. Don't get me wrong. This is good for these girls. You have to keep going, keep your poise, all that kind of thing, just to be able to play. But baseball teaches you what you need to know. Anybody can run. Anybody can kick. But hitting a baseball is a test of character. Nothing's hidden."

"Like steroids?" I said, inspiring a steely look from him. Then I asked, "Tell me how." I had the feeling he was going to tell me regardless, but I was anxious to hear his equation of baseball as the soul's barometer.

"Keep it up! Keep it up!" he called to the team. "Something I'd rather ask you, Cameron."

"Anything, as long as you don't ask me to hit a baseball."

Gelb had a weird way of smiling without smiling, a way of acknowledging a joke without a perceptible wrinkle visiting his face. I recognized this was, in a way, a compliment. "My wife is in a bad way."

"She sick?"

"Worried sick for days. Her rabbi went missing."

"Oh, I'm sorry."

"No, no. It's not like that."

"You say *her* rabbi?"

"Yeah. She goes. I avoid. Nice guy. Russ Mendel. In his mid-fifties. Got a few grown kids. Big, booming voice. You know the kind. I mean, not like you have a rabbi, but..."

"I know."

"My wife's a nervous wreck, not sure what to think. People from the temple are out looking for him, passing out fliers, setting up search teams in the woods. Police were asking his wife about whether he's got any enemies, anybody might want to see him dead. They ask the neighbors if maybe she wasn't too crazy about him. Nothing really sticks." He shook his head, as if in disgust for what he was about to say. "The guy drives to the Wal-Mart or whatever and never comes home. His wife calls the police when he doesn't come back, tells them where he was headed, and they go there and find his car. They figure he's missing. Maybe he's been kidnapped? Who knows." Gelb then involved the girls in a drill to make them pass the ball to each other, showing them to do so when a shot was open for a teammate. "Anyway, it's about two, maybe three days, and the store pulls its surveillance tapes from the parking lot. And there's Russ, getting out of his car, and he's carrying a bag. No problem. Maybe he's got something he needs to return. But it's a big bag. And he walks into the store. They look at the other tapes inside and they see him walking into the men's room, then coming out a few minutes later. Only this time, he's got on a ballcap and he's shaved off his mustache. You see him walk back out to the parking lot, wait a few minutes, and a cab comes driving up. He gets in, rides off."

"What happened?"

"What happened is he took the cab to the airport and bought a ticket to Mexico City. Turns out he had a passport in a different name. So now, he's got to answer to the U.S. government and to his wife. He's lucky he already shaved his mustache because she'd rip it off his face."

"What's in Mexico City?"

"God knows! Probably got something going on with somebody else, but I doubt it was to appeal to the Hispanic Diaspora."

"And your wife?"

"You'd have thought God had died. We had Russ over every month or so for supper. I once thought maybe he had something going with her. And...hey! You got an open shot right there! Look at it! It's right there in the face!"

The girl began arguing with him.

"What are you yelling at me for? I've already told you everything. You got everything you need to master this game. And what are you doing? You're telling me you don't need my help?"

The girl skulked off with a perplexed look, as if she wasn't sure what he had said to her.

"Anyway, she keeps asking what he was thinking. What he's thinking now. He had all this, and he just walked away from it. Spit on it. The contempt. That's what upset her."

"What was the question?"

"The what?"

"You said you wanted to ask me a question."

"Oh, that's right. Glad you remember. No. Yeah, the thing I was going to ask you is this — is that sort of thing common?"

"What? A wife going to pieces..."

"No, I mean, a religious guy leading a double life. Guy who just packs up and leaves and shocks everybody who thought they knew him."

I could tell by the look on his face, a sort of baiting, expectant smile, that the question wasn't quite so innocent. How much did he know about Prescott? Or me? Was this his way of letting the veil down a little? "Seems to me like you know the answer to this."

"Well, maybe I know what I think, but I was wondering what you thought."

I was suspicious for reasons you can probably understand. Gelb quickly added, "That doesn't mean it's true. I mean, I'm more of a hostile witness, a witness for the prosecution."

I chuckled. "When you say common, do you mean just among clergy, or..."

"Not necessarily."

"Well, you know, we *all* deal with that duality of man thing." I gave the phrase quotation marks in the air with my fingers. "Some of us have a tougher time than others." There was no use in trying to guess what he was thinking, then tailoring my answer to the occasion. "What do you think?"

He blinked hard and swallowed hard. "I think a guy like that is putting on an act."

"It's all an act," I said, as though agreeing.

"That's right. The whole thing. He has this job because he's trying to do the right thing, but the whole time, he's conscious that he doesn't really mean any of it. So he keeps a lid on things for only so long until he jumps on a plane for Mexico City."

"Just because he jumped on a plane to Mexico City, that means it was *all* an act? He didn't mean any of it?"

"Nah, no."

"But that's what it seems like. To your wife, right?"

He nodded. "She starts wondering if all these things he said really means anything."

"Well, you know what Forster would say. That we're all leading a double life."

"Who's got time for just a double life? You're standing there as a soccer coach. How much do you know about…"

"Nothing."

"Right. Well I don't think very much of religion. I think what it wants is something unnatural. In a way, it disgusts me."

"Unnatural."

"It forces on people this idea of what is permissible and what is normal and what is admirable, then it makes them conform to it. You know. Sinners in the hands of an angry God. Do unto others or I'll do unto you."

"Of course you resent it. Because it's not what you want to do. But then, what are you doing coaching soccer for Ben Forster?" This was an answer I was ready to receive. I stood there not sure of what I was doing, wondering who I might be satisfying. What did this coaching business have to do with *anything*? Who was Benjamin Forster and what possible difference could it make if anyone taught these girls how to play soccer? Anyone else would have done a much better job.

Why me?

Gelb sighed. "I'm doing the same thing you are. I'm doing it for myself, not him or his ideas of right and wrong. I have an idea that this is, somehow, admirable and worthy. But somebody else can have their own idea of what is worthy. Religion is different. The tyranny of the idea is that it makes us unnatural."

"By religion, you mean Christianity."

"Not just that. You know what I'm saying. Conventional morality. It's unnatural."

"That's the whole point," I said.

"You mean you're admitting that?"

"No, I mean it's the truth. We're supposed to be unnatural, fallen people. What we think is normal is not really even admirable. And we don't really want to be near God, because He only reminds us of what we aren't. How far we are from Him. That sort of thing. We don't have a choice though. We need Him." I was sure if Gelb ever talked to Forster, he would relay all of these pretty words I was saying, and it would be sufficient to convict me in a court of law if I was ever accused of being devout.

He shook his head, as though he had heard this one many times as well.

"That's if God is paying attention. I'm not sure He is, if He's even there."

"Then how would we know what is worthy?"

He wouldn't take the bait. "You do that pretty well," he said, smiling. The only sound, for a moment, was the squealing girls, kicking for the goal at last. "Really believe any of that? You can tell me."

The way Gelb said this made me suspicious. I thought, it must be obvious to him, at least, that I'm not really what everyone thinks I am. I wondered what had tipped him off. Was he just perceptive or were they *all* on to me, just humoring me with the idea that I had fooled *them*? Then there was the possibility that I was being testing myself. They had dispatched me to find out what I could about Prescott, but now they were trying to make sure they had sent the right man.

"What are you up to?" I asked him, smiling.

"You know," he said. "I mean, you know what I'm talking about. Some people allow others to do their thinking for them."

"Don't you?"

"No. I do my own thinking."

"You sure you didn't hear that some place and figure it sounded good?"

Gelb laughed.

"I think people want to believe that what they do makes sense, that they think about it and weigh the options carefully and then act. But, I mean, who does that? You see what you want, you go after it, and then you try to justify why it's a good idea, even if it isn't. Sometimes it helps if you've heard somebody do the same thing. You just use their words."

Then Gelb, shaking his head, rescued me. "Look, I work for Ben Forster and I spend a lot of time doing what I think is the right thing to do. What *I* think is the right thing to do. But then I think that maybe what I think is right is due to what Harry and Frieda Gelb thought was the right thing back in my childhood, and that I'll be carrying them around with me until the day I die. And so did they for their parents, and so forth. And all of this goes back to rabbis and prophets and people who thought that was what God wanted them to do. But if there is no God, if we invented Him for whatever reason, I mean, then what we're doing is denying who we really are."

"And you think that's a bad thing?"

"Well, not all the time. But I think about Marty and I wonder if he figured it out, and he decided to get out while he could."

"Figured it out?"

"It. You know."

"Ever thought about taking off for yourself?"

"Everybody does, don't they?"

"If he did figure it all out, you think maybe he would have been a little more bold about it than sneaking out of town?"

"Good point." Gelb rubbed the top of his head and surveyed his team of girls, all of whom seemed intent on anything other than soccer. "I'm sure Marty believed what he said about all that. The God stuff. But just because somebody really wants something to be true doesn't make it so."

"Same thing with not believing," I said.

Why did everything I was saying to Gelb sound like one of those church signs that I drove past, the ones that gave me a weird combination of an eye roll and a shiver — "Know Jesus Know Peace, No Jesus No Peace."

I found myself thinking back to Christine Thrower, certain of her damnation until I squeezed her hand. Was I enabling a fantasy, or just reassuring her of something she should have known instinctively? Just a squeeze of the hand, a little squeeze, was all it took. How much had I helped that along?

And why had I done it? What was I saying to God? *I believe in you, but I will not follow you. I will do this for you, but that will have to do. Maybe then you will leave me alone.*

Gelb was silent and finishing rubbing his vanishing locks. "I don't know. Mexico City's looking pretty good to me right now."

I shrugged. "Maybe."

"Good answer," he repeated. Gelb struck me as a man who wrapped ambiguity about himself as one might a comforter on a wintery night.

"And there's no denying that I am not a soccer coach," I said.

"Amen."

And the bouncy girl with her flying wrists laughed a split second before someone kicked a ball that went hurtling, with supersonic force, into my face. It came so suddenly that I fell to the ground with the sound of all of the girls on the team laughing. Gelb never moved from his spot.

"You okay?" It didn't take long for me to perceive by the tone of his voice that Gelb would later get a good laugh out of this too. I came to my feet, my eyes still closed, rubbing my nose in some ridiculous attempt at gaining sympathy. There would be none, I understood.

"Sorry, mister," I heard a voice say, and I opened my eyes to see a teenage boy come bounding up to retrieve his ball. He was probably fifteen or so, and the outlines of the man he would become were already apparent — the broad shoulders, a firm chin. He looked familiar to me for some reason.

"Uncle Cam?" he said. It was Peter's son.

"Ricky?"

The boy's brow wrinkled at the name. "You okay? I didn't hurt you too much?"

"No, no, I'm fine," I said. "How are you?"

"Okay," he said. We stood there for what seemed like a long moment, but probably was only a few seconds. I had not seen him in a long time. Cecelia always contrived to have Ricky some other place when I was around. Even when she called, she was certain he was asleep. As time went on, I should have realized that her appointed times got later and later, because Ricky was staying up later. She didn't want to run the risk of him picking up the phone by mistake and hearing his mother carry on a conversation with his dead father.

Ricky looked like he wanted to say something, but didn't know what. I desperately wanted to say something, to make some kind of connection.. I knew a great deal about him, because Cecelia felt the urge to tell "Peter" how his son was doing. But as far as Ricky probably knew, I had very little contact with his mother.

Memories came to me that I had forgotten. I would always stop off and pick up a toy for Ricky before I ever came over to Peter's house. Consequently, he was always happy to see me, going from giving me a hug and greeting to the more familiar "what did you bring me this time?" I doubted the boy remembered any of this, but I could still see a conditioned response long buried, as if his brain was telling him to expect some kind of surprise when he saw his uncle.

"Sorry," he said. "See you." He had to run back to his team. I opened my mouth to say something, but nothing came. Gelb had my attention in a minute with some drill of which I had very little understanding, but it kept practice moving toward the cutoff point at six. I was so interested in what was going on, that I didn't notice Cecelia walking up behind me. I detected her scent a moment before I turned and heard her voice.

THE WITNESS

"Cameron," she said.

I turned to see her, once again perfectly drawn in spotless business suit and with pristine hair. Her eyes hid behind sunglasses. Her lips were tightly drawn together.

"Stay away from him," she said, and walked off.

25.

I probably should have enjoyed, even relished the prospect of following Prescott to catch him in the act of whatever it was Forster suspected of him. I should have taken a camera and prepared lavish notes. I should have planned an entire web site. The truth was, I didn't know what I was looking for. And in a way that surprised me, the notion of shadowing him appalled me. Somehow, I felt sorry for him.

I woke up before Cynthia stirred because I knew that Prescott liked to leave his home before sunrise. I supposed this was part of his character, like his only-too-happy to meet you smile and his ridiculously vigorous handshake. Prescott probably rose before the sun in a cold sweat that someone might be up before him. When he bounded out of his house for his car, I could dimly make out the satisfied smile I knew would be there.

But he surprised me from the first. He had on, not the too perfect suit I expected, but ragged shorts and a T-shirt cut small enough to show a well defined chest and arms I would have gladly traded for my own. I remembered the gut that had greeted me at my first interview, now gone, banished. When he arrived a short time later at the local gym, I watched him race inside, and take his place among a convoy of stationary walkers bound for the same healthy destination. I could make him out through a window and watched him grit his teeth through a few miles and reps on some of the machines. He threw himself into the routine with the kind of maddening vigor I would have expected.

Even from a distance, for all his gusto, he did not look happy or pleased with himself. He looked like a man wilting under an impossible weight, though he couldn't have been his own. I recognized that he had been the victim of ill-fitting suits all the years I had worked for him — he had the physique of a man half his age. No, it wasn't age that he was battling against. It was something else.

I waited in my car, listening to the radio and occasionally thinking he might glance out and see me. No. Prescott was lost in his own world. For all he knew, legions of spies might be following him. Whatever I was watching was out in the open, and I wondered if perhaps this had been evident the whole time I had known him. When Prescott stepped off the treadmill, visibly unable to stand and draw breath at the same time, I heard the assured voice of Dr. Benjamin Forster in another of his feel good radio addresses reminding me that the race was not always to the swift, and I laughed myself silly listening to him wishing me his customarily exceptional day.

I had calmed down enough by the time Prescott showered, shaved, and dressed to drive on to what I thought could be work. I put on my sunglasses, waited a suitable few seconds, and drove a few cars behind him. But he went past the Forster Building and I wondered if I was to catch him in some kind of rendezvous. I felt ridiculous, then, when he pulled into the parking lot of a funeral home and walked in. I wondered what he was doing there. Even after his time at the gym, it was still too early to come to a funeral home unless he knew someone would be there. But no — I saw him come out of the place with his arm around a man who was weeping. The man was dressed in regular clothes, and I assumed he was the family member of somebody who had just been carried here, probably the night before. The man paused, looked Prescott in the eye, and draped a broad arm around him, burying his head in Prescott's shoulder. Prescott patted the man on the back. His body language indicated that he could have stood there perhaps for the rest of time or until the man cried himself out. Prescott had come out of his way to be there, on a hunch the man might be there at that moment making arrangements. All of this only served to make me feel more and more dirty as I took it in.

And there was worse to come. Prescott never made it to work that day. If he had known somebody was following him ready to take down any kind of indiscretion, he couldn't have done better for himself than what he did for most of the day. I followed him through town as he made the usual round of soup kitchens, child welfare shelters, battered wives' homes, shelters, rehab and hospice centers, and community outreaches that I would normally have on such a day. In fact, it was after lunchtime that I realized he was making my rounds for me. I was probably too wrapped up in the task at hand to understand that Prescott had probably gotten a call saying I couldn't be able to come into work today — the arrangements already having been made through Hagler for me. I was out, so he had to go and make contact with all my usual people, who were only too happy to see him instead of me. Most of the time, they were convinced they had seen him anyway, instead of me.

And still, there seemed something wrong with him. For a moment, I considered it might be that he was peeved at me for not coming in. I almost never took sick days, but Prescott reacted to those rare times I didn't come in as a personal affront. But no — there was something wrong with my boss. Something that I couldn't quite put my finger on made me suspicious that perhaps Forster had reason to suspect his surrogate of something.

I also perceived that if indeed there was something Forster was engaged in, he was the type of man who probably couldn't deal with anything that went against his own self-perception. He did not strike me as a man who could lead a double-life with any kind of assurance or panache. I wondered if this trek through the tempest-tossed of the city was some attempt at self-flagellation.

Or purification. *Maybe I'm not the only one who feels like he needs to make himself pure by solving all the problems of the world in one day,* I thought.

Perhaps that was why I saw him pick up a basketball and play a quick game in tie and rolled up shirt sleeves with a passel of kids at one shelter. Despite all his gym work, Prescott was hardly coordinated enough to take on teenage boys anxious to show off their jump shots. Though his arms were long enough to block just about anything, his timing was atrocious. But he took their success in stride, and as he left the court he mussed the hair of a few boys with his massive hands like a proud father. It was an archaic gesture. Some of the boys had shaved heads and I could tell at a distance they did not appreciate this invasion of their personal spaces. Part of me regarded all this exertion with an edgy admiration, while the other hated him that he wasn't playing the role of hypocrite to my satisfaction.

I followed Prescott out into the country about mid-afternoon and thought perhaps I was finally zeroing in on some kind of rendezvous. But no, his car pulled into the gravel parking lot of an old country church where there was some kind of revival going on. Once he was inside, I pulled close enough where I could hear the music and preaching through the open windows, and I realized this was a black church. Prescott, perhaps the whitest man I had ever met in my life, was inside clapping on the off-beat and singing, and giving an "Amen" when the preacher reached the appropriate volume. For the first time all day, Prescott looked totally unburdened. He wasn't there to speak, as I assumed at the start. No, he was merely there to listen, watch, and worship, and he couldn't have chosen a better place at that moment.

What fascinates me when I step into a church is the idea hovering in the background that God is a part of whatever is going on. This isn't a memorial service or a testimonial dinner where the guest of honor can't make it. The people there more or less operate on the idea that what is going on in that room — the off-key singers, the carpet that needs replacing, the cracked stained glass, the hoarse preacher — all of it has as much as weight as the proceedings in St. Peter's, The Holy Sepulchre, Notre Dame, St. Basil's.

Sitting there in my car, watching all of this and wondering what other indignities might be heaped on me as I tried to trap my boss, I kept thinking about what Cynthia had asked me. Why didn't I just get another job? It was good enough advice, and as the minutes ticked on, it wasn't the only voice asking me that question. For some reason, I heard Peter, tiptoeing up behind my imagination as Prescott's minister reached a staccato pitch on the wages of sin.

You know, that's a good woman you've got there.

Which one are you talking about? I asked. I was anxious to shut the voice up, even if it was in my own head. It's hard not to ignore that one form of mental illness is hearing voices and not being able to distinguish which are real, and which are fake. As Mr. Arthur Koestler wrote, when the accursed inner voice speaks to you, hold your hands over your ears.

On both accounts.

High praise coming from you. I supposed you wouldn't be too happy with your missus when she invited me over.

Let's just say I choose not to remember her at her most vulnerable. Too bad you have to play husband to two at the same time.

Your fault. Wasn't my idea for you to check out early.

Wasn't mine, either. Your better half had a good point. Why are you still working for Forster?

You getting lonely? Need me to join you?

No. Not at all. I just wonder why you think you need to stay on this job.

I don't know. It does some good somewhere.

Yes, you do know.

Then explain it to me.

You think by staying right where you are, you're having it both ways. You're satisfying God and sticking it in His craw — at the same time. Nobody knows except you.

Yes, they know. They all know about me.

Nope. You've got them all fooled. Except Him. But then, that's the point, isn't it?

And if that's true, why would I want to do that?

Probably for reasons you've never really admitted to yourself. Or even put into words.

So you do it.

I could hear him sigh. *If you insist. You blame Him because I'm not here. You took this job because it woke you up when I died. You thought you needed your life to count for something. But you wouldn't go all the way. Why should you hand over yourself when He'd already taken me away from you.*

Brilliant diagnosis. But you're wrong.

Am I? I could see your spine stiffen when Prescott told you to go out and get yourself saved if you wanted the job. That really burned you up.

And it wouldn't have burned *you* up? The guy is talking about this thing being this great decision, something to base your life on, the moment when you finally "get right with God," and it all boils down to a question of whether you want a job or not! That's so cheap! Just tell me you wouldn't have cussed the guy, decked him, and then left with his wallet!

That's not the issue.

Speaking of burning up, where are you speaking from? After all, I don't think you ever darkened the doors of a church after your wedding day.

Oh, you wound me with such harsh words. There's a lot about me you don't know, Big Boy.

Same here for me. I have my reasons for what I do. Not everything in my life revolves around you. You've been gone five years. I sort of have my own life.

So you've forgotten all about your big brother, have you?

Not at all.

Interesting choice of words there a second ago. You "sort of" have your own life. You have half a life, the other half being mine. You can't even go a few minutes without mentioning the other part.

That part is still mine.

Tell yourself what you want.

I will. Say hi to Hitler down there for me.

Say it yourself. I've been watching you. You've *been watching you. What*

173

do you call where you find yourself right now?

It's not that bad. If the worst is following this guy...

That's not what I mean. You're tearing yourself apart. And it's going to get worse. You know it will.

Maybe I deserve it, then.

Doesn't mean you have to go through with it.

There! Wasn't that your answer to life? Checking out on it. Takes a lot of guts to do that.

You have a choice, Cam. You can choose to be who you want to be.

What can I say? They sent an imposter to catch an imposter.

About this time, I broke off the conversation because the service was over. Prescott come out the front door behind the minister and proceeded to shake hands with everyone there, one after another, not as an officer of the church but as another member. Then I understood why I never saw him at Forster's church — *this* was Prescott's church. This was where he regularly attended, this church where he was the only white member, where the voice of the minister could be heard across a busy highway even if the windows were closed.

And so, I was almost resigned that my day was going to end in several revelations about my boss except the crucial one I had been sent to discover. I still followed Prescott back into town, expecting him to swing by the office. When I saw him speaking into his cellphone as he drove, I understood that he probably wouldn't, that he had been keeping up with things while carrying out his duties. But he wasn't headed home either. No, there was something he had to do.

As Dr. James Watson reminds us, important biological objects come in pairs. But for some reason, I did not suspect anything when Prescott pulled into the parking lot of a florist and went inside. I expected this was his latest act of sainthood, buying a spray for the casket of whomever he had visited that morning. When he came out however, he struggled to hold an unruly bunch of long-stemmed roses that bounced in his awkward arms. And even though Forster's genial voice came over the radio again at that moment, as if shadowing his most visible surrogate, I instead heard another voice.

If you're going to marry someone, pick a woman who's allergic to flowers.

THE WITNESS

You'll save a ton of money. That's what I did.
   "Gotcha," I said.

26.

Over time, Cecelia and I had worked out a system for her occasional calls, much like a peace treaty, or more correctly, a ceasefire. After I married Cynthia, Cecelia stopped calling my house and switched to my cell phone. But the calls would come on nights when I had to be out of the house at work, either for the Foundation or church. Cynthia was my wife, and Cecelia felt that part of me, at least, was still her dead husband, communing with her. After the fiasco of her one attempt to have Peter back in the flesh, she would only allow phone calls. At certain times, I was to call her, or she could notify me if she suddenly felt a pang of nostalgia. Peter had become one of those apparitions whose coming seems advertised at a certain hour and place.

All of this had to be worked out over time, of course. She kept her distance from me, and I kept my dates with her so that Peter could. I expected at some point that this would end, but it didn't. She kept calling, and Peter kept answering in the voice that I never had any trouble summoning.

THE WITNESS

The ancient name for ventriloquism, by the way, was gastromancy, and it began like necromancy, as a black art by which the dead could pass information they had learned from beyond the veil. Later on, like all magic, it soon transmogrified from transmitting the thoughts and observations of the late cousin so-and-so to transferring a tinny voice into the body of a wooden doll.

But like all magic, it involves a deception. When talking, a ventriloquist must make all their sounds with their lips apart, meaning that they physically cannot make the sounds for b, p, and m. In their place, they substitute the v, t, d and n sounds, and the audience fills in the blanks. The audience wants to be fooled, and so, their brains do the rest for the practitioner. Nobody cares that the dummy sitting down on the ventriloquist's lap seems to have a speech impediment. They only care that the little guy is speaking.

And so likewise, Cecelia didn't notice that as time went on, my voice did not change as Peter's would have had he lived. Nor did she care when a phrase like "Am I right or am I right?" passed my lips, something that I don't think Peter ever said in the course of his life. He was much too insecure for that. No, Prescott said things like that, and I unconsciously appropriated it from him, and without thinking, put it into the mouth of my brother, who, by the way, was dead.

No, she didn't care. Cecelia called me one night to ask advice - Peter's advice — on how to deal with Ricky's problems in school, not caring that I had no children and would not have known the first thing about it. She wanted Peter to hear when she got a promotion. She called once to consult with Peter about possibly selling the house. It took awhile before I realized she wanted my — Peter's — blessing on the idea.

"Don't be afraid to move," I told her. "Just pick up and go." I knew Peter had loved that old house, a lovely two-story Tudor at the sharp curve of a secluded circle, and I could imagine the memories that my brother and Cecelia had shared in taking two years to restore it. I thought if I encouraged her to sell, she might be forced to mentally move as well. Perhaps, someday, she wouldn't need these hand holdings by proxy. I wasn't sure what it meant when she didn't sell the house. Was she saying she no longer accepted me as her husband's stand-in, or telling Peter she wasn't obligated to listen to him because he was dead? If it was possible to feel enough offense for two men, I did. In the end, Cecelia told me — Peter — that she understood why he told her to sell the house, but she couldn't believe he had been serious. And so it was once again virtually impossible to tell just how far my hold over her sanity was. Did she *really* believe she was talking to Peter? Was it just a fiction she was adhering to because she had gotten used to it? Was she, in fact, doing this just as much for *me*, so I could hear Peter's voice again?

Even five years later, a typical conversation began with Cecelia asking for Peter the moment I answered. Not even a greeting for me, just, "Can you put Peter on?"

Who is putting who on? I wondered.

I usually cleared my throat, and gave my shoulders a hunch before plunging in. "Hello?" I said this as though I had rushed to grab Peter from some task. It was a mental picture I needed to focus on to get through the whole business. For some reason, I picked him coming in from working in a garden, the back of his neck glistening with sweat and a blade or two of grass stuck to his forehead. Sometimes, I would breathe heavily into the receiver as though Peter had been engaged in some kind of heavy labor. I have no idea what this did to Cecelia. Once, I had the perverse urge to suddenly have Peter say, "Can you speak a little louder? I can't hear you over the tormented screams of the damned down here."

"Baby!" she would exclaim, as though it was a surprise. "Just wanted to grab you for a second." Then she would launch into whatever she had to say. What was unsettling was the banality of the conversations. Sometimes she spoke of what she did in the course of a day, how grueling a trip to the grocery store had been, a television show she and Peter had been following when he was still alive. I listened dutifully, sometimes gave recognizably Peteresque utterances, judgments and pronouncements. Other times, I simply sleepwalked through the moment until she had gotten whatever she needed.

Strange how she managed to do most of the talking. Then she was gone. Sometimes, I noticed, she did not give me a desperate "I love you" so much as a "Talk to you, soon!" That made it hard to figure out whether she was getting better or worse. The temptation, naturally, was to say worse. Her husband had been dead five years and she still expected a line open to him. That wasn't normal, was it?

Then, I would remember how the famous escapologist Mr. Harry Houdini exposed mediums by going to séances and asking to speak to his mother. He would invariably have the case closed up when his "mother" would reply in English, a language she never learned. He kept going to the mediums though, legend said, not because of any benevolent gene compelling him to watch over would-be rubes, but because he *wanted* to hear from his mother. His own wife kept staging séances ten years after his death, waiting for a code phrase they had agreed he would give, if he could, from the other side. She never heard from him.

So was Cecelia trying the same thing with me? Was she waiting to hear something from Peter? The real one?

I still heard from him. Whenever I spoke to her, I would hear his voice in my head, good and strong, just as I had the first time accusing me. But his voice *did* change over time. Instead of roasting me for fulfilling this role, he instead seemed mad at his wife, at the way she seemed so easily satisfied with a conversation or the barest hint of her husband's presence.

"Put Peter on," she would say.

Yeah, you must be putting me on, sister, I could hear him say.

"Is it as hard on you, being without me, as it is for me without you?" she asked one night, when I was driving back from a youth shelter.

I don't think Cam can do your voice for me, if that's what you mean.

"You know there's never been anybody but you," Cecelia said, as though reading the sentiment from a prepared script, on the occasion of what would have been their fifteenth wedding anniversary.

And you and you and you back there in the back of Cam's mind. My, but it's crowded in here!

And yes, when I heard this voice, I didn't think of it as me doing yet another ventriloquist's trick, but the acutely real, impeccable, imperishable spirit of my dead brother. I thought this because this voice seemed offended, resentful, jealous of the time I was spending with his wife. He sounded weary, as though he could get no rest, like a wandering spirit in search of holy ground.

One day, Cecelia called me while I was at work. It was a rare day when I was actually in the office. When she asked for Peter, I said I had to walk into the conference room to speak. I didn't want everyone in the office to hear me speaking in a different voice.

"How are you?" I asked her, in my voice.

"Okay, I suppose," she said, in a matter-of-factly voice.

"Okay," I repeated. "Just that?"

"Sure. Can't complain." She gave a little laugh at the end that was either too buoyant to be believable or too detached to be sane.

"How are we doing?"

"We? As in..."

As in Cam and I? Are we satisfying all your desires?

"How are you doing with all this?" I said.

"All this?"

"Cecelia, don't you think it's a little strange that you still call me, all this time later..."

"I don't want to talk about it. Put Peter on."

"What are you going to do if something happens to me? I don't know anyone who can do *my* voice doing Peter. Because that's what you want to hear now. Not Peter, but..."

"I know what I want. Don't you think for a second that you're somebody else. You're not the next best thing, you're the only thing I've got to rely on. Don't think I'm unappreciative, I mean, but, you're not Peter."

You tell him!

Shut up, I thought to myself, the part of the self that regarded itself as Peter. *Now who are you jealous of?*

"No, I'm not Peter. I never wanted to be him," I said.

"No, you just wanted what he had."

"I'm going to hang up now," I said, clinching my teeth.

"Before you do, put on Peter."

"Just what do you think..."

"I think you owe it to your brother to..."

"Don't you talk to me about what I owe my brother. My brother is dead. I owe it to his memory to leave it intact, not destroy it, cheapen it!"

"You think it's *you* talking, don't you? Don't you understand! That's really Peter talking through you to me. He wouldn't let me down, and he hasn't. You think it's you doing a cheap imitation? No, no." She gave a mocking laugh. "That's *him*. I'm surprised he lets you go when it's all over. He was always stronger than you."

Go, baby! Let him have it! This is sooo overdue!

"Really?"

"Yes, and there's nothing you can do about it. Now, put Peter on."

She paused, and all I heard was the sound of her breath.

"I said *now*."

There was a moment where I thought about assuming Peter's voice and summoning him up, as though hazy through the smoke of a sorcerer's fire, like the shade of the prophet Samuel foretelling the end of Saul. *No, my dear, it is you that have been wrong, and you'll keep on being wrong because the only voices you hear are the ones in your head that keep telling you that you still possess me. You're torturing me and my memory, and my brother, and yourself, and you must stop before you've twisted everything I ever touched into something unholy.*

But I looked up to see Prescott just as the words came out of my mouth. And I could hear Peter saying something to me.

Don't I get a say in what I say anymore?

Prescott, a strange, beguiled look on his face, was standing there as he heard Peter's voice coming out.

"You really have to take it easy on him, Beauty. He's wrong, but he's still my brother. You can't expect him to understand." I didn't hear anything on the other end, which I understood to be satisfaction.

I looked up at Prescott, who had a startled look on his face.

"I'd better let you go," I said, still in Peter's voice, coughing.

"No, you can't," Cecelia said, in a supremely confident voice, as though I was absolutely in her power and incapable of doing otherwise. She had conjured up this spirit through me, and it would be impossible for me to do otherwise.

Apparently that was only half true. With the part of my brain that governed wisdom permanently disconnected, with Prescott looking on within earshot, I cleared my throat, and in my best imitation of Dr. Benjamin Forster said, "Have an exceptional day!" before hanging up.

Prescott folded his arms together and I tried not to look at him. "How long have you been doing that?"

"What?"

"That voice. That was uncanny."

"I was talking to my sister-in-law."

"Amazing," he said, shaking his head. As with Prescott, his expressions were sometimes so passive it was difficult to tell if he was dissatisfied or intrigued. I half expected him to know Peter somehow.

I was about to open my mouth, not sure who would come out, when he dashed out of the room. "You've given me an idea," I heard him say.

27.

So Prescott, unaware of what we all were up to around him, told me to show up one morning at a recording studio. The idea he had was for me, suddenly and without warning, to become Dr. Benjamin Forster.

Of course, he didn't tell me this up front. He merely told me to meet him at a certain address at around eight in the morning. I expected to pull into some community charity, and instead was confronted by a large brick building that vaguely resembled a barn. I thought I was in the wrong place at first, but no, there was Prescott's Lexus, with his personalized "HELP" license plate.

There was little to prepare me, once I was inside, for the crushing, stifling silence of a recording studio. I walked in and immediately wanted to clear my throat, and I didn't even know I would be speaking into the mike. When I did give a stagy cough, it sounded like an explosion. There was an impish desire within me to shout, just to see how far it would carry.

As I came into the control booth, Prescott looked up at me and smiled. He was madly fumbling with a phonebook. "Does anyone know the number for the Unitarian Universalist Church?"

Standing nearby was Gordon Marvell. Prescott was relying on him more and more now, and so he probably felt compelled to wear a suit each day to work. Gordon apparently could freelance and improvise the way Forster and Prescott wanted, and wasn't bashful about taking on work. He adjusted his tie as though looking at himself in a mirror just as Prescott asked the question. "Why do you..."

"They've got the microphone that I usually bring. I forgot to drop by and get it." Prescott flipped through a few more pages. "They're not listed where I expected them in here."

"Need me to go get it?" I asked. I still wasn't sure why I was there.

Prescott seemed not to notice my question. "Does anybody know the number for the Unitarian Church?"

"Shouldn't you be able to just dial any number and get them?" I asked.

Gordon gave an embarrassed laugh, Si Gelb a much bigger one, but not Prescott. "That's not so funny Cameron," he said. "They help us with a lot of things."

"Sorry," I said. "Couldn't resist."

One of the fastest selling recordings in history was an album called "The First Family," a parody of the Kennedy presidency recorded by a man named Mr. Vaughn Meader. Overnight, Meader's nightclub act, which consisted of a letter perfect impersonation of John F. Kennedy, spawned catchphrases and made him one of the most sought-after comedians in the country. Of course, this was before Dallas and Lee Harvey Oswald transformed JFK into the sainted icon. When that happened, Meader was at the absolute apex of his popularity. An apocryphal story has it that Meader learned the news of the murder from his agent, who immediately said, "What's the matter man? Lost your voice?" It should surprise no one that Meader died penniless decades later, unable to ever make a serious reprisal of his fame after having it snatched away so suddenly.

I thought of this when Prescott turned to me, only a second or two after chastening me, and said, "You get to be Dr. Forster today."

"Me?"

"Yes. I heard you the other day on the phone. You were sensational! You were absolutely indistinguishable from Dr. Forster. You'll do great."

"Wait a minute. You want me to do my Forster voice? For the radio?"

"Correct. We need a radio spot for him."

"Then let *him* do it."

"We can't. He's unavailable."

"Unavailable?"

"He can't do it. We need a stand-in."

Lucky me. "Why is he unavailable?"

"I'd rather not go into it. Health reasons, let me say."

"Run one of his old ones."

"We have been. Truth is, Dr. Forster hasn't recorded a new one of these in some time."

"How long?"

He hesitated and winced before admitting. "Probably six months."

"It's that serious?"

"That's something I can't get into."

Of course, I need not tell you that the first thing I suspected, long ago before my wife could vouch for it, was that Forster wasn't real. Maybe Prescott or someone else had created this shadowy figure who never showed up for some reason known only to them, like some dummy corporation formed to launder money or finance a South American revolution. If such a thing had been the truth, Prescott might simply need another voice because the old voice had skipped town. Or had been silenced, I mused ominously.

No, that wasn't it. Forster had been to my wedding. He had even approached me, though through a surrogate.

Or had he? Just for a second I wondered if maybe Hagler got to me with this message because there was some sort of power struggle going on within the Foundation. *They want to force Prescott out and they're using me for it. Can a man be trusted when you already know he's lying to virtually everyone around him?*

I blanched a bit at this question.

Then there was always the possibility that, Prescott's caginess aside, he was telling the truth. This little deception he was settling on was only a stopgap until the real Forster, recovered and transfigured, arrived back on the scene to dispense his customary wisdom to the lumpen proletariat.

"You want me to do his voice."

"Yes."

"You don't think anyone will notice the difference?"

"Not based on what I heard the other day. You got the main thing down — his closing. Better than anyone I've ever heard. You see, we've had to do this before. Dr. Forster hasn't been well for several years now. He rallies sometimes, then he falls. We have to draft somebody occasionally, but we've had to work with their voice electronically to get a partial match. In your case, I'm sure that won't be necessary."

"You know, impersonating a person is based on exaggeration."

"I'm aware of that, but you have an advantage."

"What?"

"They can't see you. It's much easier that way. You let their imaginations take it a step further. As good as you are, you ought to know that sort of thing."

I cleared my throat again. "Yeah, I guess I just...forgot."

"This really shouldn't be any trouble for you."

"If I speak with the tongues of men and angels..."

"Splendid," Prescott said, turning a knob. He reached into a folder and handed me a sheet of evenly spaced copy in large print for easy reading. It was a typical Forster homily on how virtually every choice one makes is based on underlying moral imperatives. My eyes glided over the words until I came to this quotation from Mr. Nathaniel Hawthorne: No man can wear one face to himself and another to the multitude without finally getting bewildered as to which may be true.

I looked at Prescott, who evidently had been expecting me to arrive at this sentence. He gave a chagrined look. "It's my idea of a little joke."

It gave me the idea that there was much more to Prescott than I could have guessed. I wondered if his joke was on me, on Forster, the listeners, or all of us at the same time. I detected a certain amount of impish pride in himself for arranging between all of us to give himself a laugh. He did look to be enjoying himself a little too much.

"I'm not sure I can do this," I said.

"Be another person?"

"No," I said. The man had no idea just how well I could do *that* job. "I mean be *this person*. I've never even *met* him."

"I know how it is," Prescott said, in a tone of voice that made me think there was no way he could. Then he added, "I'm a Lincoln impersonator."

"Lincoln?"

"Yeah. Our 16th president. Stovepipe hat. Fourscore and seven years ago. Perhaps you've heard of him?"

"Yeah, the name sounds familiar." I tried to assure him I was as familiar with the Great Railsplitter as Stephen A. Douglas had been. The idea kept me giggling to myself. Prescott, ebullient, feverishly industrious, noxiously positive man that he was, subbing for the grave, dark, desperate soul that saved the Union in a long, dark coat. Lincoln as the ebullient host of a children's program, perhaps if General Grant were a whisky swilling elephant in Union great coat.

He smiled, further making the image absurd. "It's actually quite simple, if you've got the right build. Tall and lean, all you need is a beard and the right wardrobe. Nobody really knows how he would have moved or what he sounded like. I used to do it before I put on weight, and when I took it off, I got back on the circuit."

He spoke as though he had a nightclub act, and again I thought of the ghost of Vaughn Meader, wandering the battlements of Martha's Vineyard in search of someone to retrieve a comedic Excalibur. "So in what kind of venue are you a Lincoln impersonator?"

"Schools mostly. They hire me to go and talk to the kids, recite his speeches. Some kids ask me for an autograph. Somedays, I show up at a store for Lincoln's birthday sales. I was at a Civil War reenactment once. I posed with some Confederates for a gag picture. Great way to earn a living. You know, Lincoln is so popular that his writing, photographs, everything associated with him has been faked over the years. But now there's a booming market for the fakes."

"That so?"

"Yes. In fact, I bought one not long ago. A man in Omaha, Nebraska sold it to me. It was supposedly an early draft of the 'House Divided' speech that had phrases in it that had been crossed out. You could read it and immediately tell it wasn't Lincoln. But it fooled several scholars for many years. I had to have it."

That he would want to do this was one thing, but I sensed something else from Prescott's tone. He did this because he needed to. It satisfied something in him, the picture of a child ambling up for the signature of a ghost. It gave me an indication of what kind of person he was inside. What was it about Lincoln that fascinated him, the same something that fascinated so many others? Well, Lincoln did sneak into Washington in disguise in 1861 to elude assassins, something that Lenin did more than fifty years later. *You can fool some of the people some of the time.*

"I guess there's more educational value in it than being an Elvis impersonator," I said.

"Actually, there's more of us than there are of Elvis."

"Is that so?"

"Oh, yeah. Makes you wonder what might have happened if Lincoln had recorded songs." I laughed. "He could have, you know. He had a high voice, like mine. What people say about his voice, I mean those who actually heard him, was that it could carry. I usually try to hit the classrooms because I think it's very important that children see Lincoln. See him. Understand that he's worth emulating. His example. If some of that rubs off on the children, who knows? And the character is in the details, like his voice. What did Lincoln really sound like? Probably no voice as interesting, unless it was, say, Jesus."

Mr. Philip Roth said that all you have to do is wait and life teaches you all there is to know about the art of mockery. Mockery, as in nothing in life is real, and even the fakes are fake in how they convey reality. And to think, that was before Mr. Roth dreamed up the character of Iron Rinn, the socialist hero who impersonated Lincoln, or Coleman Silk, the tragic literature professor whose whole life was an impersonation. Mr. Roth, of course, said he found all religious people hideous, sheep who followed a big lie.

And recording under another name wasn't exactly a new idea either. Mr. Winston Churchill supposedly used an actor during his famous wartime speeches so that the people of England would be stirred to fight to the end rather than make fun of his pronounced lisp. In the seventies, the group Klaatu sold thousands of copies of their album when fans mistakenly though they were the Beatles, recording under another name. And I remembered reading that Mr. Paul McCartney said the Beatles had actually considered touring in costume under another name, though I remembered reading this in "The Bachman Books," a collection of novels written under a pseudonym by Mr. Stephen King...

"Anything you can tell me about Dr. Forster? I mean, that might help me get a little edge? Anything to get this right."

"Oh. I forget you've never met him. Well, let's see. I can tell you that whenever Dr. Forster records these messages, just before we count him in, he always grabs his belt, like he's afraid his pants are falling down."

"That so?" Great detail, but I hardly knew what to do with it. "Loose clothes?"

"He's lost a lot of weight. In some of his last spots, you might have noticed his voice sounding a little thin."

"Not really."

"Well, it's our job to make sure nobody notices, so that's a good sign. I just noticed that he does that. Makes me think he wants to be sure about something, whether it's his pants staying on or whatever."

I nodded.

"I don't know if that helps."

"Right."

"One other thing."

"Yeah." If I had been a praying man, I would have said one so that perhaps, through some supernatural effort, Prescott might say something to help me with this impossible task.

"I remember the last time, we didn't think he'd get through the session. He tapes about 20 of these at a time, and he just didn't seem to have any stamina when he came in. Trouble...breathing...and that's all I'll say. But he came through like a trouper. When it as over, I remember he sat back and took in a big gulp of air. And then he said, in the most mild, natural voice, 'We grow old, underestimating the grace of God.'"

In Prescott's voice there was so much natural awe about the man that I felt like I understood as much about him as I did about Forster. Somehow, I would have to communicate in a voice the presence of someone who might inspire that kind of awe.

"You'll do fine, Cameron," he said, just before he went into the control booth to start. "You ought to know by now what happens. As the Lord uses you, and He has, you gain more confidence, which allows the Lord to use you even more."

So that's why I feel hopeless, I thought, again clearing my throat.

28.

We passed the day this way, in the recording studio, the silence a wall that separated us from the rest of the world. There was a television set in the control booth, and from what I could see, there had been some kind of terrorist explosion in another part of the world. The picture was slightly grainy, not as sharp as something you would expect in an American broadcast. On the picture was a car consumed by fire, jammed up against a concrete barrier or something. It was hard to make out, but they kept running the footage over and over, enough to make one wonder if this was the most important burning car in the world.

Maybe I'm like a suicide bomber, I thought, looking at that car. *I'm in the midst of these people and they think I'm one of them.*

But I'll end up destroying them, won't I?

I didn't worry about it. I was too busy trying to sound like Benjamin Forster, and at times, I think I might have pulled it off. Singers often talk about how they develop their own styles trying to be someone else, but the originality comes because they can't quite pull off the imitation, and instead create something new. Such is art, and the perpetual act of creation connects us all at some point we least expect. Michael Jackson's penchant for plastic surgery was once described by his wife as his attempt at making himself into a work of art. His wife at the time was Lisa Marie Presley, whose own father Elvis was transformed into a work of art, by among others, Andy Warhol. Warhol did virtually the same thing to his protégé Edie Sedgwick, who fell in love with the singer Bob Dylan, who modeled his persona after Woody Guthrie and Elvis, the art object whose son-in-law was briefly Michael Jackson.

I am he as you are he as you are me and we are all together.

The spots made nominal demands on my borrowed voice, and I found myself adopting the easy cadences of Forster's reassuring voice. As I found out, Prescott wrote most of these radio spots, but not all of them. Prescott's were very neatly typed in large letters with helpful pronunciations spelled out after potentially difficult words. But he also handed me one that was written out in the most appalling, illegible scrawl I had ever seen. The hand that wrote those pages couldn't possibly be sober, I thought, the way the line of letters veered up and down along the pages, with curly bits of attempted cursive shooting out like tracer bullets. I took out a piece of paper during a break and began writing out the words, but some were impossible to figure out. I called Prescott over and asked him.

"Oh," he said. "I forgot I'm the only one who can still read his handwriting."

"Dr. Forster's?"

"Yes," he said.

I looked down at what I had transcribed thus far. Though I couldn't quite make it all out, I understood he was writing about evolution. He mentioned a recent article about two sets of African fossils which challenged the conventional picture of man ascending through various strains of hominids to his present incarnation. He was particularly amused by a scientist who was quoted as saying the discovery would be seized on by creationists, but it was just science further refining an idea.

"This is what science, unlike religion, constantly does," the scientist said. "It's always compelling us to test ourselves and our assumptions."

I found myself laughing, much in the same way Forster must have. I could see the Boss' point. Anyone who expected a believer to swallow a line of unchanging shibboleths without so much as a peep had more faith than the average believer. It gave me the barest look into the mind of this man I had been serving for so long. There was something else here — the voice of a mocking, provincial rebel who probably would have sneered at the easy assurances Prescott had been putting in his mouth all these years.

But Prescott evidently couldn't see his boss's point.

"I don't think we need this one," he said, sniffing at the badly written words. He shook his head and I could hear, ever so slightly, the sound of the paper wrinkling in his fingertips, as though he was grinding it.

"What's wrong?"

"Oh, he does this every now and then. It's one of his pet causes. He seems to think that evolution needs to be challenged just for the sake of challenging it. He just wants his point of view out there, but I think this sort of thing can be misinterpreted."

"How do you mean?"

"I tell him he's got his image to look after. If people heard him going on and on about evolution, when it's pretty much established science, then they're just going to associate him with the same things they always associate Christianity with."

"Which are?"

"Ignorance. Intolerance."

By the tone of Prescott's voice, perhaps for the first time, I understood that these views he meant for Forster were actually his own. "I don't think that's what he means though. Not from what I could read."

"Of course not."

"I mean, he's simply saying not that it is wrong, but that it's not something to base your life or your soul on."

"That's not how it will be heard," Prescott said.

"I didn't think *we* were supposed to care about what others thought about us. Shouldn't he be allowed to say what he wants to?"

The great English comic actor Mr. Peter Sellers, a devastating genius at mimicry, famously said that there was nothing really interesting about him, unless he was being someone else. *There is no 'real me.' I no longer exist. I had it surgically removed*, he was quoted as saying. Perhaps the problem that Hagler had hinted at so darkly was this — Prescott did not merely believe that he was working for Forster. He had come to believe, in some strange way, that he *was Forster*, that together they had created this third personality that was half of each man, and that as such, he had every right to determine what opinions that man had a right to have. It was a hard job, I understood. Prescott wasn't just trying to be two men. That was way too simple. One of his personas was also trying to be two men — a dedicated worker *and* a philanderer — and the Forster he created as a benevolent civic spirit was threatening to prophesy, which was a danger. Prophets turn most vehemently on their patrons.

Then I saw a gentle smile pass over Prescott and he took another step forward.

"What do you think, then, about evolution?"

"Me? Personally?" I asked. Prescott nodded.

I didn't know if he was drawing me out in order to let me hang myself on my opinion, or curious. My voice, so suddenly not my own, dropped back into its familiar octave. I told myself I must say something, so that no one would be suspicious of me.

"I could swallow it all ...except for one thing, really," I said.

"What's that?"

"Jesus," I said. I had been in a church long enough to know that this choice that Forster was wrestling with, uncomfortable and seemingly irrational, maddening, frustrating, unnerving and eviscerating as it was, could only be the work of one figure. "I can't account for Him any other way than the way He speaks about Himself. Unless you ignore who He is, or make Him something He's not, you can't explain Him."

This was the truth, by the way. I had by this point explained away virtually everything that one might use as a basis for the soul-saving decision I was supposed to have already made. But my close reading of the Bible for employment purposes had not been totally clinical, and when I got to the Gospels I suddenly understood all those columns of instructions for sacrifices in Leviticus. The great vastness of the void separating God and man ...God from me ... was plausible to me, an impossible distance that only God Himself could cross. The pale Galilean had stirred something inside me that bordered on fascinated dread.

Yet I did not, could not, give my life to Him. I could not let Him *win*. I could help others, perhaps, blunder their way toward Him, but I told myself I would step casually out of their way. In all reality, my casual steps were more like frantic footfalls.

A character in one of Miss Flannery O'Connor's stories once said that Jesus threw everything out of balance. Consequently, it was probably no surprise that Prescott resumed his odd dance of obsequiousness, stepped back twice, looked at the paper with Forster's words, and handed it to me.

"Thank you," he said, a bit unconvincingly, grudgingly, but definitely. He had perceived the choice, as I had, and surrendered. I understood it was not something he was used to. His face looked hot and hard, and he wiped his forehead quickly, as though we might not notice. "I suppose I forgot for a moment why we're here." He then made a signal to Gordon Marvell in the control booth that we were about to record. I saw the look on Gordon's face that told me he had never seen anyone stand up to Prescott like I had and win.

I looked down at the sheet, resumed copying out the words and tried to figure out what he meant. When Prescott told me I had twenty seconds, I realized that I was going to have to make up what I couldn't decipher anyway, so the words that I imagined Forster carefully crafting where changed anyway. I interpreted it the best I could, and perhaps for a moment, I really believed what he had to say.

29.

I should let you know as I sat for Prescott doing my Forster imitation, silently passing judgment on him the whole time, I kept the knowledge of what he'd been up to locked within me. The afternoon I saw him buy the flowers, I followed him as the sun went down to a house I knew was not his own. He drove through several neighborhoods, over speed bumps, stopping for every stop sign and yield sign, taking a deliberately roundabout way. I didn't think he knew someone was following him — least of all me. But he seemed conscious, in the way of unfaithful men, that perhaps the whole world was pursuing him to this place. Then again, Prescott was just abnormally careful about everything. And yet...

He got out of his car with flowers and walked up to a side door of the house that opened up beneath a carport. Beyond it was a three-car garage with the doors down. I saw the side door to the house open, the flowers received, and a feminine form emerge behind the door and plant a long, loving kiss on him. He looked over his shoulder in a stagy manner and retreated inside. He stayed long enough to confirm every suspicion, then skulked out in the same manner he came in, pausing long enough to blow a quick kiss as he got into his car. The whole thing was so blatant it had the effect of making me skeptical. Surely a man like Prescott wouldn't be so careless and stupid. I thought he was blatant about it because he wasn't used to being sneaky. Then I wondered if it was the arrogance of a man who had so far unaccounted for his accumulated sins. I wrote the address of the house down and drove off with every intention of calling Hagler that night with the news.

But I didn't. I picked up the phone several times that evening only to replace it and shove the address back into my pocket. I understood there was still much I didn't know about Prescott, so much so that I wasn't willing to hand him over to his own, self-created tortures. The maliciousness I had once held for him had disappeared after spending the afternoon with him at the studio. Yes, he was a hypocrite. Yes, he was an over-officious prig who took himself too seriously. But he was...more interesting. Somehow, I wanted to help him. That was the ridiculousness of it. All this assistance I had given to others I now wanted to render to him. And so, for about a week, I did nothing. I heard nothing from Hagler, who I assumed was waiting to hear back from me. The address stayed in my pocket and disappeared when my pants went into the wash. This was no accident. I would need that fact later when I honestly told him I couldn't remember the address.

When I finally decided to contact him, I knew it couldn't be over the phone. That was a cowardly way to approach the task. Hagler wanted to know what I knew. I resolved I would tell him, let him make his own conclusions, and the whole thing would go forward from there. Whatever Forster decided to do, I knew it would probably be at least fair to his longtime lieutenant. I didn't know much about Forster, but what I did know reassured me at least on that score.

I looked up Hagler's address in a phone book and printed out a map from the Internet to get there. I rehearsed and revised what I would say when I arrived for virtually all of the short trip over. The apologies and explanations I might offer for Prescott were like spider webs and just as easily cleared away with the first waves of a hand. I

understood why Forster was acting this way, but I still felt for Prescott
in a way that I never would have dreamed possible.

And then, I looked down at my map and arrived at Hagler's house,
and in a split second, I had the dawning realization that I knew this
home, and that Hagler's address was familiar, and that this was in fact
the same house I had seen Prescott enter with flowers and leave with
a playfully pantomimed kiss, and that Prescott was having an affair
with Hagler's wife, and that Dr. Benjamin Forster had commissioned
Hagler to get me because he already knew all of it, and had hoped I
would handle this in a fair way. And the fact that he had entrusted this
duty to me meant that Forster did not himself know what the correct
way to handle it might be, much as I did not either.

I kept driving around the block, perhaps as many as five times
before I worked up enough nerve to park my car under the carport, in
almost the precise place that Prescott had when I had seen him there.
I heard an engine humming some distance away and a plane passing
over. A flight out of town, virtually anywhere, seemed like a welcome
prospect. I knew Hagler was there. I didn't know if his wife was there.
I looked in the cloudy windows of the garage and saw Hagler's car
there, but not his wife's, and I coughed as I walked away. I knocked
on the door I had seen Prescott enter, rang the doorbell, and heard
nothing within. Then I went to the front door and did the same thing
with no answer.

When I came back around, I began coughing again from a sudden
tickle in my throat, and the noise I had heard earlier was somehow still
there, but less insistent. It had settled into a low hum. In the words of
Mr. Thomas Mann, not every story happens to everybody, which is
why it took me far too many valuable seconds before I had a second
sudden series of revelations. I was about to get into my car when I
noticed that sound again and began coughing, and I understood that
the sound was Hagler's car, inside the garage, that was running, and
the reason the garage door windows had been cloudy was from carbon
monoxide — the same stuff that was making me cough. Those things
taken suddenly together meant that Thomas Hagler was inside the
garage with his car running, trying to kill himself, which undoubtedly
meant that he knew precisely what I had come to tell him.

For perhaps the only time in my life I was happy I had to wear a suit with a pocket handkerchief, which I fumbled out and over my nose as I wrenched the garage door up. The fumes rushed past me and I ran to the car door. Hagler was inside, his eyes shut, foaming at the mouth and twitching. I reached in and turned the car off, then doubled him over my shoulder and carried him out onto the pavement. I reached into my pocket for my cellphone and called 911.

"Hagler," I said, slapping his cheeks, waiting for the dispatcher. I told them the address.

Of course, now *you remember it.* It was Peter's voice, mocking me. Shut up, I thought.

I wiped Hagler's mouth with my sleeve and listened for a breath I did not hear. I ripped open his shirt and the buttons sprayed away like little pieces of candy scattered across the pavement. I listened to his chest and heard no heartbeat. I checked for the absent pulse. Then I began CPR.

Good thing old Prescott had you take those courses on resuscitation.

Shut up. I had no way of knowing if I was doing them the right way. You practice on a dummy and you never worry about it having broken bones. You can't just resuscitate someone anyway you want to. You have to do it the right way.

Hagler's lips were still burbling up spittle, but I gave him the breaths and kept up the chest compressions, believing that the ambulance would get there just in time for them to pronounce him dead. I had never seen anyone die before. The sick thing, that I was fully conscious of at the time, was that I *wanted* Hagler to die. Somehow, I wanted all my labor to be in vain.

It had nothing to do with Prescott, Hagler's wife, Forster, any of them. In just a few seconds, I had resolved that Hagler would succeed in his suicide attempt and be granted a way out of his embarrassing situation. He had no reason for living anymore. This would not only condemn Prescott in the eyes of Forster, but grant me a sort of quiet, heroic patina. I would forever be the man who tried and failed to grab back Hagler after his suicide attempt. I could see Cynthia telling people at a dinner party that I didn't like to talk about it, it being such a painful memory. I don't know *why* I particularly wanted this, nor why I was disappointed when my chest compressions worked and Hagler coughed back to life for a second.

His lips were moving and I squatted down to hear him. The ambulance was just coming up the drive, its siren impossibly loud, drowning out not only the words he was saying but the ability to perceive them.

Then, finally. "Why?" he said.

I had hunched over him with my elbows bent, head down, tilted to allow my ear full access to his words. When I heard this one, I looked at him. His eyes rolled back and he spoke again.

"Why did you do that?" he asked, choking.

I felt the medic putting a firm hand on my shoulder to usher me out of the way. Two men then converged on the prone figure while the one behind me took me to one side to allow the others to work on Hagler. He shuddered again.

"He's crashing," one said to the other, with a tone that sounded like a mechanic noting a noisy muffler. A defibrillator powered up as they talked in muted, professional tones. Once again, this time a little later, his heart restarted, and once again, for some ungodly reason, I felt a vague yet palpable disappointment.

"What did he say to you?" said the medic who had walked me away from the scene, now joining the others. I suppose he thought I might have some information that could help them.

I said nothing.

"What?" he repeated.

I answered, in a voice that sounded obscenely like Hagler's, "He thanked me."

Better hope he doesn't wake up. Then they'll be working on you.

Shut up.

iii. NATURAL SELECTION

30.

The philosopher Mr. Franz Rosenzweig died of Lou Gehrig's Disease, which is interesting since he died before Lou Gehrig was diagnosed with the disease. As he gradually lost the use of his limbs, he dictated his thoughts to his wife, slowly, painstakingly, letter by letter, using sign language. His last sentence was this: "And now it comes, the point of all points, which the Lord has truly revealed to me in my sleep, the point of all points for which there—" At that point, his doctor interrupted him, and he never got to finish the sentence. It is the nature of life that it doesn't always let us get the last word in exactly as we might wish.

But by the time I recounted Hagler's attempted suicide several times, my fabricated last words for him sounded just as real as if they were the actual ones. I might have deluded myself momentarily into believing that they *were* the right words, but only for a fleeting second. But as time went on, it became apparent that while they were my version of the last words he had spoken before losing consciousness, they might not actually be his *last* words.

Just before they took him away, I reached into Hagler's pocket and pulled out his keys, thinking I would let myself in the house to call Rebecca and tell her to meet me at the hospital. The medics went on and I heard the siren retreat before I turned the lock and let myself in. The house was silent and it made me feel like a burglar to hear the sound of my footfalls on the tiled floor. The phone rang and I picked it up, expecting Rebecca's abrasive voice. It was a telemarketer. If Hagler ended up surviving, he could expect a free year of digital satellite television waiting on him when he came home. There shall be showers of blessings.

I must have stood there for a few minutes before I realized that there was no way I could call Rebecca since I did not know the number. There was nothing marked on the phone in the kitchen to tell me if her number had been programmed in as a speed dial. I looked around the house, thinking I might find something, an address book or a dry erase board with a number. Nothing. I went upstairs and paused outside the bedroom that I guessed was theirs. I thought about entering, but then decided against it. There had already been too many people in there, I told myself.

If I had ridden to the hospital with Hagler, I learned later, I would have witnessed his heart stop twice and the medics persuade the dogged, reluctant organ to beat to life again. When I got there, the police were waiting on me in a small room. *Had he been depressed? Did I see anything out of the ordinary or suspicious?*

No, I thought. Of all the attempted suicides I've witnessed, this was the most commonplace one by far.

I did get a call in to the church to have someone notify Rebecca, since her cellphone number was probably on file. But by that time, I was already impatient for her to arrive. There was a nagging sense growing in me of being inconvenienced, that my actions in this, no matter how benevolent I might see myself, were keeping me from being somewhere else. I had nothing else to do, nowhere else requiring my presence, yet I was being put upon by this man who didn't even have the courtesy to kill himself in the correct manner. When I finally correctly understood these feelings, I tried to tamp them down. The man's wife would be arriving soon. She would know instantly that she was the probable cause of what had happened. There was no mistaking that Hagler had meant to kill himself. What would she do? I prepared myself for the possibility that she might need someone, and I observed that this would only be my latest attempt at filling the void for an absent man while standing next to his woman.

The actor Mr. Alan Alda states that in a comedy people get what they want, while in a tragedy people get what they deserve. I found it hard to understand which I was witnessing, when Rebecca Hagler arrived just in time to be told by her husband's doctor that he was alive but in a coma, and it was not yet possible to tell how much damage had been done to his brain. His heart had stopped several times, and while it was beating now, there was no way to know how much vital oxygen it had been robbed of.

She listened carefully to the instructions, nodded with a sort of open mouthed acceptance, heard me explain how I found him, then asked to be admitted to see him. We were taken up to a ward with several beds separated by glass partitions and curtains. Heart monitors beeped and ventilators rose and fell in varying rhythms interrupted only by the squeaks of hustling nurses' shoes. They drew back a curtain and I saw a new Thomas Hagler, different from the one I had last seen, with a tube shoved in his mouth, his eyes closed, dressed in hospital robes and lying motionless. He seemed not prone but rigid, as though he really had died but they were keeping him like this to satisfy somebody's quota.

I stood toward the back, near the curtain, thinking it indecent to intrude on the two of them, but she kept looking back at me and speaking to me.

"Look at him," she said. Her tone had no pity in it, but instead seemed to be stymied by the sight. "Just look at him. I should have known this would happen."

She shook her head, and she spat on him like I had seen people do in movies. I couldn't tell if she was copying them, or if the gesture just rose up inside her. The words that followed, though, were hers, undeniably.

"You couldn't make me stay with you any *normal* way, could you? You think *this* is going to keep me here? You think I care enough to stay here and hold your hand while you get over this?"

I had stood there and heard the doctor say there was a fairly good chance he might never "get over this," that what they could see of his brain function was minimal at best. She had heard it too, but somehow, she was convinced that he was in there, inside that stiff set of limbs, listening to her every word.

She looked back at me. "This is just like him. Look. He can tell what I'm saying. Can't you see it?" She turned back toward him, as though expecting him to answer. "You're just listening to all of this. You're enjoying it! You expect me to sit still for this, don't you? You expect me to love this? I didn't love you when you could walk and talk! You never went anywhere I wanted to go! You never said anything I was interested in hearing! Never! You hear me!?"

At least there was a questioning tone to those words, as though she might accept the possibility that perhaps he couldn't hear her. He was lucky. Her voice was carrying through the entire ward, and she ignored the instructions of nurses to stop — first hushed, then shouted, never quite conquering the ringing quality of her own words. I expected to spot security sprinting in within a moment.

"There's *nothing* that can keep me with you! If you thought you were being nice to me by doing this, you could have at least had the decency to do it right! It would be just like you to bungle the first good decision you've ever made! But I know you! It's all about *you*! This wasn't an accident! You meant for this to happen! It's your revenge, isn't it?"

I didn't really believe it when she started hitting him. The only response he gave was involuntary — the ventilator was forcing him to breathe. Otherwise, the doctor told us, he wouldn't. But she still hit him. She slapped his face and his motionless arms, his face again, and his chest, his face again, and again.

"Stop her, will you?" one of the nurses said, and I understood that she was talking to me. In the few steps it took to cross the room, she was now pounding on her defenseless husband with fists. I expected she might be weeping, but she wasn't. Her jaw was set and her lips curled and she brought the blows down until I grabbed her arms and stopped her, wrestling her away from the bed. Hagler's body remained the same, except where Rebecca's slaps had left his face red. The expression never changed, which Rebecca probably took as some sign that he was playing his part to the hilt. And she was laughing at him.

"What are you doing?" I said. I realize it was a ridiculous question, but nobody ever says what they're thinking at a time like that. They only say what they expect others expect them to say. My question probably should have been, *He finally does what you want him to, and you're beating him for it?*

"Let me go!" she said, but I didn't until I had hustled her out of the ward. A security officer and a policeman were rushing in and took her from me. A nurse was standing by to make sure she was escorted out.

"Was that his wife?" asked another nurse, who had been watching but hadn't acted.

"Yeah," I said.

"No wonder," she said, under her breath.

I didn't say anything. I still had that feeling of creeping time, that I was needed desperately anywhere but where I was, and it was imperative I leave immediately, because I was being inconvenienced by all of this.

"Are you related to him?" the nurse asked.

"No."

She ventured another guess. "Her?"

"No," I said, turning to look at her.

"Do you know any of his family?" the nurse asked.

"No, I don't," I said. "I can check."

"Good," she said, and I walked out of the hospital with no intention of doing so. It was raining outside and the people coming into and going out of the building ran as though the raindrops contained something lethal. By the time I got to my car in the parking lot, my cell phone rang.

"Cameron?" the voice at the other end, oddly familiar, called out.

"Yes. Here I am," I said, like I was responding in the dark.

"Good to know," the voice said. "This is Dr. Benjamin Forster."

31.

His voice was not as I expected — it *did* sound like the one I had recorded for Prescott earlier. For a second or two, I had a bout of ridiculous skepticism — as if I expected to be talking to myself mimicking him. Then it was overtaken by admiration at how well I had done the job of being him.

"Hello, sir," I said, stammering out the words.

"Good to talk to you, Cam," he said, in a voice that sounded as though we had spoken every day of our lives. "Are you well?"

"As much as can be expected," I said, clearing my throat for no discernable reason. It was getting worse. I had to consciously remember what my own voice sounded like. Was it the magnetism of his personality or the fact that I had forgotten? I was so shocked I was standing in a hammering rainstorm, oblivious to the water soaking my clothes, hair and skin. *So this is what it means to be transfigured,* I thought.

"I understand," he said. "You must be at the hospital with Thomas. How is he?"

To fully appreciate this, you have to realize that by this particular moment, it had been barely an hour since I had found Thomas Hagler, at most an hour and fifteen minutes. I looked around nervously, expecting to see someone standing nearby with a cell phone who I might recognize as Forster. No one. Just the sound of passing cars in the parking lot and water rushing out of gutters. Then again, there was the possibility — quickly dismissed — that Hagler had not in fact attempted suicide and that Dr. Benjamin Forster's many charitable and evangelistic outreaches merely concealed the diabolical master criminal within, slowly eliminating enemies perceived and overt, by way of suspicious "suicides."

"He's unconscious," I said. "It doesn't look very good right now. They've brought him back several times but there may be brain damage."

"Rebecca there?"

"Well...yes. I mean, she was."

"A scene, I take it?" Though I didn't know him, I thought I detected a knowing amusement in the question.

I swallowed hard and looked around again. "Yes, sir."

"Cam, this is a delicate situation, which I'm sure you're aware of."

"Yes, sir," I said. "I didn't get a chance to tell Thomas what I..."

"I know," he said.

"You know," I repeated, unsure what he meant.

"I know about *that situation*," he said, and I understood he meant the connection between Prescott and Rebecca Hagler.

"How do you..."

"Cam, I'm afraid I'm going to have to ask you to take over things for Charlie Prescott," he said. I had the feeling he knew what my next question was, but his tone made it seem that any query about how he knew what he knew was unnecessary. The only thing *I* needed to know was that it was no longer possible for Prescott to do his job. "I've asked him to step aside and he's already agreed to do so. I hate this, but it's undoubtedly necessary."

"Dr. Forster, I..."

"I know you'll do the best you can," he said. "That's always been more than sufficient to whatever task we gave you. Actually, I've had my eye on you for a long time. I have no doubt..."

"Sir, what about Prescott?"

"He can't continue to work for me," he said. "I'll make sure he's taken care of, but this is something I can no longer ignore."

"Did it..."

"Did it what?"

"Did it, well, surprise you, sir?"

The question seemed to stop him. I had a picture, hastily assembled in my mind, that Forster might be sitting at a table with a checklist of things to do, and a timetable for how long he could budget for this particular conversation, and suddenly, I had upset things with my question. I have no idea how many seconds I consumed. It was one he wanted to answer, I guess.

"No," he said. "No, not really."

"Why?" I was surprised at his answer. For some reason, I expected Forster to argue vehemently at the moral rectitude of his lieutenant, and to wave away any concerns about his private life, based on their long association. In the book of Genesis, Abraham detains the Angel of the Lord (or perhaps, God Himself, the scripture is vague) on the way to destroy Sodom and Gomorrah by asking if what He intends to do is not right. What if there are righteous people in the midst of all that unrighteousness? He apologizes, but he asks the question, nonetheless. "Shall not the Judge of all the world do right?"

"Because he's a man," Forster said, as though that should be enough. Mr. Alexander Solzhenitsyn said that the line that divides good and evil cuts through the heart of us all, and yet no one is willing to destroy a portion of their own heart. I wondered if Forster was trying to do this. Instead, he was inscrutable. "It was good to talk to you, Cameron. I'll be in touch."

And the line went dead and that was it. Whatever misgivings I may have had were inconsequential. Whether this was meant to inspire me or simply because he didn't have time to spare on my problems, I couldn't fathom. I was simply alone, left wet in the rain standing by my car.

32.

Perhaps you've heard of Alger Hiss. If he was a spy, then he might have been the perfect spy, since there are those who will still argue he never was one. Richard Nixon, who knew something about new identities, who went on to a perpetual career as a popular Halloween mask long after his death, made his career by unmasking Hiss as a spy for the Soviet Union. Hiss went to his grave some fifty years later denying he had ever been a spy, even after serving time in prison for perjury. Historians pouring over Russian archives have found threads of evidence supporting either position. After all, who would believe a spy could work in the State Department and help in the formation of the United Nations at the Yalta Conference in 1945?

It's always the people you never suspect, isn't it?

And so, I was now Dr. Benjamin Forster's alter ego, as well as his voice. Within minutes, my cell phone was ringing from the office. Gordon Marvell wanted me there. Someone was on the way to the hospital to stay with Thomas Hagler. I was needed back immediately.

I drove back expecting some kind of catastrophe, curious as to what it was since I had just spoken with Forster. And yet, it was nothing other than the most mundane kind of paperwork. I was marginally familiar with it but I had managed to avoid it thus far. I supposed I had the job because I knew Prescott better than others, and Prescott knew Forster. Gordon, who had been working more and more with Prescott over the last few months, kept thrusting documents in my face to sign that had to do with simple payroll and other banalities. They were the sort of things that would still proceed along with or without me or Prescott, but they took on supernatural importance with Gordon. I began to wonder if it was just fear that the tap might be turned off from Forster's foundational largesse, and we would instead all find ourselves out of work. Did Gordon need that last paycheck so much?

Gelb came in with some of the same, only with a much less frantic mien about himself. For him, it was getting the scheduling right for a dinner party and community fundraiser Forster was giving in two weeks, a counseling program that needed a new chairperson, and ordering the appropriate trophy for the youth soccer league championship.

I listened to all of this for long enough until I thought that I was being held hostage. I had asked myself why I didn't simply look for another job, and now that question was resounding inside my skull like an accusatory drum cadence. I tried to tell myself that it was like being kidnapped. Then I modified that idea. This was actually Stockholm Syndrome, the psychological condition where a captive identifies emotionally with his captors. *They didn't kidnap me*, I told myself, *but I feel like I can't leave.*

What was most appalling was their seeming lack of concern for Prescott. They had worked with him almost as closely as I had, and for longer, yet they didn't seem to be agitated in any other way than that work might suffer if these other matters were not attended to immediately.

Finally, I had to stop them. "Don't any of you even care about what's happened?"

They both paused. Part of my question had to do with what I perceived as my utter lack of business being in Prescott's office, which smelled musty for some reason, like a neglected library. They said nothing, as though they expected I wasn't finished with them.

"Did you both know what was going on?"

Neither man moved, then Gordon shrugged. "Sort of, but I didn't want to ask." I had the feeling he was fudging a little bit, keeping something back.

"Oh, I asked," Gelb said, waving his right hand for effect. "I definitely asked."

"What did he say?"

"Charlie said what you'd expect, that stories about him were mistaken."

"Stories? So this had already gotten out?"

"I figured you knew. We all did," Gordon said.

"No," I said. "I mean, I always figured there was more to him, just not this."

"More to him?"

"Yeah. That he was deeper than all the optimism and punctuality and everything. A guy just can't be that enthusiastic about everything. He's got to force himself to be that way. And if he does, it's probably because something else is going on with him."

"Why did you think there was something wrong with his optimism?" Gelb asked.

"Because it's just too depressing for somebody to be *that* happy." The two men laughed, a little joylessly. I realized how ridiculous it all was. Prescott's behavior — the part that they somehow had known about — had the curious effect of humanizing him to us, making him more sympathetic, and yet his behavior was shameful. While the rest of us knew him as a man who kept Forster's empire of care functioning smoothly and efficiently, we did not know the aspect of him that was willing to place a delicate man who relied on the perceived love of his shrewish wife in an impossible situation, and was willing to do so for his own dimly perceived pleasure.

But I know you, that you have not the love of God in you.

"So it was more or less an open secret," I said.

Finally, Gordon seemed to relax. "I'm surprised you didn't know," he said. "It was an open secret that the two of them have been going at it for some time. I always thought Thomas knew. I just thought he didn't care. Lord knows if it had been me married to her, I would have wanted something on the side. Prodigiously."

As he said the words, Gordon's voice lapsed from a carefully polished, neutral cadence of words into that of a black man talking candidly, the words rolling out effortlessly, a strong accent on the first syllable of "prodigiously," his mouth opening and closing to great effect. Mr. W.E.B. DuBois said that a black American always feels he has two souls, two thoughts, forever unrecognized, and that it is only his individual strength that keeps him from tearing himself apart. The way Gordon slid between the two voices, the two dialects, with the ease of a soldier filing into step on the parade ground secretly made the mimic in me envious.

"Did Prescott ever say anything to you about it?"

Gordon was quiet for a moment. "Yeah. I mean, not in so many words. He never would have done that. No, he just asked if I thought it was getting in the way."

"Of what?"

"The work," Gordon said. "I think he was more scared of that than anything. He looked like he was going to cry. I told him I didn't think so."

"Was it getting in the way?"

"Why do you think he had everybody else working so hard? Freed him up."

"Did you ever say anything to Forster?"

"I didn't figure I needed to."

"Is this *it*, Boss?" Gelb said, something that took my breath away.

"What *it*?"

"Are we done for? We closing up shop?"

"No!" I said, somewhat frantic. "No, not at all. What happened is bad, but it isn't *that* bad. I think I know what Forster would say. We still owe it to the lost to see what can be done for them."

"The lost," Gelb said. "They sound irretrievable."

That was Gelb's way of reminding me that even though Prescott was not there, it wasn't my responsibility to begin talking like him.

"I was just wondering if my family might start talking to me again," Gelb said.

"What do you mean?"

"It's a joke. I got a few cousins who think I converted when I started working for Forster. They haven't been to my house in years."

"I know what you mean," Gordon said. "My brother thinks I vote for Republicans because I work here." He bit the words off angrily, as though the only fruit of equality in America was the right to be misinterpreted by his closest family members.

"And they don't talk to you?"

"I was joking," Gelb said. "I didn't want to see them anyway." Gordon didn't answer.

"What should I do? I mean, about Prescott?"

"What do you mean 'do?'" Gelb asked.

"I feel like we ought to do something for him. Help him out. Get him counseling. See about getting him a job."

"Don't think that would be a good idea right now," Gordon said.

"Dr. Forster said he'd take care of it, but I don't know what that means."

The two men moved toward the door. "I wouldn't worry about it," Gelb said. "Believe me, you probably want to stay away from that right now."

"Why?"

"Better for you. Better for him. When you get things squared away, get out of here. Go home."

Gelb made a thumbs up sign and smiled, if a bit unsurely.

"Were you trying to tell me about this that day at soccer practice?"

"What?" Then it hit him. "No. But I guess maybe I had it on my mind, somewhere in there. You never know. Don't let it get to you. Remember, go home. Relax." He turned to face the door, then remembered to say one thing. "Make a new man out of you." He smiled as though I had never attempted anything like that, and then shut the door behind him.

I thought of my words to him about the lost, and the annoyed, amused look that passed over his face. I could hear him saying something in my mind about those annoying Christians, forever hovering over people, perpetually more concerned with saving souls than the people they belonged to.

Standing alone in Prescott's office, I began walking around to look at things my eyes had seen many times but never really perceived. It was if the residue of the man's personality was here, a remainder that had simply evaporated off him like a mist and coated the furniture, the file cabinets, the pictures on the wall, the Greek masks. The photograph of Monique Prescott, which I had noticed the first time I came into the office, was gone. I wondered if he had taken it with him. In another corner was a picture of Prescott standing next to a man with a signature underneath. I wondered if it was Dr. Forster.

All I felt at that moment was an absence. I felt outraged that Prescott, who had occupied this office for so long, so ... *faithfully*...was practically dead given the reaction of the men who worked so closely with him. It was true — what he had done was wrong. There was no way to excuse it. But the whole reason we did all of this community service work was about forgiveness, wasn't it?

Then I corrected myself. A man who cheats on his wife and conceals everything from his employer — especially an employer with a demonstrated interest in moral circumstances — may be forgiven, but he should still expect some consequences.

But did that mean that Prescott was, to use my earlier word, "lost?" Was he irretrievable? Did that mean that he, too, was a mimic? No, I thought. There was something genuine about him, much more so than me. Maybe he had been sincere sometime in his life, before he ever met Rebecca Hagler. Maybe his double life explained why he was so adamant that others adhere to an elevated standard that seemed insane. It shocked me that, all the time I had been killing myself on this job trying to convince everyone of my sincerity, the one person who might have understood was the person driving me. I wondered, at that moment, how many Christians lived in mortal fear that their "cover" might be blown?

Prescott's mimicry was simply doing what people expected of the "godly." He did those things against his nature, fighting them the whole way, which explained why he always did them overzealously. The depressing part of it was that this dark patch that had seemingly creeped out by mistake was actually who he really was under all his own mimicry.

And the words? That was easy. That was the Holy Spirit, giving him something to say instead of what was really on his mind. Because the nobler parts of Prescott, small as they were, were magnified by the Spirit until the watching world assumed the one picture where the other was the reality. As imperfectly as I understood it all then, I was sure that was what had happened. What made me less anxious to claim any superiority over Prescott was the knowledge that he was at least one up on me. I did not have the Spirit in me. I was just a damned mimic.

Mother Teresa's verdict was that if one wants to be a true believer, one has to be willing to be a victim of God — that was her word, *victim* — and to face the anger of God. Perhaps Prescott had also been a true believer in himself, and he was now his own victim.

Which was supposed to be good news for me, except for one thing:

I had now evolved into Prescott, and into his office.

"Splendid," I said to myself.

33.

I saw Richard again at the Mall when I was posing as Santa Claus. Posing is perhaps not the right word. More like filling in. I should have realized that in taking over Prescott's many unspoken duties, taking time to ring a bell dressed as St. Nicholas while standing in the open air asking for donations would be among them. I had been out there for four hours, occasionally shifting my weight from one leg to the other and walking aimlessly about, shaking the bell as though chasing away evil spirits. Christmas was more than three weeks away, and the pace of shopping had not yet reached its critical mass. I occasionally touched the fake beard through my heavy gloves to readjust it against the wind, and remembered to carefully repeat the mantra-like laugh of Kris Kringle to keep the children entertained. It was simple. I had once done it in a maximum security prison for a gaggle of inmates about to receive care packages. My Clausian bulk on that occasion was supplied by a bullet-proof vest. That visit hadn't been Forster's idea either. I had suggested it, after Cynthia gave me an idea for it. As always, it was a way to impress the boss.

Richard came walking up in a leather jacket and new jeans, wearing an old army cap that looked like a special from a surplus store. He had on sunglasses for no discernable reason, since it was late in the day and overcast, but his face bore the blank look of someone whose eyes are hidden from view. He seemed to have grown a little since I had last seen him at soccer practice. A strange thing happened when I saw him. In some corner of my mind, I never forgot that I was supposed to be Santa Claus, so that meant I couldn't acknowledge knowing anyone or risk spoiling the illusion for some little boy or girl who came up to place a coin in my bucket. And yet, when I saw Richard, I somehow forgot that I was in costume, so I waved at him in the manner of a jolly old elf, my fake jellied belly shaking awkwardly.

Richard saw right through the beard, as though the sunglasses had some special surveillance equipment attached. "Hi, Uncle Santa," he said, smiling devilishly.

"Thanks for not blowing my cover, ho-ho-ho," I said, in the old, booming, manly voice of the dime store Santas of antiquity.

"No problem," he said, pulling the ear buds out from his iPod. "What are you doing? New job or desperate cry for help?"

"It's just..." I started to say, and then I understood what he had said. It surprised me. It was funny. I was sure he had heard it somewhere but it was just like his earlier needling shot at me on the phone. It filled me with pride, a father's pride, and made me happy that he felt he could say something like that. I don't know if he could see my smile underneath the beard, but he seemed satisfied with himself. "This is part of my job, believe it or not," I said. I wouldn't acknowledge his joke. Denying him his due might spur him on to say something else and repeat my admiration.

"You keeping the money?" He was really trying, wasn't he?

"You know the foundation I work for? This is part of the job. Helping out people at Christmas time."

A little girl of about eight came walking up and placed a rolled up dollar bill in the kettle. She patted my false belly and gave me a hug. I expected her to say something, but she walked on. Her parents, at a safe distance beyond, nodded at me and caught up with her.

"At least you're popular," Richard said.

"It never lasts," I said. "They get what they want and then they're gone. What are you listening to?" I pointed to his iPod.

"Nothing," he said. I understood this was his way of politely telling me to mind my own business. It made me think of Peter, and the way he would always deflect any question about how his home life was. "Fine," he would say, and nothing more.

"You like music?"

"Yeah." He nodded as though I had asked him if he liked eating and breathing.

"Video games?" I asked. This was a guess. I didn't know if he was too old for that or whether the question itself showed how oblivious I was to what his life might be.

"Yeah."

"What do you like about them?"

"I dunno. Kills time, I guess."

"Must have a lot of it," I said.

Mr. Tom Wolfe said the present is only a movie of the past. By the time we figure out what's happened, it's already over. I wondered about Richard's life, filled with memories of wars that never existed, enemies dispatched who never breathed, races on terrain that never appeared on a map, songs of passion never savored. I wondered if we all stuck the ear buds in and turned the televisions on and flipped through our fantasies in a mad dash to avoid the fear of death. This boy knew his father was dead, but he didn't know perhaps totally that the same thing was going to happen to him one of these days. And to everyone else he knew. We all have our ways of dealing with the relentlessness of human cognition.

"What?" he asked.

"I'm sorry. A guy I knew is in the hospital. He probably won't make it. Being artificially jolly doesn't help."

"Sorry. Who says you have to be jolly?"

"The suit?" I said, gesturing with my hands toward the enormous belly and white beard. "When you're standing in like this, people expect certain things."

"It's funny," he said.

"What?"

"You're Dad's brother. I couldn't picture Dad doing this."

I thought about it a moment. "I couldn't either. Not unless he was playing a joke on somebody."

"You doing that?'

"No. Joke's on me, I guess."

You're right about that, big boy.

That was Peter's voice. I felt him there, not in Richard but more as a prodding presence at my elbow, trying to impress something on me that I already felt. I was responding to what I could see of Peter in Richard, but they were different. I couldn't picture Peter involved in video games or his son's music. He, like Gelb, would have had his son playing baseball. He would have been offended that his own son would be playing soccer, as though it was a betrayal, an unpatriotic act, an abomination.

But I could feel anger at some thing else too, anger that I perceived was Peter's and not mine. Peter would have felt guilty, embarrassed that he was not there for his son. I felt a sense of that myself, knowing that Richard was growing into a version of his father that his father was not there to witness.

But I can see it, I heard him say.

"I guess it's hard," Richard said.

"What is?"

"Being Santa Claus. Having all those people depend on you. Say the right thing. All that stuff."

"Well, you just remember you're imitating him. That's something your dad taught me."

"Yeah?"

"Well, he taught me about imitating people. He said you can do somebody's voice, but your audience doesn't respond to that as much as what you bring to the performance. The voice, the act — that has to be there, but it's you they're looking at."

"You mean he was an actor?"

I laughed at the question, and immediately felt embarrassed. I think he expected me to be able to name a movie his father was in. That would be comforting. "No. He was just a character. He was a performer. He loved to make people laugh. Everybody was an audience."

He wordlessly nodded his head, as though he appreciated this version of his father he had never before encountered.

"It's like this," I said, gesturing toward the costume again. Another family approached with a child, and I gave them the jolly laugh and patted the boy on the cheek. His mother gave me an annoyed look at my touching her child, but the boy threw a good-natured fist into my belly. I feigned a pained expression that made him laugh and seemed to satisfy his mother, and on they walked. "See that?" I said. "I gave them Santa Claus. Didn't say anything. Just did the laugh. They took care of the rest. Just like your Dad said."

"You're not him, you know?" Richard said.

Was that, in his slightly knowing, slightly annoyed accusatory, pimply voice an accusation? How much did he know about his mother and me? "Who?" I asked, gingerly.

"Santa Claus," he said, as though he felt no need to clarify. "He's not real." He smiled. "Were you naturally this clueless, or was there surgery involved?"

"Why do you say that, little boy?" I replied, in my best jolly old elfin voice. "It wasn't so long ago that you believed in *me*."

"Grew up, Santa," he said. "Toys got bigger. You got smaller." There was an insinuation in what he said that I didn't like. He was old enough for drugs, but I didn't pick up anything from his appearance that I associated with that kind of disconnected apathy. What particular toys did he mean? Just the video games and music or was there more? I remembered Peter's brief wild streak and tried to remember all that he had experimented with, wondering if there might be some kind of genetic component. I wondered how much

225

Cecelia knew about her own son, who he had found to fill the vacuum left by his father, who he might be trying to copy.

"Doesn't look like I'm any smaller," Santa said through me.

"Guess not. What's in there?" He pointed to the fake belly.

"I'm not sure. I just got the costume a few hours ago. Strapped all this on and headed this way. I get off work in a little while. Have you eaten lately?"

"I'm not going anywhere with you dressed like that."

"Wouldn't dream of it. Maybe later?"

"Yeah, sure," he said.

"Just call you?" I said. I figured it would be ridiculous to expect the boy to remember to call me, or it wouldn't adhere to that week's definition of cool, whatever it might be.

"Sure."

He was about to walk on, without saying anything, when I stopped him. "Richard."

"What?"

"Do me a favor and don't say anything to your Mom."

"About what?"

"About... about seeing me."

"You mean like this?" he said, pointing to the costume.

"No," I said. "It's a long story, but I don't think your Mom likes me too much."

"Sure," he said, and I could tell he had no problem with it. In fact, I sensed he was happy to have an excuse not to tell her anything. It made me wonder once again how much she really knew about his life.

"You don't mind?" I asked.

"This is part of my job, believe it or not," he said, only he was returning my own words to me in a pitch perfect rendition of my own voice. He did it much better than Peter would have.

"You'd make your Dad proud," I said. He smiled and entered the mall, still wearing his sunglasses.

34.

Cynthia sat across from me in the restaurant as the lunchtime crowd hummed around us. After we said the blessing at her request — I kept forgetting to do this — she munched on her shrimp and imitation crab salad and occasionally dabbed her mouth with a carefully folded napkin so as not to disturb her face. She had violet lipstick on and her eyelashes looked so full as to be artificial. I thought I could hear the sound they made when she blinked, like the fall of a snowflake on a windless day. She was smiling at something I had said. I can't remember what it was.

I remember feeling a sort of silent anguish. For some reason that I cannot explain, I didn't trust her smile. Cynthia was the kind of person who smiled often — generous, thoughtful, knowing smiles that invited you into her space and promised to listen to whatever was on your mind. I had seen her disarm many people with that smile, including me. But for perhaps the first time in our marriage, it didn't seem genuine to me.

She was unaware of this. She spoke to me and took another bite of her salad, and her eyes looked around the room, sizing up the couples, groups and individuals sitting around us. When she did look at me, it was only for a second or two and then she was back to the salad or the room, or stealing a glance at one of the televisions stationed around the place. It gave me a chance to stare at her without her noticing.

Why did I suspect that she wasn't *really* happy? Maybe it was the rest of her face away from that smile, that smile that maybe concealed anger or apprehension or some discontent. Her nose was bigger. The tip had swelled and when she breathed I noticed the nostrils flare in a way I didn't remember before. There were the beginnings of crow's feet around her eyes, big enough that the makeup couldn't conceal them. I noticed lines forming around the corners of her mouth, and worry lines around her eyebrows. No, they weren't deep. I was close enough to see them. Was that a little swelling around her eyes? Lack of sleep? I wouldn't know. I didn't sleep more than two or three hours a night, and hadn't for the life of our marriage. I usually slept on the couch after making sure she was asleep. Had I been wrong some of those nights? Was something keeping her up?

I understood that my wife was getting older. She had started dying her hair red to hide the gray. I knew that the same thing was happening to my face. Occasionally there was a gray hair around my temples and my hands were beginning to grow slightly meaty. No, there was something wrong with Cynthia. Something that she wasn't telling me. She may have been smiling, but it was a lie, I was sure. She wasn't really happy only she didn't have the nerve to tell me. It was like those mincing bites she took of the salad, as though it was her duty to consume the food and she was going to be as thorough as possible, but somehow she didn't relish this meal. I wondered if it was the food or the company.

"What's wrong?" she asked me, jarring me back to her conversation. Wasn't it somehow impossible that I could be thinking about her and somehow be called away in my imagination while she was all the while sitting in front of me?

"Nothing," I said.

"No. What's wrong?"

"I thought there was something the matter with you?"

"What?"

"I don't know."

"What?"

"I said I don't know. I thought maybe something was bothering you."

"I thought something was bothering you," she said, and she smiled. And again, I thought the smile was too perfect. Cynthia's looks always had a way of breaking my heart. *This moment will not last*, I told myself. *She will change and grow tired of me, or I will alienate her, or one of us will no longer be here, or something horrific that neither can see coming will render this moment nonexistent.*

That was Peter's fault. I didn't trust anything anymore because of my brother. Lives did not last. Moments did not last. Happiness, in whatever form we thought it might take, did not last. Maybe it did not exist.

Just then a woman interrupted us. This was happening more and more. There were scores of people from church or who came in contact with the Foundation who knew me. I did not recognize them, could not recall a name, was basically left grasping for any help in order to acknowledge them. This woman, in his mid-sixties, had worked with us in getting imitation designer clothing to underprivileged children. I wasn't quite sure, but I thought this woman has some connection to organized crime because she was able to get the clothes, along with fake label sunglasses, at scandalously low prices.

But it may have just been my cynicism. People were willing to go to such extremes to help Forster, and they seemed to pop up in the most unlikely places, until it made one feel like working for the Mafia. It was hard not to be cynical about the people giving help — either perpetually, irritatingly positive or jaded and sullen and silent. The people receiving help were the same, hovering between embarrassment and resentment, either protesting that any help they took was at best temporary or complaining there wasn't enough food or clothes or assistance, and what little they got was terrible. It made you wonder what any of them were doing, wherever they were, how they got there, where they might end up. Perhaps my cynicism was a defense, as it is with other people. We all go through life mistaking cynicism for knowledge, knowledge for wisdom, wisdom for righteousness.

I made conversation the best I could with the woman without ever admitting I couldn't remember her name. Finally she walked away, to my relief. After a moment, Cynthia spoke up again. "Have you heard from Prescott?" Cynthia asked.

"No," I said. "He's probably smarter than that. If he's had any contact, it's been with Dr. Forster."

"I saw Monique the other day," she said. "I brought her some food and sat with her for awhile."

"What did she say? What's she been doing?"

"She was embarrassed. The other day she went to the church website and started signing on under different usernames, and she started telling stories about Charlie. Made up stories about what a terrible man he was. Started a chat room about it until the webmaster got on and told her not to do it. He sent messages to all her usernames, and each time, she said, she posted something else nastier."

I laughed. It was a phony laugh, and I perceived the smile she gave me was just as phony.

"She was proud of herself for doing that. That's why she was embarrassed."

"I know how she feels," I said.

"I don't think you do," Cynthia said.

I looked at her, and she didn't look away. *She is unhappy*, I thought. *She's unhappy with me. She won't come out and say it, but this is her way of telling me.*

"Charlie left her for probably the worst woman in the world, and she knows it. It's killing her."

"I can imagine."

"Why do you keep saying that?"

"What should I say?"

"Cam, how could you let that go on?"

"What?"

"You're telling me you didn't know? About Prescott and Rebecca Hagler?"

"No," I said. "I didn't know. Prescott didn't tell anybody. You remember that day I came to see you. I had no idea what they wanted me to find out."

"But you worked with him."

"I worked *for* him. The less I knew about him the better. Prescott wasn't the easiest guy in the world to work for, and prying into any of his business always left me uncomfortable."

"But he trusted you."

"To do a job. That's about it. You've got to understand, Cynthia. With Prescott, the job was *everything*."

"Not all the time."

"It was as far as I was concerned."

"What is she supposed to do?"

"What do you expect me to do? I get the feeling you're mad at me because somebody else cheated on their wife."

"Talk to Dr. Forster," she said. "Monique feels alone. He hasn't been by to see her. It's like she's been cut off from everything she knew."

"He probably doesn't know what to do."

"You can help with that."

"I've talked to the man *once*. When he told me to take the job."

"But you *can* talk to him."

"I don't think that's a good idea. This isn't a good time for him."

"You think it is for her?" People were starting to notice our conversation. We had never raised our voices above a sharp whisper, but that has a way of attracting more attention in the right setting. The noise around us never subsided, but we were aware of a sudden amplified interest in us among the other diners.

"What is this?" I asked.

"I'm sorry," she said. "I just wanted you to be aware." She said the words in an exasperated voice, as though it wouldn't matter if I had known because I would have been indifferent anyway.

"About her."

"About *things*," she said. "You're working for him now. I thought you'd be able to fix it." The way she said *him* made me think of some golden squatting statuesque figure of transcendental peace who elicited faithful prayers from a robed mass of followers.

"It's a little bigger than me, and a little bigger than Dr. Forster."

"I think you're just telling yourself that." Her head wagged and it secretly enraged me.

"I think you're telling yourself that I can do something because you want something done."

"She feels powerless, and so do I."

"How do you think I feel? I don't even really know how to do this job."

"The job. The job. You'd drive through a blizzard to feed somebody at a soup line but you can't look somebody in the face and just listen to what they're saying, can you? It's just a job. You don't care about any of these people as long as they're grateful and quiet."

I could see she was mad, and specifically mad at me, though I had no idea why. I wondered if she suspected me of something. I wondered even more after her next question.

"When's the last time you talked to your sister-in-law?"

"Cecelia?" I asked.

Cynthia nodded. I had always kept Cecelia at arms' length in conversation with Cynthia, for several spectacularly obvious reasons. I had been secure over the years that with my discretion and Cecelia's wish to keep her surrogate Peter's voice intact, our shared secret would remain that way. I tried, in the half second or so between her question and my response, to size her up and guess whether her question had any agenda other than well-founded suspicion that something connected the two of us.

"No," I said. This was actually true. The last time I had spoken with her was months before at the soccer practice when she had told me to stay away from Richard. I knew that Cynthia sent her

Christmas cards every year and a birthday card on both her's and Richard's birthdays. I had once come home to find Cynthia in an animated conversation with someone at the other end of the phone, laughing and sharing stories about our life together. After she hung up and I asked who it was, she said, "Cecelia. Your brother's ex-wife. I mean..." I saw her go from a smiling woman in the afterglow of a rich conversation to sudden embarrassment and punishing shame, like an ice cube wilting under an angry sun.

She probably thought I was mad when I dashed from the room. Instead, I was headed to throw up. The idea of the two of them talking to each other terrified me. As did my next words to her in the restaurant:

"Why do you ask?"

"I just...I thought maybe she could talk to Monique. She sort of knows what it's like."

"How? I mean..."

"I don't mean she knows what it's like to have your husband cheat on you. I think what bothers Monique more than anything is that he's gone. She doesn't feel whole. I think that shocks her. She seems embarrassed that she's not as strong as she thought she might be."

"Strong as in..."

"Monique is a strong woman. She just doesn't feel that way right now. She was crying and she told me if it had been different, if Charlie had just died, she would be devastated, but she would get over it. But this way, she's mad at him, and she's mad at herself because deep down, she just wants him back. She hates herself for that."

"So she feels weak. Because she doesn't feel whole without him."

"Yeah," she said, surprised, as though perhaps I really did know how Monique felt.

"Being a widow, I would imagine, is different from..."

"I don't know. Cecelia seemed like she had herself really together, the times I've talked to her."

In those words, I found some measure of restorative calm. Cynthia obviously suspected nothing, especially if she considered Cecelia a strong woman. And yet I felt my own anger rising at the prospect. I wanted so much to pound the table and assure her that, no, Cecelia was not at all a strong woman who had herself together, and that her ability to snow the world into thinking so was one of the reasons I almost hated her, because she wouldn't admit that she needed me to keep her going. I felt like a drug, an unacknowledged one, and the hellish part of it was that my ego wanted the recognition for working with her in an enterprise which sickened me deeply and desperately.

Instead, I took a bite of my sandwich, about the time my cell phone beeped with a text message.

Meet me at DeMara Hotel. Richard. 1:30 p.m.

I looked at my watch and saw it was already 1:15. I was grateful. It offered the chance to see Richard again. Maybe he wanted lunch, or just to chat. And what was more, it would allow me to flee this conversation with Cynthia before something came out that neither of us wanted to hear me say. I said my goodbyes, left money for the tip, and reassured Cynthia that somehow I would mention this to Forster, and that I really was a human being who could sympathize with others. She gave me that same smile that I did not trust, and I was out the door.

The DeMara was only a few blocks away, so I walked. In the short time it took to get there, I wondered why a teenage boy would ask me to meet him there. The DeMara was an old-time bellhop and desk clerk luxury hotel that had begun welcoming people in the era of train timetables. In fact, there was an old wooden board that hung on one wall which had once informed passengers of the next arrival and departure times for the nearby railroads.

As I walked in the lobby through the revolving door, I tried to remember the last time I had been in the DeMara. It had a nice restaurant that I was sure I had taken Cynthia to over the years. I walked past the polished player piano and tried to recognize the tune. Rich, red carpets shone against the white marble floor beneath. I found a leather chair and sat down, the surface making a crackling, rubbing sound as I filled the chair.

I looked at my phone again and recalled the message. *1:30 p.m.* Not how I would have expected a teenager typing out a text message to put it. Maybe he was downtown instead of in school. Maybe there was trouble. An argument with Cecelia. Maybe he was skipping school to see me. I sat and waited and considered the possibilities until I heard someone call my name.

"Call for Mr. Cameron Leon," said the voice over a loudspeaker. I turned to look at the front desk where a black woman with short dreadlocks wearing a burgundy vest spoke the words into a microphone.

I came to the desk. To the side of the clerk was a little can with a picture of a small girl on the side who I recognized from soccer practice as a member of one of the teams. A card said she had been diagnosed with brain cancer and her family needed money for the operation. I emptied out my pockets of change to dump in and looked up to see a security camera, recording all of this for the moment. I hastily looked at the clerk and asked for the phone. I was directed to an antique desk nearby with an old simulated rotary phone, which I picked up.

Standing in a pay phone, across the room, looking at me, was Cecelia. "Hello, Cameron," she said, as I heard the words through the receiver. "Thanks for coming."

35.

Cecelia was a tall woman, which is why I never saw her that the word "proud" didn't pop into my mind. It was like one of those epithets that proceed the name of a character in an epic poem. Thunderhurler Zeus. Grandsire Priam. Proud-striding Cecelia. She was customarily beautiful. As Mr. William Shakespeare put it, God gave her one face, and she made for herself another.

As she hung up the phone and came walking toward me, I might have been tempted to forget every memory I had ever had of who the two of us were. She would no longer have been my late brother's wife, and I no longer a man who had been married to another woman for five years. If that had been the case, I would have wanted to know her very intensely and very soon. But I resisted that temptation for many reasons.

The chief reason was that, in seeing her, it suddenly made sense why Richard had called me here. He hadn't. It was her. And she had a purpose.

In the movie "North By Northwest," Cary Grant plays the advertising executive Roger Thornhill, who is mistaken for the master spy George Kaplan in a hotel lobby. A bellhop goes through the hotel bar asking for George Kaplan just as Thornhill sticks his hand up to ask an innocent question. Two men standing nearby see this and assume that Thornhill is Kaplan. Why is Thornhill mistaken for the spy? Because no one has ever seen George Kaplan, because he does not exist. He is a decoy moved from hotel to hotel in order to draw attention from other spies.

The DeMara Hotel was where Cecelia had met Peter, and the whole thing would never happened if not for me. Peter was already driving when I applied for my first job, which was at the DeMara. I was sixteen and needed a ride to the interview. Peter took me, and walked me inside. He had just graduated a month or so before. By the time we got there, I walked into the hotel in search of a bathroom. As Peter stood outside in the lobby, a desk clerk called for the name Cameron Leon. It was a phone call from our Dad, though I can't remember why he felt the need to call.

Because I was in the bathroom, Peter walked up to the counter to take the call. The desk clerk who called my name was Cecelia. By the time I came out of the men's room, Peter had already asked Cecelia out for a date. But she didn't realize that his name wasn't Cameron until midway through their first date. She had assumed, since he took the call, that he was me. "My wife fell in love with my brother first," he would say later.

What Cecelia was doing, I guess, was what they call repetition therapy. Sometimes when someone undergoes a life experience, positive or negative, they either consciously or unconsciously repeat it, hoping it turns out differently a second time. It's the superstition a ballplayer adopts after sinking a shot or pitching a no-hitter, or the action one avoids to cut short a losing streak.

"You were expecting Richard," she said. There was a smile in her voice if not one on her face, a self-satisfaction that the fiction she had used to lure me here had worked.

"What do you want?"

"I told you to say away from him, but you didn't listen to me."

"He asked...I thought *he* was asking me to meet with him."

"He's a kid."

"What do you want Cecelia?"

"I want you to come with me," she said.

"Where?"

"Just follow me," she said.

After a second or two of hesitation, I lifted my arm and motioned her to start walking. I would follow. We got on an elevator and Cecelia pushed the button for the fifth floor. In the short ride, she did not look at me, except a glance and a nod to reassure me somehow that all was well. I stood there racking my brain as to whether the number five had some significance between her and Peter.

We walked down a hall until we got to a room and she put a card key in the slot. The door beeped and she opened it. She stood in the doorway and motioned me inside. I walked in. The door shut before I turned around.

She was standing there, leaning against the door. I had no idea what she wanted. A host of possibilities came to me — she was going to kill me. No, I thought. She had finally decided to have a rendezvous instead of wanting me to talk. No, her clothes were dressy and formal but not alluring. There was a part of Cecelia's personality that never wanted to cede control of a situation, in any fashion. That was why Peter's death had been so horrible for her. That was also why I saw something in her similar to some of the recovering alcoholics I had met through Foundation programs. They all had the same personality traits, hiding the dark part they could not control, exercising the fullest measure over every other facet of their lives, until even that slipped away.

The silence was too stifling for me. For some reason, I didn't want her to be in control of this situation. I didn't trust her. "Why did you want me to stay away from Richard?"

"I don't know," she said. "I just kind of lost it."

"What..."

"I didn't want you..."

"You didn't want me taking Peter's place?"

She nodded.

I didn't say the obvious thing — that she hadn't had a problem with that in other emotional areas. I was only good for the occasional fantasy but nothing more. "I'm just his uncle. I know that."

"I know," she said, as though she didn't feel in the mood for a lecture. She quickly changed the subject. "Cam, I wanted to see you."

"Why?"

She walked toward me, and without thinking, I started backing away from her. The closer she attempted to get to me, the more I wanted to run away.

She opened her mouth as if about to say something, then closed it. A second or two passed for her to reconsider what she was going to say. "I hope ... I hope I didn't interrupt anything with this."

"I was having lunch with Cynthia." I added, "She asked about you." The whole thing sounded absurd.

She touched her hair, or rather, she reached up as if to brush away a few locks, but there was nothing there.

"I think," she began. She cleared her throat. "Cam, I think... there's something I want to tell you. I think ...I think I've been hearing Peter's voice."

I didn't know if this was some kind of joke.

"His *real* voice," she said. "It's like he's speaking to me."

"When does this happen?"

"Lots of times. At work. When I'm alone. When I'm trying to sleep."

"What does he say?"

"Do you think it's really him?" she asked.

"What does this voice say?"

"I ask because you go to that church and you're involved with all these people..."

"Go ahead and tell me," I said. "What does this voice say?"

"I never did understand any of that stuff," she said, looking away from me. "Peter did, but I didn't."

"What stuff?"

"Churchy stuff. You know, I never went when he did."

"Peter went to church?"

"Sometimes. Lots of times really. I think he kept it to himself. I don't think he knew what you would make of it. He knew what I thought about it."

The voice I heard in *my* head was saying *I have come to set a man against his...*

"He never told me that."

"I don't think he knew what to tell you. He probably wasn't sure what you would think."

"What I would think?"

She gave a searching look, as if it was something she still didn't understand about him, all this time later. "Peter put great stock in what you thought about him, Cameron."

He did?

"He probably was afraid you wouldn't think he was sincere."

"Was he?" I found myself wondering, as though I was Charlie Prescott, whether Peter had been saved. "Why did he start going?"

"Richard," she said. "I think he was ...praying for Ricky. He should have been praying for himself."

For whoever wants to save his life shall lose it...

"There's something I want to tell you, Cameron," she said.

Her using my full name shocked me, for some reason. There was no formality about it. In a strange way, it was intimate, as though she was acknowledging after a long time of denial who I really was.

"I've been thinking about it, and I think we should be together."

I let out a derisive snort. "Is this why you wanted to see me?"

"Yes," she said, though her voice was not warm or inviting. She sounded as though she was resigned to something and had prepared herself. The words sounded like muffled drums at a state funeral.

"Why should we be together? I want to hear this," I said.

I expected at some moment she might take a step forward, draw closer, try to show me what it was on her mind. But she stood there, as though I had drawn a gun and threatened something at a false move. "It just seems natural. I mean, think about what we've been doing all this time."

"We haven't done anything, Cecelia."

"Yes, we have. I mean, we..."

"I'm married, Cecelia."

"I know that, but I know what we have together."

"What we have together..."

"...and I know what we both mean to each other."

"Each other."

"It just makes sense." Her voice was cold and logical and I didn't want to believe a word of it, that she might be serious, but that's all she was. Deadly, emphatically serious.

"Cecelia, how can you..."

"I think we should be together, Cameron. I think you believe this too. We've been playing at something for a long time here, and it's time we owned up to it. Because of Peter, we both share something. I think it's time we honor that."

"Because of *Peter*."

"We both know him. We know each other. What we've shared. It's like being here at this place. If things had been different, I would have met you instead of Peter that day. I thought I *had* met you. Maybe it was *meant* to be."

"How did you arrive at this idea, Cecelia?"

She took a deep breath, and for the first time, she seemed to relax. "It's like I heard his voice, Cam. Like I said. His real voice." Cam. This was the Cecelia that Peter fell in love with. Not the proud, strong, tall woman who duped me there. This was a warm, vulnerable woman that Peter had spoken of. Of course, she felt relaxed speaking about *him*, about him talking to her.

"What was he saying?"

"He said, 'It's okay. It's okay.'"

I laughed. If I had struck her, it wouldn't have shocked her as much. "Of course he said it's okay!" I shouted, sarcastically. I looked down on the floor and scratched above my right eye. "You think that was his voice? You think that's what he would really say?"

She seemed stupefied at my question. "You're his brother. Why wouldn't he say that? Haven't you been saying that, all these years?"

"It's a lie!"

"But you keep saying it!"

"Because that's what you wanted! It's still a lie! My God, Cecelia, where is this going to end?"

"But I heard his voice!"

"Cecelia, we're talking about my brother. Before he was your husband, he was *my* brother. He was a living, breathing man, not this shadow ghost you can just call up with a few words! He was a man and you've made me make him into a puppet! What do you want him to say? All I have to do is make him say it! But that's not who he was. And what's so disgusting about all of this is that you know it!"

"Stop it."

"I want to! I've wanted to for five years. You tell me you heard my brother's voice. I've heard it every day since he died. You don't know what his voice is anymore. All you hear is mine, or the voice you carry around in your head. You don't need me. You just make it say what you want it to say!"

"I said stop it! Shut up!"

"He's dead, Cecelia! He's dead! Peter Leon is dead! You know that!"

"Alright. So he's dead!" She said the words as though some organ deep inside her was being ripped apart. "What about what's going on between us? Don't we owe it..."

"What *us*? You don't know me, Cecelia! You don't *want* to know me. I'm just a medium for you to bring him back. You don't even want me around your son."

"You know why I don't want that. I didn't want him to have to deal with *this*."

"But it's okay if we want to be together? He'll just have to deal with it then? Is that what you're saying."

"I didn't say it made sense. I'm just willing to try..."

"What? To make this insanity somehow make sense?"

"But what about what I feel for you?"

"You don't feel anything for *me*! I'm like that door that you walked through to come into this room. Just a lifeless, meaningless thing. I can't be Peter. I'm not Peter. This *relationship* we have isn't even a relationship. You don't love me."

"Why can't I love you?"

"Because you love Peter. You *still* love Peter. I know. I understand. I love him." I heard my voice catch in my throat. "I loved him. But he's not here anymore. He's not a part of this. And you know it. That's why you'll only go so far as this illusion will last, and no further. If we ever did anything, then it would be about us. But it isn't."

She turned away from me, and then twirled on her heel to face me. "What about you, you coward?" she said. "This isn't all my fault. You took advantage of me. You certainly didn't mind that Peter wasn't there. Don't kid yourself. You were there all along because you wanted what he had."

I clenched my teeth. My hands turned into fists. I was about to do something that would have convinced her I wasn't Peter once and for all, and the phone rang. For a second, the two of us couldn't believe it. It was as if the anger in us stopped and fled instantaneously. One of us might have laughed. She was standing closer to the phone, so she picked it up.

"Yes," she said. After a second or two, she rolled her eyes. "This is a hotel room, not a house." There was noise on the other end. "Sure. Same to you." The line went dead and she looked at me. "Telemarketer."

Her shoulders relaxed. With her back still to me, she took the receiver in both hands and jammed it into the phone. I was sure the thing was broken. Her shoulders began shaking violently. I thought she was crying, but there were no tears. She was just trembling.

I walked toward her and my hands went over her shoulders. She wheeled around again. She bared her teeth in a canine snarl and hit me in the chest. She pounded my chest mercilessly, as though she might beat me into a different person. I let her for awhile, then I grabbed her arms to stop her. She was hitting me for the same reason she had been calling me all those years — because she couldn't hit Peter. She had called me because she couldn't call Peter. She hated me now, because she couldn't hate Peter. That part I could accept. I would rather she hate me than hate Peter.

The Peter that I carried inside of me, the shadow of all of those encounters throughout our lives, the one I assembled from all the firing neurons in my skull, was at my side throughout that moment. If I could have conjured him up in some tangible form, he would have had his arm around me, thanking me, reassuring me, apologizing that I was having to be there for her instead of him. When she finally ran out of energy, anger, whatever had been driving her, she sat down on the edge of the bed, looked at me as though she might have expected a different face, got up, grabbed her purse, and walked out of the room. The door slammed behind her. I sat down on the bed for a few minutes, turned on the television for a minute or so, used the bathroom, splashed water on my face, and walked out.

36.

I finally met Dr. Benjamin Forster at the Foundation Christmas Party. I had been invited before, but the party always fell on some evening when I was out doing the Foundation's business. Prescott usually went in my place to celebrate and he usually found me later with a plate of food from the party. One year, I was driving teenage children to sing carols at nursing homes and Prescott walked up with a plate of turkey and assorted chocolates, wrapped in cling wrap. The teenagers spotted the food and in minutes I had nothing but an empty paper plate. Prescott shrugged and said I might make it next year, but of course, I didn't. There was always something else — toy drives for poor children, packages for overseas families, arranging for gifts for servicemen. Yet Prescott would show up with food and an apology, and the relayed gratitude of Forster.

But Prescott was gone, and I was in his place, and I would never have known which man's hand to shake had Cynthia hadn't pointed him out to me. We arrived at his home on a hill decorated with lights and trees with artificial snow sprayed on the branches. Inside were a good four or five hundred people, milling around with food and drink and enjoying the music provided by an orchestra. I was dressed in my best suit. Cynthia looked wonderful, as though she had been rehearsing for this for some time.

"You're trembling," she said to me.

"Aren't you?"

"I've met him, remember. He's a wonderful man. I'm sure he'll be as crazy about you as everyone else is."

Cynthia smiled as she said the words, smiling as though I was about to open a gift that she had picked out herself.

"You're happy?" I said, not meaning for it to sound like a question even though it did.

"Yes," she said. "I'm happy for you." The unpleasantness of earlier was, for the moment, gone.

"I'm glad that you're happy."

"*You* make me happy."

Somehow, that didn't cheer me up.

He looked familiar, but I couldn't tell why as I approached him. Forster sat in a wheelchair, and I noticed an oxygen tank next to him and the nose piece through which he received his air. He was balding, with white hair at the temples. He had bushy eyebrows concealed behind glasses. His mouth hung open, but I guessed that was from the need for breathable air. From the distance across the room, I thought he might be wearing makeup to improve his color, though I got the impression whoever had put it on him had overdone it. Yet in spite of his appearance he shook hands with everyone vigorously and looked almost in command of the situation from his seat.

As long as I had been working for him, I knew Forster had been in some kind of physical distress, though the details were always vague. I understood him to be a proud man who disliked having to be seen in any kind of disability. Gelb once said something about him having to "deal with the truth," which I took to mean his condition. "And the truth is almost always an unpleasant truth," he said. I wondered if the man's pains — to his body and his ego — made it easier for him to go about the work of dissolving his fortune in pockets of dispersed plenty.

So he really exists, I thought to myself. *Prescott didn't just make him up.*

I approached him from behind and the people whose hands he shook saw me coming. I recognized one of them as Jim Janssen, my prayer switchboard buddy who ducked out early the night I met Cynthia.

"Somebody's here to see you, chief," said Jim, looking at me.

Forster looked like he knew who would be there and grabbed the wheels of his chair himself — I understood without ever being told this was not normal for him — and turned around to see me.

"Cameron," he said, like a father catching sight of a child home from school. He reached up to take my hand in both of his.

"Sir," I said. "An honor to finally meet you."

"Oh, you've met me," he said. "I'm sure you have. But it's so good to see you again."

"I appreciate that sir. You know..." I motioned to Cynthia.

"Dear girl," he said. "Give an old man a hug, why don't you?" Cynthia smilingly obliged. "Splendid!" I heard him call, and I knew immediately where Prescott picked up that phrase. The voice was as I had imagined, as I heard so many times on the radio. Its resonance was a bit shaky but still intact.

"It's good to finally meet *me*," Forster said. I could tell by his expression, he intended for me to laugh.

Finally, it came to me. "Oh, you mean the radio spots!"

"Yes! I was astounded! You sound more like me than I do. I couldn't believe it. I kept thinking, now I didn't record this. I didn't remember doing it."

"I hope you didn't mind. I felt uncomfortable..."

"Not at all," he said. "My boy, that was a brilliant performance! I don't even think my wife could have told the difference. How does it feel to have that kind of talent?"

I shook my head.

"Have you had anything to eat?" he asked.

"No sir," I said. "We just got here."

"Help yourself," he said, waving toward a table nearby. He took me by the arm, and we understood he meant for Cynthia to get her some food while I was meant to stay there with him.

"Thanks for having us. It means a lot."

"Doesn't mean a thing. Shouldn't to you. Think of everything you could have been doing tonight instead of coming to see me. I couldn't believe you were coming. I half expected you would be out about the business."

"To be honest with you, sir, I wanted to see you."

"What about?"

"Nothing sir. I just don't remember ever having met you."

"Certainly you met me."

"When?"

"Come now, Cameron. I should think it would stick out in your memory. It certainly does in mine."

"It does?"

Benjamin Forster, as old as he was — and I had no idea how old — still carried about himself the air of a boy caught with a bat after his baseball has broken the neighbor's window. He gave a devilish smile, full of embarrassed amusement, his head bobbed down, and I expected him to tell me something that I would later figure out had happened to Prescott, and that he had merely confused the two together.

"It was not long after you got hired," Forster said. "You washed me at the nursing home."

"At the nursing home..."

"The nurse left you with me. I had just had my stroke and I couldn't talk."

I looked over his eyes. That was where the difference was. There was something in his eyes that had been murky and lifeless that day. That was why I didn't completely recognize him.

"I don't think it's too much to say that I had given up, Cameron," he said. "I thought I would never walk or talk again. I was incapable of even bathing myself. I had all this money and people doing my work, but I had never guessed they would have to do that work to me as well as for me."

"I had no idea that was…"

"Of course you didn't," he said. "No way you could have known. I wasn't about to tell you. I couldn't. That was the whole point. You came in, and only later did I understand that was you. I thought you were just some man who came in by mistake."

"That's about how it really was, sir."

"I can't tell you how much that meant to me, though. I won't say it's what turned me around. That credit goes to a lot of rehab work and some very dedicated people who wouldn't let me give up on myself. A lot of answered prayers, I can tell you." This wasn't what I expected from Forster. I expected a more forceful declaration of his faith than just answered prayers. But I got the impression from what words I was getting from him that Forster felt uncomfortable. He didn't like passing himself off as an example of anything other than an old man who threw his money in some benevolent directions and hoped it did some good. There was a dash of larceny in him, an awe that he was giving a party for people who thought of him, somehow, as a good person. "But I can tell you, Cameron, that I thought about you sometimes when I would get down. The fact that you were there for me. That the Lord provided somebody there for me right then."

"But sir…"

"You did what you did. What can you say about that? What can anyone say?"

"I was just there, sir."

"Nonsense. You saw a job that needed doing and you did it. That's been your hallmark, the thing that distinguishes you. You know, when I started this thing, I had no idea how far it would go. Any success it's had…"

"Is due to me," said a voice behind Forster. It was Si Gelb, in tuxedo, thrusting his hand out.

"Of course it is," Forster said.

"Don't let him fool you, Cam," Gelb said. "I know what he's going to say. He's going to say whatever success we have is due to 'the

Lord.'" Once again, Gelb said the words making quotation marks with his fingers.

"I was. Nothing wrong with that, you reprobate."

"Well, there's not much we would be able to do without Cameron here. You remember that." Gelb patted my back and walked on, as though he didn't want to intrude on the conversation.

"As I was saying, Cameron, when I started this thing, I thought, 'Well, Ben, you've got all this money, and there's all these things that need to be done. Why don't you just pay people to do them? The work will get done, people will be happier, somebody will get a paycheck, and the world will be a better place. The Lord will be happy with that.'"

He gripped my arm, forcefully, in such a way that I had to keep myself from saying something.

"I know now, Cameron, that you've got to *want* to do it. You've got to need to do this work effectively. You've got to believe in what you're doing. *You* convinced me of that."

"Look sir, you're wrong," I heard myself saying. I knew in a second or two what I was going to say. I was going to admit everything. This would be the confession. This would be the moment I should have had so long ago in the church. I wasn't going to take his money anymore and not at least reveal what had been going on in my heart for so long. But how do you make that kind of confession, especially to a man in a wheelchair who has just told you how he used your example to gain back his speech, his feeling, his motion, himself? *No, Dr. Forster. The truth is that this whole time, you've basically paid me a salary to be a Christian, and I'm afraid that once you find out the truth I'm going to lose my job. But this whole time, I've constructed my entire life around doing this job. Oh, I believe, I truly believe, but I will not follow. Don't ask me why. You wouldn't believe it. Just believe me when I tell you that everything you know about me is a lie. You've heard that Satan masquerades as an angel of light? Well...*

"Wrong?"

"Anybody could have done this job," I said. "Anybody."

Forster seemed offended at first by what I'd said. I wondered if there was anybody left to contradict him. I wasn't even sure Prescott had ever done that. He looked wounded. Then that smile came back, that boyish smile that was somehow fatherly at the same time, and he patted my arm.

"That's the truth," he said. "Anybody can accomplish anything as long as they believe. Cameron, you're a miracle. You've just shown me once again how special you are. I salute you, sir." And he did. He wheeled backward a foot and threw me a crisp salute with his right hand.

Woe to you when men shall praise you...

"I never did get a chance to thank you too, for the way you handled that whole thing with Charlie," he said, his voice dipping down under the noise of the orchestra at the mention of Prescott. "That's what I'm talking about."

"I didn't do anything there sir. I wished I could have done more. I didn't even know anything was going on."

"Oh, I don't mean that. I know. I had my suspicions, but I thought as much work as you were under, you wouldn't have known anything about it. But you were in a prime position to find out for sure. And if Charlie had done something wrong, I trusted you would act against any interest you'd have had in keeping his nose clean. You would have understood how important the whole thing was. To me. To him. To all of us."

I shook my head. He probably thought I was being humble. I was amazed at how a man this unable to read human nature had ever accomplished so much. His infirmities could only explain a little bit of it. There was an element of being too important, too busy, to be troubled by the details of a person's true character. It was only enough that he assume the admirable and good was in there somewhere, and it would manifest itself because of his personal power.

"What about Prescott?" I asked. "Charlie. What's to become of him?"

"That's up to him," Forster said, an ache of resignation in his voice. "I don't know what he thought he was doing all this time, but I don't think I've ever been as disappointed in anyone."

"I don't think he understood what he was doing," I offered.

Forster nodded. "He didn't understand the good he was doing, or the bad." I was about to say something, but he held his hand up. "I know we all are, but that doesn't excuse the damage a man can do by just not using his head."

"It doesn't destroy all the good he's done either."

"No," Forster said. "But it can keep him from doing any more." The way he said the words, I had the feeling Forster saw his old surrogate in much the same way he saw himself. Prescott was a man who could no longer carry himself where he wanted, though in a different way.

Forster encouraged me to look around the place, to get some food, to enjoy myself. I milled around, the man's words still banging around in my skull like bell clappers, so much so that I didn't even really pay attention when Jim Janssen came up to shake my hand. He said that one night with me at the switchboard had stayed with him the past five years. When I had told him that — you do what you have to do — I had somehow given him so much guilt over leaving early that I had spurred him on to something that had changed his life. I had no idea what it was because I was no longer listening, but I didn't bother telling him it wasn't even my idea. He went away happy and glad to have finally told me what effect I had on his life. And the rest of these people, milling around, shaking my hand, congratulating me. None of them were aware of what was going on.

Didn't they see what the enormously damning result of Forster's foundations and charities was? They condemned people! You can only feed so many, which means some will go unfed, and then you must account for the unfed ones. The ones who don't get it. What do you tell them? What do you fill eternity with when God demands an explanation? There was no end to it, really. You could heal the sick, but somebody else gets sick. The old die, and they are replaced by the young who slowly turn old. Men and women are sent to jail and released only to return or be replaced by others who will repeat the cycle.

There will *never* be a moment for me to relax, I told myself.

And I somehow felt myself jealous, walking through Forster's house. I wasn't jealous of him. No, I was jealous of all of those people I had been helping all the years before I came to his house. They all had problems, terrible, horrible problems, seemingly inexhaustible ones, but I felt like they could be solved, much like Forster thought, as long as there was someone there to do the job and to believe in the work that was being done. Tragedy doesn't always come to harm us.

But what about me? Didn't any of them see that I was an imposter?

What about God?

You know what's going on with me? Why are you letting this go on? Why don't you do something?

Did I care?

It turns out I did. I was just passing a conversation when I happened to hear Prescott's name. A woman with earrings the size of fists hanging from her ears said his name in a derisive little voice and I turned in her direction.

"I always knew something was going on," she said. "I think everybody did. You can't keep an act like that up forever."

A man I thought was her husband, a sixtyish man with a paunch and eyeglasses like windows standing next to her, smirked. "You had to expect it would happen. I mean, the man was so difficult to work with. To be around."

There was another woman standing nearby. It was Melissa Garvey, from the office. She was holding on to a man in a tuxedo who I supposed was the man she had been dating. It was the first time I had seen her smiling since her divorce. "He was so...unforgiving. He could be horrible if you made a mistake."

"It probably takes that kind of demeanor to run an office, especially for a man like Dr. Forster." This was the earring lady's husband. He sipped his drink and coughed.

Melissa cut in. "Cameron Leon doesn't need that to get things going. The office runs so much better with him in charge. No, Charlie

Prescott was a cancer. Dr. Forster is hardly ever there."

I wondered who Melissa thought had kept her on the job during the many absences prior to her divorce. I knew Prescott had made allowances for her, made sure she got a raise, a few other things that she probably had no knowledge of. It was a measure of Prescott that he never would have let her know any of what he had done for her.

"It just goes to show that a person gets what he deserves," the woman said.

I couldn't have agreed more with that statement. I stepped into the crowd and in a second saw Melissa go from a smiling greeting to a screaming realization that I was about to punch the earring lady in the face. This woman, who had no idea what Charlie Prescott deserved, would probably bring my life crashing down once I connected with her face, but I didn't care, because I deserved it. All my lies, I surmised, were going to end.

Except for one thing. God, so silent for so long, suddenly decided to intervene in the form of the earring lady's husband, who calmly stepped in front of her and swatted away my awkward punch. He was fast, I'll give him that, which is why I just caught sight of the punch he delivered to me a split second before it arrived and knocked me out.

37.

For a brief moment I could picture my own funeral. It only took a few seconds of time I suppose, but my imagination fleshed the whole scene out in such detail that I was left with little doubt about the words said, the scents of the flowers, the tears left shed and unshed.

It was a vision, you might say. It arrived fully-formed. There was no second or two of revision where the picture readjusted itself to the limits of my imagination or my expectations of what might happen. I was an observer at my own funeral.

I saw myself, Cameron Edward Leon, lying in a wooden coffin, something much more ornate that I might have guessed for the occasion. That was Cynthia's choice. I was dressed in an old suit, one that Cynthia bought for me awhile back but had grown worn in a way only I knew. The inside jacket pockets were torn and threadbare and the left pants pocket had a hole in it that I was constantly forgetting. The lining of the jacket had also become unsewn so that when I put one sleeve on I sometimes had to reach inside the sleeve to pull the lining back to where it should have been. I could picture an undertaker trying to get it on. Indeed, it was bunched at the sleeve on my body in the coffin, and it was one of the touches of this particular vision that gave me a chill. Cynthia would never have known any of this. I had always meant to take it to a tailor but I never had time.

I saw someone step toward the casket and reach out to touch it. When he did, his hand became entangled in the spray of flowers that covered the bottom part. It made a strange, artificial scratching sound that made my skin creep.

What surprised me was the size of the crowd. There was a long line of people waiting to get in, to shake hands, to meet Cynthia. I recognized most of the faces from church, people I had met over the years and ministered to. There were many people I had known through the Foundation and still others I didn't know but assumed where there because of Forster. I thought of all of these people I had visited, grief stricken when I saw them, or infirm, and how I had always rushed away from them and washed my hands so that their smells did not attach themselves to me. The only thing I could smell now were flowers, and their scent turned my stomach.

Cynthia was regal. That was the word that best fit her. She stood with her back straight through red misty eyes with a small ball of tissue curled in her fist. She was the picture of brave grief concealed behind a dignified air.

I saw her flash gentle, knowing, grateful smiles at people who shook her hands, not always sure who these people were but accepting them as witnesses to the kindness of her departed husband. Her lips drew up in acknowledgement of their attentions and her head dipped as though giving reverence. Men shook her hand. Women hugged her and patted her hand. She reached out to touch children who happened by and directed them on if they stared too long at my silent body. I understood this wasn't really her. She was merely doing what she had seen other women do in the same situation.

I saw Forster there as well. He was in a wheelchair and shook hands from grateful admirers. For a time, I understood he considered their attention to him embarrassing, wanting them to shift their eyes away from him to the casket and my family. He shook hands and nodded his head as well, but he would casually, with knowing looks, direct any well-wishers back to the young widow. I was surprised to see him wipe his eyes behind his glasses several times and to hold his head down, his fingers concealing his eyes. Occasionally his shoulders shook and I perceived that my passing had wounded him in a way I could never have imagined.

His head shook as though he might use all his power to wipe away what he was experiencing, like Zeus grappling with a headache, unaware that it will produce Athena. I could picture the same sad trek to the graveyard as I had experienced before, especially when I saw Cecelia.

She was much like Cynthia — brave, grave silence though no one was bothering her for a handshake to acknowledge they had come to the visitation. Instead, she stood against a wall and watched Cynthia and occasionally shot her eyes toward my casket. I wondered what she might be thinking, if she missed me or if she felt some sort of double funeral in that she could no longer hear even a cheap imitation of her husband's voice.

Richard was standing next to her. His suit was a little too big and it appeared newly bought. I could see his ubiquitous ear buds in and could make out a faint drum beat but his head didn't bob with it as I might have expected. His appearance may have been the second most troubling of the whole scene. He had a strange, bewildered look on his face, not like a teenager's groping for a general understanding of the world around but as though something inside him had been shaken by what he was seeing. His mouth was tight and his brow low and I saw him bouncing his back off the wall in an insistent, angry gesture, his shoulders low and his hands thrust in his pockets.

And then someone put his arm around Richard and rubbed his neck, and I saw him relax and convulsively bend himself inside the crook of the man's arm for comfort. It was Peter.

There's was no mistaking my brother. He looked exactly as he had the day he had been killed in the accident. He had an understanding, patient look on his face. There was grief in there somewhere, and he would cater to it later. At the moment, he was serving his family with the understanding that there was a job to be done and it must be seen through to the finish. He nodded his head at his son's grief and patted his back. I saw his hand reach out and grab his wife's. It was a gesture I doubt anyone else would have paid attention to except me. I had a strange sensation seeing that, something like jealousy though not entirely.

Peter then looked at me. No one else up to that moment had even been aware of me, I suppose. But Peter was staring at me, not through me at some other shadow on the far side of the room. He nodded his head, as if to tell me that he was there when I couldn't be, just as I had been in the same place at his funeral. He said nothing to me, since it wasn't required. But I had no explanation for his presence there, or the look of reassurance he gave Cecelia. It was as though he was saying, without words, that he had returned and all was well. She did look shaken, as though she would have to answer for all she had done to herself and to me, but she was willing to put up with it as long as he was there. Did I see in him the look of someone wounded more by this than by my passing? I couldn't tell.

Maybe it was like one of our last conversations, a few months before he ceased to exist, when he seemed particularly and uncharacteristically weary. For some reason, he was sarcastic and cutting and rueful, and it surprised me. "You don't need anybody, do you?" he asked me, for some reason beyond anything I might have said to provoke the question.

"Why would you say that?"

"Look at you. You're not married. Seem pretty happy."

"Things aren't always how they look."

"O-ho, a chink in the armor after all?"

"You fishing around for angst? Don't you have enough of your own? I should think you were about due for a mid-life crisis by now."

"I don't know. You know how it is."

"No I don't. Tell me."

He struggled for the words, as though remembering a second language only rarely used. "You get older, but your brain doesn't feel it. You feel the same way you always have, but you know time is passing. When people ask you how old you are, you have to correct yourself. You start to think and..." He shook his head. I knew enough about Peter to realize he was dissatisfied with his own explanation. Whatever was on his mind was somehow much larger than the unsatisfying phrases he heard coming from his own lips. It was embarrassing for him to believe that what he was experiencing could inspire nothing more than a few weary clichés.

I tried to help him out. "Bought yourself a gold chain? Sports car? Scouting for a trophy wife?"

"I already have a trophy wife, thank you very much. My car is fast enough and I don't have enough hair on my chest to display with one of those open necked shirts."

"What's wrong, man?"

He grunted, wrestling with something nameless, faceless, not wanting to admit whatever it was had any power over him. "Nothing. Just...nothing."

Those words, and the lack of them, stayed with me. What couldn't he say? Maybe that was why, improbably, my brother had started turning up in church pews, so fearful that I might find out. He probably couldn't explain it, much as he hadn't explained his feelings to me that day.

But as for my funeral, I had the feeling one gets, I suppose, when one leaves a room expecting a conversation to begin about one's self, anxious about what might be said but knowing it won't be heard. Where was I if I wasn't there? I don't know. It was a vision, meaning it didn't necessarily have to make sense. But it gave me a moment to think about all the things I'd been hearing so long about eternal life. If you think about it long enough, the idea of it is quite horrifying, isn't it? Even in this life, we can expect some occasional sleep. But eternity? When do we get a break? And yet, the idea of action, activity, reality, continuing on without us is equally horrifying. At least, it is to me. We might like to think of the solace of non-existence, the bliss of oblivion, the idea that at some point we will cease to be, but that solace does not exist in the Christian church. Jesus is a reminder that death is merely the name we give to the end of one face before the slipping on of another.

I had the feeling that I should be going, though I didn't quite know where to. Did I have some new face waiting on me, or would I finally come face to face with ultimate Truth? Was the sum of all the sermons I had patiently sat through waiting for me beyond these crowds, or had I finally switched places in totality with my brother? If we were drawn up on the x and y axis of reality, was I simply his multiplicative inverse?

If he had said something to me, perhaps it might be, "Et in Arcadio ego." But as Mr. Mark Twain said, himself a purveyor of alter egos, reports of my death were greatly exaggerated. The voice that I did hear, not my brother's, not my own, said, "I'm not through with you..."

Did I hear Him also say, after just a moment's hesitation, "yet?"

38.

"What did you think you were doing?" Cynthia's voice was clear and crisp and reasonably sane, even though her tone was like that of a tourist in a foreign country who doesn't speak the same language as the person they've stopped for directions.

Ah, things were certainly different from the last time I had thrown a punch at someone. She had married me knowing I was a danger to people who tried to witness to me. That made me dangerous and a little exciting. Only she could somehow tame my unfathomable rage, the secret pain that drives the angry young man. Now she knew I was also a threat to people at dinner parties who indulge in catty conversation.

"I was standing there talking to Dr. Forster's wife, and they came to get me to tell me that you had been knocked out. They said you had tried to hit to an old woman."

"She wasn't old. She was middle-aged."

"That makes a difference?"

"Doesn't it to you?"

"Cameron, why? You should have seen poor Dr. Forster. He's so proud of you. He congratulated you! He relies on you! He's given you his best position, invited you to his party, and you take a swing at one of his guests? And you know all the people there are *somebody!*"

"If I didn't know better, I'd think you were mad because of what happened to *you.*"

"Yes, I am!" she said. "That was so embarrassing! Can you imagine what it was like to have to pick you up off the floor and get you out to the car, by myself? Nobody would touch you! They were afraid you'd go off on somebody else!"

"She had it coming," I said.

"The old woman?"

"She wasn't old! She was talking about how Prescott deserved what had happened to him."

"You don't think he did?"

"It's not her place to say something like that."

"So she deserved to have a man hit her in the face?"

I shrugged.

"And besides, think of all the things you've said about Charlie Prescott!" she thundered. "I've heard you say things much worse. And they were true!"

"I don't care. That's not the point."

"What is the point then? I'm just dying to know."

"Cynthia, we do all this work for these people, and what does it get us?"

"Cam, how can you ask that? You of all people. You know we're not doing this work for anybody, not Dr. Forster. It's for the Lord."

"No it isn't," I said. "It's about *us.* We feel better about ourselves because it makes us feel good to know we're doing something. *We're* making a difference. Besides, I didn't do any of this for free."

"You're just mad, that's all. Besides, this isn't about you anyway."

"I thought it was. I thought we were trying to find out why I took a swing at an old lady."

"I thought you said..."

"They pay me to feed people. They pay me — he pays me — to do the work that he can't do. It's all a big bribe, a big show. I've been doing this all this time, but I don't believe in any of it."

"Yes you do."

"No, I don't! I'm not a believer, Cecelia!"

She looked mystified. A beat passed before I understood I had called her by the wrong name.

"I'm sorry. Cynthia. I'm not a believer."

"You don't believe what?"

"Don't you understand! I've been doing this, all of this, because of the job!"

"Stop saying that. You don't believe that."

"No, that's just it Cynthia." I stopped to make sure I had called her by the right name. "I'm not a believer. I never have been. It's all been about keeping my job."

She stared at me. I couldn't tell from her expression whether she believed me, whether I had confirmed her long-held suspicions, or whether she even understood what I was saying.

"Cynthia, I joined the church — Forster's church — so I could get a job with the Foundation. That's all it was about. It had nothing to do with salvation. I didn't believe any of it. I just walked up there and they took me at my word that I did. I am not a Christian." I said the words with such relish that I half expected myself to break into some kind of mad, maniacal laughter.

"Yes you are."

"No, I'm not. I did not give my life to Jesus Christ. I have never given my life to Jesus Christ. If I gave it to anybody, it was Dr. Benjamin Forster."

"You don't mean any of that. Nobody's that good at faking anything."

"I am, Cynthia. I fooled everybody. I even fooled you."

"You're proud of yourself?" she said.

I shook my head. "No. No I'm not." As she had so many times, she had astounded me with her confounded goodness.

263

"You're also wrong, Cam," she said. "Just think of all that you've done. I should say, all that you *think* you've done. You couldn't have done that unless God was working through you."

"But how can he work through me when I don't want Him to?"

"See, you *do* believe."

"Do I? What does it mean if I believe and I won't give Him what He wants?"

"Something's wrong, Cam. You're trying not to tell me what it is. You try to hit a woman, but you say it's because you're not really a Christian. You're saying your life is a lie. You're mad about something. Is it me? That we haven't had children yet?"

"No," I said. "That's why *you're* mad at *me*."

"No! I'm not mad at you. Why would I? You're..."

"It's all a lie," I said. "My whole life."

"Stop saying that! If your life is a lie, then so is mine!"

"Whatever truth there is in your life is what you've made there. It didn't come from me."

"What are you saying now? Are you saying that that you don't love me?"

If there was ever a moment in my life when I needed to sound like someone else, to have someone else's words to use, this would have been it. If I could have lapsed into Peter's voice, or Forster's, or Jesus', I would have done it. There were so many things I could have said, instead of the gasping, groping, ridiculous admission that came bounding out.

"It was...it was...for the job."

"What?"

I didn't look at her. I wouldn't have said it if I had. "They told me I needed a wife."

"A wife?"

"For the job. They told me I needed to get married to hold the job. I happened to meet you."

"I don't believe you when you're saying this. You only say this because you love me."

It has always amazed me how people can hear someone say

something totally callous, unfeeling, evil, and arrive at a conclusion which seems to contradict everything they have just heard. Yet she was clinging to this because to accept what I had said as the truth would have been beyond her ability.

"Cam, don't you understand what's happened? Forster doesn't know what to do with you. I mean, how is he supposed to put these two things together? This is not who you are."

"That's what I'm telling you, though. It *is* me. Everything you know about me is wrong. It's an act. It's a lie. I've only been playing at being a good man. I'm not a good man."

I expected her to keep reaching into the air to pull back a denial, anything to keep from admitting to herself that I knew what I was saying, and that I meant it all. I knew my wife, the way she had of making the world conform to her view of it regardless of the facts. But if there was anything else underneath that, it was a realism at what she had to work with. The expression on her face suddenly leapt from denial to understanding, a flaring around the eyes that reflected clear, unobstructed vision at what she might have avoided before.

"*That's* why you're so uptight," she said. "That's why you can't relax, why you're so unhappy. I always thought it was because you just pushed yourself. No, you think people expect you to be uptight."

I nodded my head, though she didn't need any reassurance that she understood.

"You really don't believe in anything."

I shouldn't have stared at her, but I did. I couldn't get over how I was saying these things to this wonderful woman, who should never have come anywhere near me. She blinked and I saw a twisted smile creep into her face, as though she had finally come to the end of a long practical joke involving hundreds of people and places and moments. I had thought that she might never grasp the truth — that my inadequacy had nothing to do with her. It was a creature apart from our marriage, nurtured and feeding on my many masks.

"Do you even care about me? Do you even know if you do?"

"I don't really know anything," I said.

"Was it so hard to keep on doing it? To keep faking? Why now?"

"I thought you deserved the truth."

"Thanks a lot," she said. "Thanks a whole bunch."

The truth, Jesus reminds us, will set you free, which is why my wife at that very moment decided to leave me. I had no voice to stop her, no words to say to undo what I had done, and no idea how I could possibly have made the situation worse.

39.

After awhile, I had nothing else to do. I picked up my keys and drove to the hospital and sat next to Thomas Hagler's bed, watching his chest rise and fall with mechanical hopelessness, fully aware that no one else would be coming to see him. The nurse looked in a few times, checked his vitals, and gave me an approving look. After all, I was doing what I was supposed to do, the accepted visitation of the sick, the lonely. Isn't that wonderful, she might be saying to herself. That man is here to look after Mr. Hagler when his own wife has abandoned him, when no one would want to be with a man who's tried to kill himself.

I came because I had no other place to go. By this time I was convinced that nothing I did was my own idea. I was incapable of original thought or action. I had done so much posing as a righteous man that any attempt I made at righteousness was somehow a sin.

I could feel the simulacrum of pride in my heart at being there when no one else could be compelled to do so. And that was the condemnation. That was the evil within me. I put my face in my hands because I was afraid to show it.

I thought back to Hagler, slipping the money from the collection plate into his wallet, inviting my judgment as well as God's. I wondered if perhaps all of this could have been avoided had I just said something to someone at the right moment. He would have been embarrassed, perhaps admitted his problems to Rebecca, perhaps been stronger at the crucial moment or forced into being stronger for long enough to keep going. That was the problem now. He had deprived himself of the ability to merely keep going.

He laid there. The heart continued to beat, the chest rose and fell because of the respirator, but that was all that remained of him. I thought of that vision — me in the casket. *Is that how fragile I looked?* I thought, looking at Hagler. *Is that how fragile I always look? Even when I'm well?*

All has been taken from me, I could hear Hagler saying in my mind, like some character from an ancient play wandering on stage ahead of a chorus. This is the sum of who I am. There is no more disguise. I have used up my faces. Mr. Haruki Murakami reminds us that human beings cannot survive for very long without some sense that their story will continue. If you lose your ego, you lose yourself. There was no more disguise. I had used up my faces.

I leaned forward far enough to smell Hagler, over the aroma of hospital cleaning fluids and gauze and antiseptic mysteries, and what I took to be his cologne.

It didn't seem real. The man had been bathed and rebathed and ministered to countless times since he had entered the hospital, but yet there was still a trace of his scent. I stole a sideways look to make sure no one was around, then I took his hand and sniffed it, just to make sure I wasn't imagining the whole thing. No, there it was. It was just hanging on after so long, a reminder of the personality that had dressed himself and shaved and presented an identity to the world before he tried to take his own life. I had the feeling when that scent faded, so would all that had been him.

Where was his soul? I wondered. Had it already gone on, or was it just hovering somewhere around, looking down on me and on himself? Or was it trapped in there, busting to get out of that confining shell incapable of movement.

Perhaps he could have gotten help in time. But no, I thought. Recent events had only accelerated a slow, looming process. It was just that living with two lives had become unbearable. There was a lot of that going around.

Not long after that moment when Peter snapped at me, then was unable to explain himself, I saw him in a different light. Actually, I couldn't see him. Like many of our conversations, it was over the phone. I could tell something was different about him.

"You sound happy," I said.

"Really?"

"Am I wrong?"

"No. I guess I hadn't realized I was happy."

"I was just remembering your conversation where you wouldn't tell me what was wrong."

"Which conversation was that?"

"You know. You were talking about getting older and time passing and..." My voice slowed down and shook as imitated an old man, as though I acquired a century in a few milliseconds.

"Oh, yeah," he said. I heard embarrassment creeping out in a knowing smile, like a dieter caught sneaking another dessert. "Well, I guess I *am* happier." He thought about it a second or two. "Yeah, happier. Everybody gets older. Not everybody gets happier."

"What's your secret?"

He laughed. "Nothing," he said. "Just...nothing." He laughed again, and I probably did the same.

I knew I could trust this memory. It was not my attempt to resurrect him and stick an explanation in his mouth. It was typical of Peter that both moods were inexpressible and evidently not all that far removed from each other.

What might he have said, I wondered. Would he have told me

about this investigation of faith Cecelia had hinted at? Peter probably would never have felt comfortable telling me that, even if that was the case. A mumbled hint at a warm feeling in a pew wouldn't have been in his character anymore than glossolalia.

But I wanted to believe that he wanted to believe, and maybe that he wanted to tell me about it.

I heard the sliding door of the ward open and a few footsteps toward the bed. I looked at my watch and figured it was time for the doctor to show up, or perhaps it was time for a test or something. Instead, a hand came down on my shoulder, and I looked up to see Prescott.

"How is he?"

"He isn't there. He just doesn't know it."

"How long?"

"Who knows? It's hard to tell. I would imagine there's probably a cut off point, but why should something good happen to him? It would be out of character."

"You know, I'm not surprised to see you here," Prescott said, and there was pride in his voice.

"I'm surprised to see *you* here."

"You should be. I don't know why I came. Rebecca would kill me if she knew."

"Well, she's already done enough of that lately."

"She didn't drive Thomas to do this," he said, shaking his head.

"How do you know that?"

"Because I did. I knew he was a weak man. He had to be to put up with her for so long. He had to love her to stay with her for all that... humiliation. So I guess I thought he deserved what I did to him. Look at that man. Has he ever had a happy day in his life? I think of what I've done to him, Cameron, and I..."

"You make it sound as though it was willful."

"It was."

"You never knew he was going to try to kill himself. You never knew he would end up like this."

"And you think I would have stopped had I known? But I wouldn't have. I would have made the same decisions, pushing him, pushing him and knowing."

"Then why are you here right now?"

"I'm here because I feel bad about what I've done. But when it's over, I'll go back to her."

"Rebecca, you mean?"

He nodded. "Yes. If she's killing anyone, it's me." He rubbed his face. "I should have known it would be like this. Before, we were too scared to ever bring it out into the open. Now, I'm seeing her around other people. It's impossible."

I shook my head. It was the only way I could keep from laughing, and I would have hated for him to see me laughing at him. I almost expected Hagler to bolt out of bed with a knowing smile on his face for that reason.

But I was no better. I don't know how long it was before I decided that on top of everything else, I was mad because I expected Cecelia to call me. She hadn't since the episode in the hotel. That fact was a relief. After so long being both myself and my brother, I was relieved to have returned to only screwing up one life. But I was convinced she still needed me — not Peter, but me — yet she didn't want to admit it to me or herself. *That's just her style*, I thought. *She'd rather die than have to admit how weak she is.* There wasn't much difference between Prescott and me, just different excuses.

Then Prescott spoke again. "I never thought you'd make it, Cameron."

"Make it?"

"The job. Between your attitude in the beginning and what I thought about you, I though you'd wash out. But you're the real deal."

"Not everything is what it seems."

"No, Cameron. I ran that man's business for a long time. I've seen a lot of selfless acts. I was never as good as you, Cameron. Even at my best, I still had this hanging over me. I was never as good as you."

Then I've fooled you too. Perhaps this is how God judges you, by allowing you to judge yourself.

"You know, all that stuff we teach people about living an abundant life. I had it. I see now that I *did* have it. Perhaps there was too much for me to adequately appreciate."

"What are you going to do now?" I asked.

"It's too late to do anything else. This is who I am, what I am."

"You really believe *that*?"

He gave another laugh, more devoid of any genuine happiness than the previous one. "No, but I cling to it. The belief that I had no real choice in any of this. That way, I may be able to sleep." He coughed and looked at Hagler. "We do not preach ourselves."

I pointed to Hagler. "He doesn't have any of that trouble."

We sat there silently, one on either side of the man, thinking that the other might give up after awhile. The noises of the hospital continued around us. I found myself concentrating on them instead of the sound of the ventilator or the heart monitor or the squeak of shoes or the hum of the air conditioner. I closed my eyes and the noises continued, and they seemed to grow louder than even the sound of my own breaths. The world continued on at its pace without so much as a second lost. Miss Helen Keller wrote that not until the blind child weighs his life in the scale of another's experience does he realize what it is like to live forever in the dark. I thought perhaps these noises would eventually overwhelm the man in the bed who could not see anything, who was not awake enough to wonder, like us, at the point of it all.

40.

Back at the house later, I thought about everything that had happened. A few hours before, I had been Dr. Benjamin Forster's prize possession, the heir of his disgraced adjutant.

Now, I had basically forced him to fire me. My wife had left me. I had a hard time believing she might forgive me, let alone take me back.

And tucked in my stacks of bills was a notice from my credit card company informing me my card had been suspended. I had exceeded my credit limit with my tithing, which had continued to compound itself. I felt a pang of disappointment going over the bill recognizing I had no Caribbean vacation or flat screen television to show for the thousands of contributions I had made. The interest on my generosity with borrowed money would eventually destroy me.

BRILLIANT DISGUISES

I suppose I knew from personal experience that believers sometimes doubt their faith. I doubted my unbelief. Did I ever not believe?

Had I ever been anything?

You are merciless, I told the voice — the Voice — inside me. I didn't ask for any of this, any of these people, and You forced it all on me. Everything You have given me has been taken away. I thought maybe You would go with them, but I can see that You're still here. Why did You give me these things if You were going to take them away? Why must You *make* me care about You? What am I without all of this?

The Voice answered: *Is it them you miss? Do you miss the man you think you are?*

Or do you miss Me?

The phone rang. I wondered who it might be. Forster to fire me? Cynthia, perhaps wanting to take me back? I even thought about Cecelia, whose previous offer of another life suddenly seemed viable, if still unthinkable.

I was afraid to pick up the receiver, afraid to speak, which is why Peter's voice came when I spoke. "Hello?"

There was a pause, then a voice that sounded nothing like Cynthia, Cecelia, or Forster. It was a man. At first, I thought it was a recording. "Hello sir. How would you like to receive a digital satellite television system, absolutely free?"

"Tell me about it," I said, still answering as Peter. *I could use some entertainment.* I thought of a TV show Peter never missed. What would he think now that one of its main characters had died. They had no choice. The actor, a respected veteran of the movies, had dropped dead in the studio after taping, and in his case at least, the show couldn't go on. But they had explained his absence with "a very special episode" full of crying children and poignant music and the ratings had been shaky but the show was still afloat.

The voice at the other end gave me the features of this television deal, one that would perhaps change my life. He was obviously reading prepared words, but he was good, my phone salesman, and he laid out the possibilities that stretched out before me if I merely said yes.

I listened with all the enthusiasm I could muster for my dead brother. It was a welcome change from hanging up, which is what I usually did. Most people excuse such rudeness because they consider telemarketing rude, but I knew these people had a job to do.

"Sport," I said, mimicking Peter's phrase for a man he had only just met. "I appreciate what you're saying, but I'm not interested."

"Is there any reason?" Once again, he was reading but attempting to sound spontaneous. I knew the strategy. Like a chess grand master looking over a board, the man had several different suggested responses for any answer I might give.

That is, until a thought struck me through the middle of his programmed response. I knew how to get rid of him.

"What's your name, sport?"

"My name?"

"My name's Peter," I said, as programmed. "What's yours?"

"My name's Gerald."

"Gerald, have you ever been born again?"

I expected him to hang up. There was a long pause, and I could hear phones ringing in the background and other people using the same automatic responses to other refusals from other phones across the nation. I could picture my new friend Gerald, frantically looking over his sheet of responses, aware there was probably no answer for this to draw on. I yawned. For the first time in awhile, I was sleepy.

"Born again?" There was something in his voice that reminded me of myself speaking to Prescott so long ago.

"Have you given your life to Jesus Christ?"

"No. I don't suppose I have."

"Would you like to?" The phrase flowed out of me, unexpectedly, in Peter's generous voice. *Why don't you go ahead and hang up on me!? Why must you make me talk on? Why must you make me care about you?*

"Let me get you straight. You're talking about Christianity."

"Yes. Do you consider yourself a Christian?"

"Well, I've been to church, if that's what you mean. But no, I'm not a Christian." His candor was unexpected and refreshing. It also inspired a sudden note of panic in my voice, which I'm not sure he picked up on. At some point in the conversation, I ceased using Peter's voice and began using my own.

"Ever thought about it?" I knew he had, somehow, based on his response.

"A little, I guess."

"You didn't want to make a decision?"

"Yeah, yeah," he said. "It was easier to just keep going on."

"And was it?"

He cleared his throat. If he was ever going to hang up, I thought, it was now.

"No," he said.

"Can't get rid of that feeling, can you?"

"Listen, I..."

"Being born again means giving your life to Jesus. Do you value your life?"

"Well, yes."

"How old are you?"

"I'll be twenty-two this year."

"You married?"

"No."

"Still looking for what you want to do with your life?"

"I'm studying law."

"Is that what you want to do?"

"I thought I did. Now I'm not sure."

"You regret it," I said, guessing.

"Yeah. I don't think I've ever thought about it in just that way, but yeah, I do regret it."

"Anything else in your life you regret?"

"Wh.."

"Because we all do," I said. "We all have things we're ashamed of. Things we'd rather wipe away, get as far away from us as possible. But they follow us and stick to us and we can't seem to shake them. They feel like they will be with us until the day we die. When you're born again, it's like you become a different person. The person you're meant to be."

"Well, I'm a good person..."

"No, no. There's nothing you can do on your own to get closer to God. Even if you were to work the rest of your life and die without a moment's rest, you'd still fail. Even if you'd give up your life for a little peace of mind, you won't find it. That's why Jesus gave up His life for you. He died on a cross for you, so you wouldn't have to."

"To take it away," he said. He wasn't asking a question.

And what about me? Did I really believe this? A man who had presumably lived two millennia before me wasn't just a man, but was, in fact, God. And He had died, somehow, knowing that in some distant time, a confused man who couldn't quite shake Him would be speaking to another confused man about Him and what their lives both meant.

Did I really believe this?

"You see, you understand what I'm telling you," I said. "You've probably considered this at some time, and you wanted to know more, but your life or responsibilities or whatever came along got in the way." I paused. "He still wants you."

"That's what being born again is?"

"Jesus said unless someone is born again, he can't enter God's kingdom."

"Well, what do I have to do?" Somehow, he still sounded like he was reading his response from a card.

"Just give your life to Christ. Right here. Right now."

"What? Over the phone?"

"Why not?"

"Don't I have to read up? Study? Prepare?"

"Would it do any good? If I told you that you can't do it on your own, then what could you hope to accomplish, if you wanted to?"

"What did it mean when you did it?" Gerald asked.

"To me?"

"Yeah. What were you trying to get away from?"

Peter's voice, suddenly reasserting itself in my mind, taunted me.

277

Didn't expect that one did you, Big Boy?

But there was someone else there. *What do you hope to accomplish with this, Cameron?*

Was it Prescott's voice? No, it sounded surer than Prescott, that lonely, broken man had last sounded. Cynthia? This voice sounded more vulnerable, corrective and yet understanding.

What do you hope to accomplish without me?

Perhaps I had run out of voices. I was trying to hide. I suppose I did believe, because I was trying to hide from Someone. Not an idea. Not something my brain constructed out of irrational impulses and the illusion of someone on my shoulder. It...He...was real. I knew He wanted me. The voice couldn't be mimicked.

But I don't want *You*, I felt like saying. I didn't trust Him. I guess I never had. It was much easier to say things and try to be someone else as long as I didn't have to find out who I really was.

Don't you understand? I love you even more because you're fighting me.

"And who are you?" Gerald asked.

"Maybe some day I'll find out," I said, giving a laugh that he returned. I sighed heavily, my heart throbbing beneath my shirt. My body was responding as though someone had pulled a gun on me.

This is my life.

This is my life.

And I'm going to give it away.

This decision is mine. These words are mine. No one else's. Mine.

"Tell you what, Gerald, if you pray along with me, I'll pray right along with you. And we'll find out together on the other side what happens."

I heard a sigh like mine, then silence.

"Want to try it with me?"

"Okay," he said. I wasn't sure if he genuinely wanted to, or he was trying to get me off the phone politely, just waiting me out, as I had with so many other telemarketers offering free credit reports and extended warranties and other temporary securities. I suppose he could have hung up. I could have too. Whatever sliver was holding us together might just be strong enough.

How tenuous everything in life really is.

"Let's pray then," I began.

As I closed my eyes, I thought I saw something. It was like nothing I had ever seen before.

DISCUSSION MATERIAL

BOOK DISCUSSION GROUP QUESTIONS

SPOILER WARNING: These questions may hint at key elements in the plot, so be sure to read the book before looking over the questions.

1. From the first sentence of the novel, Cam often speaks as though he is an observer in his own life — not actually living his life but someone else's. Yet he resists the Christian life because he wishes to preserve some measure — or illusion — of control. Is he always *consciously* trying to be someone else? How much control does he really have?

2. Cam often quotes writers, philosophers or famous figures from history. Do the meanings of these quotations have anything in common? Do the people being quoted have anything in common?

3. Cam mentions the Bible's impact on his life, but the novel has few Biblical quotations, such as Matthew 13:30. *"Let both grow together until the harvest. At that time I will tell the harvesters: First collect the weeds and tie them in bundles to be burned; then gather the wheat and bring it into my barn." (NIV)* What do you think the significance of this is in relation to Cam's life and how he lives it?

4. Peter appears only briefly in memories, dreams, and impressions. We learn about him through Cam and Cecelia, and briefly, Richard. How does Cam deal with Peter's death as the novel progresses?

5. How would you characterize Cam's feelings toward Cecelia? Cecelia's feelings toward him? Does Cecelia care for Cam, or just for the memory of Peter she feels survives in him?

6. Who has more effect on Cam's life — Peter or Jesus?

7. How is Cynthia like Cam in the way she grows into her role as his wife? How does Cynthia influence Cam?

8. Who is the stronger figure — Cynthia or Cecelia? How are they alike? How are they different?

9. Death appears in several scenes — dealing with its aftermath, the process of grieving, how loved ones are remembered, how our lives will end. What is Cam's attitude towards it? How much do you think it affects his decisions?

10. In Cam's final decision during his phone conversation with Gerald, is he still playing a role when he decides to follow Christ? How honest is he being in the book's final moments? Were you satisfied with the ending?

BIBLE STUDY TOPICS

"Dear friends, do not believe every spirit, but test the spirits to see whether they are from God, because many false prophets have gone out into the world."
- I John 4:1

One of the recurring themes of the novel is that of situations — and people — that are not what they appear to be. John tells his readers that the most exciting, revolutionary, or inspiring movements may not necessarily be the product of God's direction. Cameron Leon, at times, refers to spies or figures from history who are known for their betrayals. Another one of the continuing issues of "Brilliant Disguises" is that the people around Cameron don't seem to pick up on his "act," but he can pick up on their's. While he can spot falsity with the assurance of a mimic, the job for a Christian is know which voices to listen to, which impulses to follow, recognizing what is God's and what is the world.

The rest of John's epistle tells us that spirits which do not acknowledge Jesus as Lord cannot be trusted. Cameron understands this intuitively, since his own conflict is that he will not "confess." Though John is talking about spirits, this can mean spiritual movements, political movements, or even simple friendships.

"All of us have become like one who is unclean, and all our righteous acts are like filthy rags; we all shrivel up like a leaf, and like the wind our sins sweep us away." — Isaiah 64:6

At the beginning of the novel, Cam tells us that recent events have made him feel "unclean." He notes this while sitting for his interview with the Forster Foundation. No matter what Cam does through the rest of the book, he can't seem to shake this feeling of unseemliness, even through all the acts of kindness his job dictates.

Isaiah's discourse on the power of God — how nations tremble in His power — is important to remember. Though our daily lives sometimes allow us to avoid acknowledging God's presence by cloaking it with a veil of routine, God is all-powerful and all-knowing and we "are the work of His hand."

"I am the vine; you are the branches. If a man remains in me and I in him, he will bear much fruit; apart from me you can do nothing." — John 15:5

Cameron hears Prescott assure him that as he grows in knowledge, God will be able to use him more (of course, not realizing the truth that Cameron hides.) And toward the end of the novel, Cameron begins to wonder just what kind of effect he has had on all the lives around him.

Jesus' words reinforce how central He is to any enterprise done in our lives. If we attempt something without Him, our measure of success may be fine by our standards, but not by His. And if we trust in Him, we will be able to accomplish many things. Of course, the question central to the heart of the verse becomes what "fruit" we wish to bear, and whether our wishes line up with His.

DISCUSSION MATERIAL

"Let both grow together until the harvest. At that time I will tell the harvesters: First collect the weeds and tie them in bundles to be burned; then gather the wheat and bring it into my barn." — Matthew 13:30

Cameron quotes this verse when mentioning the power of mimics to insinuate themselves into a natural environment undetected, much in the same way Jesus described it in this parable. Cameron quotes the verse during the scene at the nursing home when he unwittingly meets Dr. Forster for the first time.

Jesus' words declare that destruction awaits the weeds which have grown alongside the wheat, since they are no good to eat. They must be separated and burned. The words illustrate that there are consequences for behavior, in both time and eternity. Eventually, there is a harvest.

"Nothing in all creation is hidden from God's sight. Everything is uncovered and laid bare before the eyes of Him to whom we must give account."
— Hebrews 4:13

Cam constantly tries to stay ahead of "the truth" about himself. He joined the church to get a job, and finds himself working overtime on both his job and his church activities to avoid attracting attention. Yet the spotlight follows him, and eventually forces him to reveal himself to his wife.

At other times in the novel, this eternal scrutiny is illustrated — the idea that God knows and sees everything. Yet we live our lives with little thought to the fact that everything is laid bare. Though God requires an accounting, we would be wrong to forget that He offers grace. The accounting shows that He cares about our actions. The grace shows that He cares about us.

"Come to me, all you who are weary and burdened, and I will give you rest."
— Matthew 11:28

Midway through the novel, Cameron accuses the Voice he identifies as God of being merciless because He will not leave him alone. Yet Cameron is weary and burdened, and the rest he seeks is elusive because there is always one more task that needs to be done, whether in life or in his imagination. In the end, he chooses rest.

BRILLIANT DISGUISES

The words of Jesus are personal, not only on our part but on His. It is not a promise of peace postponed, but one of rest from the burdens of life and the strength-sapping quality of mere existence. Jesus personally extends the hand of creation down in the service of the individual. The most crucial decision is whether we will draw closer to Him. As I Peter 5:7 says, "Cast all your anxiety on him because he cares for you."

All quotations are from the New International Version Bible.

ABOUT THE AUTHOR

WILLIAM THORNTON is an award-winning
writer living in Alabama with his wife and
daughter. This is his first novel.
Read his blog, discuss this book
and contact him at
brilliantdisguises.blogspot.com

LaVergne, TN USA
17 December 2009
167329LV00003B/9/P